17 first kisses

RACHAEL ALLEN

An Imprint of HarperCollins*Publishers*

HarperTeen is an imprint of HarperCollins Publishers.

17 First Kisses

Library of Congress Cataloging-in-Publication Data
Allen, Rachael, date
    17 first kisses / Rachael Allen. — First edition.
        pages cm
    Summary: Claire Jenkins has finally found a boy worth kissing, but when she
discovers that her best friend Megan also has feelings for him, Claire must decide
what she is willing to risk to get what she wants.
    ISBN 978-0-06-228134-0 (pbk. bdg.)
    [1. Dating (Social customs)—Fiction. 2. Best friends—Fiction. 3. Friendship—
Fiction.] I. Title. II. Title: Seventeen first kisses.
PZ7.A4364Aah 2014   2013021525
[Fic]—dc23   CIP
                                                                            AC

Typography by Ellice M. Lee
14 15 16 17 18 LP/RRDH 10 9 8 7 6 5 4 3 2 1
❖
First Edition

To my sister, Bekah.

Stephen King says every writer has an ideal reader,

and you have always been mine.

chapter

1

Finding a guy to kiss in this town is next to impossible. First of all, I have to find a guy who isn't secretly pining over Megan McQueen, the most popular girl in school and my best friend.

And second of all, I live in Pine Bluff. Which would be fine if I wanted to kiss guys who chew tobacco and wear flannel. But I don't.

Tonight, however, I may have to make an exception. I weave through the crowd at Wranglers, a country bar that has teen night once a week, careful not to be taken out by a rogue line dancer in the process. I'm looking for the boy in the white cowboy hat, the one Megan pointed out a few minutes ago. I find him leaning against the rails of the mechanical-bull arena. He's actually pretty cute, in a Pine Bluff kind of way. The type of guy who would have no trouble getting a girl. I don't see why he had to lie.

I strut right up to him. And lick my finger. And touch it to his shirt. "Let's get you out of those wet clothes." I wink as I say it.

For a split second he looks terrified, and the words *Abort Mission* flash in my head, but then a lazy smile spreads across his face. I've got him.

"I'm Claire," I say, unsure if we've ever officially met, even though we go to the same school.

"I know who you are. I'm—"

I put my finger over his lips, leaning in close so I can whisper in his ear, "I know who you are too."

I take him by the hand. Lead him to a bathroom that says Fillies on the door.

He stops short. "What if someone's in there?"

"It's empty. Trust me." I push him in first, locking the door behind us. The telltale ring-shaped silhouette of a tobacco tin marks his back pocket. He dips. Ew, I hope I can pull this off without kissing him.

I press him against a wall of cold tiles, a southwestern mosaic the backdrop to this seduction. Cowboy Hat tilts my chin up, but just before my lips touch his, I pull away.

"I can't do this."

His eyes are hungry and confused. "What?"

"I can't hook up with you," I say, tucking my brown hair behind my ears. "I mean, I want to. So badly." I rake my fingernails down his chest. "But I can't. Megan's my best friend."

"Megan?"

"Because you guys had sex, right? At Britney's party last weekend?"

That's what everyone's saying, anyway. Even though they were only in Britney's pool house for five minutes. Even though Megan swears they didn't. She has first period with his vengeful now-ex-girlfriend, Amanda Bell, and it's been really awkward.

He glances from side to side like he's expecting ninjas to pop out of the ventilation system. "Amanda said I had to."

"Sleep with Megan?!"

"No! I was just talking to her about how stressed Amanda's been about homecoming nominations. When Amanda found out, she got so pissed. She said I had to say all that stuff, so Megan would be the Angelina and she could be the Jennifer."

I frown. "But why would she break up with you if she knows you didn't do it?"

"I think she's going to take me back next week." He shrugs. "Um, are we gonna hook up now?"

A laugh sputters from my mouth, but before I can say anything, Megan's voice rings out from the handicapped stall. "No. You're not."

She swings open the door.

Cowboy Hat looks like he's going to be sick. Good thing we're already in a bathroom. "Oh, crap."

"'Oh, crap' is right," says Megan, pushing buttons on her phone. "Your little confession is going to hit Facebook. Right. Now."

We run out of the bathroom before he can process what happened.

"You were amazing." Megan can't stop grinning, and I'm so glad. The last time I saw her this upset was after Chase Collins. She gave him her heart and her virginity on a platter. And he dumped her. She's totally over him now, but still. The Chase-Megan era was epic.

"Well, you owe me. Especially for that 'wet clothes' line," I say.

Then I run face-first into Amanda Bell.

"Slut!" she screeches, throwing a cup of what smells like Diet Coke at me. "I saw you go in there with him."

Amber droplets soak into my shirt, trickle down my arms. Everyone within a ten-foot radius turns to see what the commotion is. Megan marches up to Amanda, their faces inches apart. She's very intimidating for someone so petite.

"Listen. Claire didn't touch your boyfriend, and neither did I. And your pathetic little plan to win homecoming isn't going to work, so stay away from me and my friends or I will ruin you."

I'm really glad I'm not Amanda right now. Whenever that tiny wrinkle appears between Megan's eyebrows, it is a signal to be very, very afraid. Don't get me wrong. I love her like she's my sister. But when Megan and someone else want the same thing, it gets . . . ugly.

"Whatever." Amanda glares at me before walking away. "You're still a slut."

I wince. I thought I was past this. I've never even had sex.

I've kissed thirteen guys. *Thirteen*. And somehow that makes me a slut for life.

"Hey, you know that's not true, right?" Megan says as she wipes me down with napkins.

I nod.

"Good. But I'm still not letting her get away with it." She walks over to where Amanda is riding the mechanical bull. In a skirt. "Tell Amanda to check her Facebook," she says to one of Amanda's friends.

We're about to leave when Megan pauses to pick up a pair of black sandals. The pair Amanda was wearing before she took them off to ride the bull. Megan shoves them into a nearby trash can with a wicked grin.

When I wake the next morning, the trundle bed is empty. Megan sleeps less than any human I know. On my way downstairs, I hear a shuffling in the kitchen. Something smells ungodly good.

"Do you want cream and sugar?" I hear Megan ask someone.

"Yes, please," Mama answers.

She's awake already. Which means today could be a good day.

I peer around the corner. Mama sits at the kitchen table in an old bathrobe, her hands fragile and jittery. Megan gently sets a mug in front of her, her other hand hovering over my mother's shoulder like she can't decide whether to squeeze it.

The oven beeps.

"I made quiche," says Megan. "Do you want some?"

"I'm not hungry right now." She's not eating. Which means today could be a bad day. "I'll eat something later when I'm at my group," she adds.

If she's going to group, it's definitely a good day. As good as it gets anyway.

I walk into the kitchen. "I'm starving."

Megan and I scarf down plates of her quiche Florentine, which tastes every bit as good as it smells.

quiche Florentine (*noun*)

1: *Spinach, onions, Gruyère cheese, and egg baked inside
   a crust so magically flaky you'd swear it was made by
   pastry elves instead of my best friend.*

2: *Something Megan just whips up for breakfast in the
   morning. On a whim.*

Mama drifts into the living room with her coffee mug and stares out the bay window, a ghost lurking among the curtains.

"How is she?" Megan asks.

I look down at my lap. "The same."

"We don't have to talk about it," she says quickly.

I nod, grateful.

Mama used to be like one of those moms from the black-and-white TV shows, the kind that only exist on the TV Land channel and in small southern towns. Sometimes I want to shake her and yell, *Why can't you be like you again?* But we never had the kind of relationship where I talked to her about serious stuff. And we don't live in the kind of house where you yell and cry about your problems out in the open.

Sometimes I wonder if that's part of the reason she's like this. She kept her feelings hidden, and they ate her from the inside out.

"So, thanks for helping me last night," Megan says.

"No problem. It's probably the most exciting thing that's happened to me all year. Which is pretty sad. I am literally going to die of boredom."

"You are not. Hey, I need your opinion on something." Megan holds up a couple of shirts that she brought over yesterday with her overnight bag. "Do you think this BCBG top says, 'I'm a really good dresser but I'm friends with everyone' or do you think it says, 'I'm snobby and I'm judging your ugly shoes'?"

"I don't know." It's not like anyone at school will recognize the brands anyway. We live in the town that fashion forgot. I mean, yes, we get magazines like everyone else, but looking through them is like trying to read a book in a foreign language. Like flipping through an Ikea catalog and finding that *spoflugin* = coffee table.

"Claire!" Megan snaps her fingers. "This is important! Nominations for homecoming court are tomorrow."

"You know you have no competition, right? You could show up to school dressed in holey jeans and everyone would be like, 'Oh, Megan's gone for a distressed look. I wonder where I can get those.'"

She giggles.

"Why do you care what people at school think of you, anyway?" I ask.

"Because. If I'm going to do something, I'm going to be the best at it."

I think about soccer. And my grades. I get it.

My grades are my ticket out of here. I know it sounds like a simple thing: Leaving Pine Bluff. Going away to school. But you've got to understand. This place is like quicksand. It sucks people in and never lets them escape. Girls with big dreams find themselves knocked up and married to a construction worker before you can say "dashed hopes." Even people like my parents, who got out and went to school, came back. I am *never* coming back.

"So," Megan says, breaking me out of my thoughts. "What you were saying about being bored and all? I think we need to make another pact."

"Yeah?"

"Yeah. Because I can't handle another year of your whining."

"Hey!" We both burst into giggles.

Megan and I are always making pacts. Some silly, some vitally important.

Pact #1: We will be best friends forever (sealed with a pinky swear in seventh grade).

Pact #2: We will never let each other kiss dorky boys (decided after I confessed the whole horrible experience with Steven Lippert).

Pact #3: We will escape from Pine Bluff and live out our dreams in the wide world beyond (we went through a poetic phase in tenth grade).

Pact #4: We will do everything we can to remedy our reputations as sluts/bitches (made after the Yoko Ono Incident—we've pretty much fixed our reps since then).

Megan clears her throat. "Pact number five will be all about making something different happen. So for you, that means meeting a new boy. Someone worth breaking your no-kiss streak for."

"Sounds good to me. What are you going to do?"

"I'm going to win queen for homecoming and prom."

"You're on homecoming every year."

"Yeah, but this is more than just homecoming court. This is queen. For both homecoming *and* prom. People almost never get the double crown."

I snort. "I can't believe we're about to make a pact about the double crown."

"Wait a minute. Wait a minute. Your half of the pact is about boys, and you're mocking me about prom queen?"

I hold up my hands. "Fair enough."

"Anyway, you know how much I love winning. So. Pact number five: I will make something different happen this year," says Megan, as we arrange our hands in the pinky-swear position.

"Pact number five: I will make something different happen this year," I repeat. Then I add, "Before I die of boredom."

Kiss #1 xoxo

The Summer Before Second Grade

My first kiss was with the most popular guy in school. For most girls, in most towns, this would be a good thing. Not for me.

Every high school has that popular boy who is not only an all-American athlete and devastatingly hot, but also a genuine, nice guy. Well, Buck isn't like that. I mean, yes, he *is* good at sports, and he *does* look like an Abercrombie model (for a parallel-universe Abercrombie that sells rebel flags and jorts), but he's a jerk. He's the guy who still thinks it's funny to tape "I play with my instrument daily" signs to the backs of the band kids. He's the guy who tried to crawl through the ceiling *Mission: Impossible*–style to place a video camera over the girls' locker room (fortunately, he crashed through the tiles and landed on a desk in Mrs. Frankowski's history class). He's that guy.

Every time I see him, I ask myself why (Why?!) my first kiss had to be with him. It was the summer Megan McQueen moved into the neighborhood.

I'm with the boys riding our newly de-training-wheeled bikes, while the other girls play with Megan's Barbie Dream House on a blanket in her driveway. Our subdivision is one of the very first developments in town, the kind with nearly identical houses arranged neatly among the dogwood trees. We circle the cul-de-sac, sometimes popping feeble wheelies, sometimes letting go of the handlebars for a hot second. Then Buck gets the genius idea that we should try to ride down The Hill.

In reality this hill isn't even that steep, but in my seven-year-old eyes it looms like Mount Everest. Many a kid has ridden up The Hill, only to have to turn around and walk their bike back down in shame when they chicken out. It is common knowledge that Glenn Baker's big brother broke his leg on The Hill. The youngest person to ever make it down was a third grader, and a biking prodigy at that.

But before we know it, all five of us are at the top, staring down in petrification at the meanest stretch of blacktop we have ever seen.

"Who wants to go first?" Buck waits for one of us to respond. "Nobody?"

My best friend, Sam, looks from Buck to the street, then back again. "I don't think this is such a good idea."

"Well, we knew you weren't going to try it. You wouldn't make it ten feet. Chunker," says Jimmy, his chest puffed out.

"Do *you* want to try it?" asks Sam.

Jimmy's chest deflates. "No." He doesn't want to look like a wuss in front of Buck, so he adds, "What about you, Glenn?"

"No way. I'm not doing it. That's how my brother broke his leg. Mom would kill me."

"Fine. I'll do it." Buck hikes one leg over his bike.

"And I'll go next," I say.

Jimmy laughs. "CJ, you can't do it. You're a girl."

"So? I'm still tougher than you."

Before Jimmy can reply, Buck kicks off. Our eyes glue

themselves to his bike as it plummets down The Hill. He is going fast. Maybe too fast. I cringe. Just when I think his bike will skip over the curb and into Mrs. McQueen's azaleas, he pulls his handlebars into a turn that sends him careening in the opposite direction across the blacktop without falling. He's done it. The four of us jump up and down and holler.

I decide to push off before Jimmy can start in on me. My bike gathers speed quickly until the neighborhood whisks by in flashes. My hair whips around my face. My heart rate is going off-the-charts crazy, but as long as I don't crash or pee my pants, this will be a raging success. I can't let the fear take over, or I *will* crash. After what seems like an eternity of free fall, I slingshot around the cul-de-sac and skid to an ugly stop beside Buck. No crashing. No peeing.

"You are the coolest girl I know," Buck says, which is pretty much the highest compliment you can get from a seven-year-old boy.

I blush and look at my sneakers, and when I look up again, Buck's face is right in front of mine. He kisses me. Right on the lips. Right in front of everyone. I think maybe he is my boyfriend now. I can't stop smiling. Until I hear it.

"Ah-woo-woo."

Followed closely by the K-I-S-S-I-N-G song.

And "Buck has a giiiirlfriend."

Jimmy runs toward us, leading the insult parade with Glenn at his side. Sam trails behind, huffing and wheezing but not yelling anything. The full weight of what he did seems to sink into Buck's brain all at once. The look of glowing admiration on his face twists into one of discomfort, and then anger.

"She's not my girlfriend. She's just a stupid girl."

He grabs me by the shoulders and pushes me. Hard. I stagger backward, the heel of one sneaker catching in the spokes of my bike, which is lying on the ground behind me. My butt hits the road with a thunk, and the asphalt scrapes all the skin off my elbows.

"You're not supposed to push girls, doofus," says Sam, his chubby face red from the run down The Hill.

"What are you gonna do about it, lardo?"

Sam shakes his head, then helps me up and pushes my bike back to my house while I walk alongside him with tears welling in my eyes.

"I hate Buck," he says.

I can't even answer. The mortification of being kissed, teased, and knocked down in a span of two minutes is just too much for my seven-year-old psyche to handle. Sam and I clatter downstairs to Mama's basement studio, where she photographs other people's babies for them. She has a knack for making even the ugly ones look cute.

Later, while my mom applies Neosporin, she explains that sometimes boys are mean to you because they like you. If I knew then what I know now, I would have called BS.

chapter
2

All day at school I think about the pact I made with Megan, right up until the last bell rings and it's time to go to soccer scrimmage. I weave through packed halls, past Buck Bronson (Kiss #1), who is shoving some scrawny freshman boy into the girls' bathroom, and Steven Lippert (Kiss #7), who is picking his nose and wiping it on the bottom of his tuba case. He's a complete tool, and I never would have let him kiss me had I not been under extreme emotional duress at the time of said kiss.

I change clothes at warp speed because I like being first to the park and having extra warm-up time. I've vowed to make this year different, to make my next kiss count. But seeing Steven and Buck just reinforces how desperate and impossible my situation is. I shake my head as I walk through the entrance to Salt Lick Park, a Christmas tree farm on my right, acres and acres of unused fields on my left. I have no idea how I'm going to pull off my end of the pact.

And that's when I see him.

Bouncing a soccer ball from foot to foot and looking so perfectly gorgeous, I half expect to see a halo of light descending over midfield. What can I say? Nothing is hotter than a boy in soccer gear. I think it's the shin guards that do it for me.

He's wearing this black, vintage Felix the Cat tee, totally different from the redneck-prepster look most of the guys at school have. In fact, he doesn't look like he's from around here at all. I start to wonder if I've wished him into existence. Then I realize that (a) I've stopped walking, and (b) I'm staring (in what is probably a really dorky and obvious way), so I jog over and say hi.

"I'm Claire."

The boy kicks his ball into the air and catches it with one arm. "I'm Luke, uh, Dawson."

He smiles and holds out his hand. I try to ignore the giddy feeling I get when our palms touch.

"Are you here for the scrimmage?" I ask. Maybe he goes to school in the next town over.

"Nope, just messing around." He shifts from foot to foot and flicks his strawberry-blond hair out of his eyes. "Is there a game starting soon? Do I need to clear out?"

"No! I mean, it's fine. It's not an official game or anything. The high school girls' and guys' teams get together and play pickup games during the off-season so we don't get rusty."

"You mean Rutherford High School?"

"Uh-huh. There's just the one."

"Cool. I'm starting at Rutherford tomorrow." He tosses the ball into the air and maneuvers under it so it bounces off his forehead.

"Oh, yeah?"

"Yeah. Just transferred in from Miami," he says, still heading the ball.

Score. A new student means he's never dated, crushed on, or stalked my best friend. If you made a Venn diagram of all the hot guys at school and all the guys Megan has dated, you'd have about three guys left. And speaking of hot-guy Venn diagrams, if you made one with all the hot guys at school and all the guys who are smart, there'd be, like, four guys who are in that middle overlapping section, two of whom I already kissed in a debacle that earned me the nickname Yoko Ono.

"What year are you?" With my luck, he'll be a really tall freshman.

"I'm a senior."

"Me too. Wow, you had to switch schools in the middle of your senior year?" We only started a few weeks ago, but still.

He nods, and the ball bounces off his head at a funny angle. He starts passing it from hand to hand in circles around his waist, and I can't help but smile at his inability to hold still.

"Yeah, it kind of sucks, but my dad's in the military, so I'm used to making friends fast." He shrugs. "At least I got to spend middle school in Germany."

"You did? That's awesome."

I am genuinely impressed. Our eight-stoplight town is half-way between Atlanta and Alabama and all the way redneck. Most of the kids at school have all the culture and ambition of sea monkeys, so it's nice to meet someone else who realizes there's a whole world out there.

"So, do you think it's cool if I stay for the scrimmage?"

"Definitely. It's not for another twenty minutes, though. We could play one-on-one while we wait? First to five wins?" This guy may be cute, but the true test is how he performs in this soccer game.

He gives me a confident shrug and tosses me the ball. "Sure. Ladies first."

I don't like the way he's standing there, all cocky and sure of himself, so I set the ball down and give it a few dainty taps. His stance relaxes, the way it would if you suddenly realized your opponent was five years old.

This is going to be too easy.

I cut to the left, and before he has time to think *I just got beat by a girl,* I'm past him and I kick a straight shot to the back of the goal. Too. Easy. His eyebrows rise into his hairline. I know that look. It's the face people make when they realize how good I am. I live for that look.

"Ohhh . . . ," says Luke as I run to retrieve the ball. "I didn't realize I was playing with a shark."

I hand him the ball with a smirk. "Maybe."

"It's cool. I like a girl who can play." He winks at me, and I'm momentarily startled by his eyes. They're blue and dreamy and everything, but there's something else, something shuttered, and that's the part I find myself strangely drawn to. If my life were one of those paranormal romances, he would be the guy that turns out to be a were-manatee or whatever.

And because I'm so busy mooning over said manatee eyes, Luke gains the split-second advantage he needs to get around me and score. Oh, it is on.

I have to earn my next point, with fakes and spin moves and every trick in my arsenal. Luke isn't cutting me any slack, and I'm glad. I could never respect a guy who did. Plus, I kind of like the way he's all up in my personal space. I finally psych him out with a quick Cruyff turn, and my shot just makes it.

Then it's Luke's turn. He manages to maneuver around me and, not to be outdone, crosses one leg behind the other when he kicks the ball into the goal. It is a showy, showy move.

My mouth hangs open. "Seriously? Did you just Rabona me?"

He fixes me with a charming smile, dimples included. Whew. Any second now his new-guy glow will wear off, and I'll realize he has poor dental hygiene and a hunchback, but I'm swooning over those dimples until then.

I fake glare at him. "You just wait."

I drop the ball and take off, juking from left to right, racking my brain for a move that will top his. Luke's on me in a second, stealing the ball away. Crap. I should have been more worried about winning than getting fancy. Crap, crap, crap. I mark him with my hand against his shoulder, determined to steal the ball back. He makes a tiny mistake, and I lash out, kicking it away from him. He'll be on me again, so I have to hurry. I turn, putting on a burst of speed, my arm flailing behind me . . . and I feel something crunch against my elbow.

I turn to see that the something was Luke's nose. It's bleeding. Like a faucet.

"Ohmygosh, I'm so sorry."

"It's okay," he says with his hand cupped over his face.

I run over to my bag, scrambling for something, anything, to stop the bleeding.

A crumpled receipt, some gum wrappers, a couple of movie tickets. Useless. My hand brushes against something in the side pocket, but I can't use that. It would be mortifying. I give my bag a second sweep, hoping a Kleenex will magically appear, but there's nothing. I know what I have to do.

I reach into the side pocket, cringing as I unwrap it.

Luke's eyes bulge. "Is that what I think it is?"

"I don't have anything else!"

And then I wrap one hand around the neck of the cutest boy I've ever met and shove a tampon up his nose.

"I'm *really* sorry," I say for the billionth time as Luke and I shuffle through the tall grass lining the road.

He lives on the opposite side of the park from me, past the Christmas tree farm, but it's not *that* far, and I couldn't very well let him walk home alone after doing him bodily harm, even if it does mean missing the first part of the scrimmage.

"It's okay," he says, gingerly patting at his swollen face. "I promise. I'll be fine."

So we walk past row after row of Fraser fir and Leyland cypress that seem so out of place in the September sun, me feeling extremely mortified and him plodding along with tampon strings dangling from his nose. Eventually we talk about things other than Luke's face and my apologies for elbowing it. I'm surprised by how easy it is, talking with him.

He makes an abrupt stop at one of the first driveways off the main road. I stop too, automatically. Neither of us speaks for a minute, and he looks oddly uncomfortable.

"So, this is me," he says, gesturing to a ranch-style brick house with green shutters.

"Oh. Um—" I take a tentative step into the driveway, and he squares his shoulders.

"I should go." He turns toward the house. A house I am apparently not invited into. I thought things were going so well.

I hear people talking inside.

"I know I packed it," says a woman's voice, sweet and quiet.

And then a man's voice, so angry it makes me shiver in the summer heat. "Well, then FUCKING FIND IT. I can't work without my laptop."

My eyes meet Luke's. The darkness I thought I saw before is back. It all makes sense. Stopping at the driveway. His stiff posture. I act the same way when I'm trying to keep people from meeting my family. I feel a burst of sympathy, but also relief. That I'm not the only one.

Luke's shoulders slump. "I better go."

I can't let him leave like that. Before I can even think about what I'm doing, I grab his sleeve.

"It's okay," I tell him. It's just two words, but I'm trying to say so much more. *It's okay that I just heard your dad yell at your mom. It's okay that your family might be every bit as screwed up as mine. I get you.*

Before he turns back to the house, the right side of his mouth curves into a smile. "Cool."

I think he gets me too.

Kiss #2 xoxo

Sixth Grade

I grab another Cherry Coke from the cooler. It's one of those old-fashioned bottles, the glass frosty and flecked with ice like in the commercials. Sam and I take turns sucking down huge gulps and letting out exaggerated "ahhh" sounds after each one. It is our first girl-boy party, and I'm wearing my best Adidas shorts and matching flip-flops for the occasion.

I look around the finished basement, at the guys in one corner huddled around the PlayStation like it's a golden calf, and the girls in another corner huddled around Megan McQueen. At my middle school, there are four girls from each grade who are the appointed royalty over the rest of the school. They're called the Crown Society, or the Crownies for short, and each class has them. Well, the seventh and eighth graders have them. Sixth graders are too lowly to get royalty. So all year, all the sixth-grade girls (the dumb, superficial ones, at least) spend all their time sucking up to the seventh- and eighth-grade Crownies because, on the last day of sixth grade, they'll pick the four new Crownies. And then you're pretty much set for life. Or at least until eighth-grade graduation.

The picks haven't gone out yet, but Megan is obviously going to be on the list. She has perfectly long, perfectly straight, perfectly blond hair and huge blue eyes, and she wears the coolest clothes, and sometimes the seventh-grade Crownies even let her sit with them during assembly. The competition is getting desperate now that it's the final month of sixth grade. Last week Britney even dyed her hair a hideous platinum color—probably in an attempt to look more like Megan.

So the girls are falling all over themselves trying to see who can scoot their bar stools closest to Megan's. I know Sam's cooler than any of them, but sometimes, when they cluster in a circle like that, I kind of wish I weren't on the outside. I was expecting a lot more from my first boy-girl party. I mean, it's all people have talked about since the invitations went out. Apparently, Amberly feels the same way, because she struts to the middle of the room with her empty Coke bottle and announces in a loud voice, "Who wants to play spin the bottle?"

"Shh!" Britney's eyes practically pop out of her head.

She points upstairs, where her mom and dad are drinking margaritas with some of the other parents. Amberly rolls her eyes.

"Who wants to play spin the bottle?" she whispers.

The boys are in. Amberly was the first girl in our class to get boobs, so they'll do anything she says. Someone's head explodes on screen behind them, and they don't even notice. They drift toward Amberly like they're zombies and she's the only person in the room with a brain.

"We can't play if I'm the only girl," she giggles, even though you know she would. That girl is tra-shy.

"I'll play."

Megan hops off her bar stool, smooths her pink shorts, and

joins the circle. Once she's decreed that it's cool to play, the other girls follow. Sam and I look at each other, shrug, and sit down too. Amberly lists off the rules.

"You have to sit boy-girl. And you have to kiss whichever person of the opposite sex the bottle points closest to. On the lips, obviously."

There's some giggling and whispering and rearranging as per the rules, and I'm relieved to see at least half of the people in the circle look as terrified as I feel.

Amberly goes first, and the bottle stops on Jimmy Marcus. I think he's grosser than gross, but I watch her every move anyway because I don't think my kiss in second grade counts for anything, and Amberly really seems to know what she's doing. She slinks across the floor like it's no big deal and plants her lips right on his, their heads tilting in perfect unison. They make it look deceptively easy, but I keep worrying about the most random things. Like how two-thirds of people turn their head to the right, so chances are the guy I kiss will too, but what if he's one of the 33 percent who turn left? Will our noses hit? Will we do a weird head-bobbing dance while everyone laughs at us?

The bottle ticks its way around the circle to everyone else. I get more and more nervous the closer it gets to my turn. I haven't had to kiss anyone yet. The boys' turns seem to magically land on Megan and Amberly. Then someone places the bottle in front of me, and everyone stares and waits for me to pick it up.

I lean over and put one hand on the neck and one hand on

the bottom. Before I spin, I think for a second about who I want it to land on, and Sam's face pops into my head. I shove the thought away. He's my best friend.

Everyone is waiting, so I hurry up and spin. The bottle loops around and around. As on every other turn, the circle collectively sucks in its breath on the last revolution. Anyone but Buck! The opening of the bottle sputters to a stop in front of Glenn Baker's kneecap. Whew. That's not so bad. Glenn is half black and half Irish. He has creamy brown skin and eyes so clear and blue you look into them expecting to see a bottom. He's beautiful even though he's a boy.

Glenn nervously licks his lips, but his eyes smile at me. My stomach does a backflip. As I crawl toward him, people lean forward on either side, but I try not to think about that.

When I kiss him, I don't feel fireworks or anything, but his lips do feel nice, and at least he isn't slobbering on me. I've never experienced this kind of kiss—a *real* kiss—and I'm starting to wonder if they all make you feel light-headed like this, when Glenn pulls away, leaving me sucking at the air like a goldfish. Then it's someone else's turn.

I catch Glenn sneaking glances at me for the rest of the game, or at least I hope I do. Now that we've kissed, he seems different, taller maybe. After the bottle gets passed around the circle once, people start drifting away from the group. Amberly pulls Buck away by the hand, and they start making out in a corner.

I could do that, I think as I wash my hands in the bathroom.

I could take Glenn's hand and lead him to a dark corner. The longer I think about the idea, the better it sounds. As I step out of the bathroom, I think about the way his lips felt. I'm wondering how his hand would feel in mine as I turn toward the party and see him sitting on the sofa with Megan in his lap. His fingers twisted into her perfect hair. Locking lips like they are the only people in the room.

All I can think is: *Guys like him kiss girls like her. They don't kiss girls like me.*

I'm still thinking about it that night at dinner. We eat at the dining-room table every night, and even though my sisters and I complain that we can't eat in front of the television like a normal family, we secretly like it. Tonight my mom made bacon-wrapped scallops and homemade mac 'n' cheese, which totally don't go together, but they're my dad's favorites. He holds my mom's hand across the dinner table in between bites.

My big sister, Sarah, puts down her utensils with a flourish and smiles broadly. "I have news!"

"What is it?" my parents ask at the same time.

"I got into Georgia," she squeals.

My parents make a huge fuss—which for my mom means chattering a mile a minute about how she knew Sarah could do it, and for my dad a wide grin and a quiet compliment. My little sister, Libby, yells "hooray" over and over, even though she's two years old and has no idea what's going on. It's a big deal that Sarah got in—school isn't easy for her like it is for me. Every redneck at her high school wears a University of Georgia hat like they're going there, but from what my family says, it's pretty selective for a state school. My family are serious Georgia fans and very southern (but we're the grow-okra-in-your-backyard-garden, drink-sweet-tea-on-your-porch-swing, go-to-church-every-Sunday kind of southern, not the NASCAR-watching, four-teeth-missing, baby-daddy-having kind of southern), so, yeah, my parents are thrilled.

I'm happy for her too—it was her first-choice school—but it's weird. Sarah won homecoming queen just like Mom, and now Sarah's going to Georgia just like Mom and Dad. Sarah's the perfect daughter. I'm just the nerdy tomboy.

"How about you, CJ?" asks my dad. "Anything new?"

"I got a hundred and five on my math test."

"That's fantastic," he says, and I can't help feeling proud. My dad is an architect, and he loves school just like me. He's always steady and he always knows the right thing to do.

"A hundred and five in math. I don't see how you do it," says Mama, but the way she says it, I can't tell if it's really a compliment.

"It sounds like we have a lot to celebrate," says Daddy. "Claire-Bear, do you mind grabbing the ice cream out of the freezer? I just bought some."

"What kind?" I ask. Mama, Sarah, and Libby all like mint chocolate chip, but Daddy and I like cookies and cream. Which pretty much describes our entire family dynamic. Them versus us. Ballet and glitter and incessant chattering versus school and sports and steadiness. Daddy likes to joke that at least he got to have one kid who's like him. "You're my one, Claire-Bear, you're my one," he always says.

"This time I got both."

Of course he did. My dad is the peacemaker in our family. Where I push against our differences, he embraces them.

"How was that party you went to today?" asks Mama.

"Fine." I push my food around my plate and try to figure out how to ask her what I've been putting off asking her all night. "Hey, Mama? Can we go shopping tomorrow? Like, for girly clothes?"

Sarah leans over and playfully ruffles my hair. "They grow up so fast."

I roll my eyes at her.

You would think the heavens had parted and George Clooney himself had tap-danced on our dining-room table. My mother's face is positively radiant with joy. She gives my sister that look all the time, but she's never looked at me that way.

"Of course we can!"

What have I gotten myself into? She's going to turn me into a miniature version of Sarah, who is a miniature version of her. I picture myself wearing a dress every day, having a flawless shell of makeup covering my breakouts, sporting perfectly styled, tornado-proof hair. Ugh. We'll have to work out a compromise. No matter how much she pushes, I draw the line at pearls and Lilly Pulitzer.

Lilly Pulitzer *(proper noun)*

A designer who makes perfectly lovely print dresses for
    perfectly lovely southern ladies . . . like my mom. Or
    Sarah. Not like me.

chapter
3

Luke Dawson. I haven't been able to stop thinking about him since yesterday. I glide from class to class to the hot-lunch line. I have been transported to a world where only Luke and I exist. The sound of mystery meat and gravy splattering from an ice-cream scoop to my tray can't touch me.

I remain in my Luke-filled fog as I grab a skim milk, pay for my food, and slip into a chair at our table. I always feel like people are watching me while I eat lunch. It's because Megan is a cheerleader and blond and waiflike and the most popular girl in school. Our friends Amberly and Britney cheer too, which means every girl at this table except me is in a cheer uniform. Amberly's wearing the regulation uniform like everyone else, but it just looks different on her. Like it's a stripper costume. She can't help how curvy she is.

And Britney, well, it's not like we've ever had a fight or anything, but I'm just not as close with her. Maybe it's because she's my best friend's other best friend, or maybe it's because she's always so quick to take Megan's side. Maybe I'm not okay with that.

"I don't see how you can eat that," says Megan, poking at my Jell-O. "Oh! But that reminds me. We're doing an eight-tier wedding cake today at the bakery. Eight!"

She gets to leave school early to go to her internship with a local cake designer. Her college-professor parents grudgingly allowed it because they're hoping she'll "get it out of her system." They don't get that food is more than just a hobby for her. It's everything.

She and Amberly and Britney talk about the bakery, about clothes, about boys, but I'm too busy scanning the lunchroom to pay attention.

". . . so hot."

Megan rattles on about whatever guy she currently likes. I drink my milk and daydream about Luke and forget to make my usual comments about how the school meat is made from roadkill.

". . . and he has the most adorable dimples."

"What's his name?" asks Britney.

"Luke Dawson," Megan says dreamily.

My eyes bulge, and a chunk of whatever animal I'm eating becomes lodged in my throat. I have to force it down before I can ask, "What did you say?"

The bell rings, but nobody moves.

"Luke Dawson. Why?"

I'm dying to scream, *Back off. I saw him first!* but before I can say anything, Amberly points across the cafeteria.

"Isn't that him?"

Megan's eyes follow her hand.

"Oh, there he is. He must have second lunch. Luke! Luke, over here." She waves him over to our table even though the bell already rang. "This is the guy I was telling you about. This is Britney and Amberly. And Claire," she says, almost as an afterthought.

"Hey." Luke gives an awkward little wave. He's wearing a shirt that says "Optimus Prime says stay in school," and I'm relieved to note his nose is only the tiniest bit swollen.

"You should come to the football game this Friday. I'm cheering," says Megan.

"Um, yeah. Maybe I'll check it out."

"Cool. See you later." She smiles at him with the tip of her tongue tucked between her teeth, radiating one million kilowatts of mesmerizing Megan energy.

And so it begins. She already likes him, and it's only a matter of time before he likes her back, so that's settled. I'm not going to make an idiot of myself chasing after a guy who likes my best friend and not me. I'm used to guys picking Megan. It sort of comes with being her friend. The thing is, I thought this guy might be different.

"I gotta get some lunch," Luke says. Messy reddish-blond hair that is a touch too long falls into his eyes, and he brushes it away. "Bye."

"Bye," they coo back at him.

"Bye, Claire."

I'm so startled by him saying good-bye to just me I can barely say it back. I start to think/hope/desperately wish things might work out after all. Until I see that tiny wrinkle appear between Megan's eyebrows.

After everyone else leaves, Megan catches me by the elbow.

"So. You like him too," she says. It isn't a question.

I blurt out everything I'm thinking. "Yeah. I mean, I know I just met him, but I really do. He plays soccer, and he's traveled the world, and, well, he's just *different*."

"He's different for me too," she says softly. "He made me feel smart."

"Aw, sweetie. You *are* smart." I want to hug her right here in the middle of the cafeteria, but that would be weird. Plus, she might take the hug as permission to go after Luke, which I am so not giving her. "So, what do we do now?"

"Have the catfight of the century?"

"Ha-ha."

"How does this always happen to us?"

You call dibs on everything in boxer shorts. "We both have impeccable taste in boys?"

Megan giggles. "True. Seriously, though, what are we going to do?"

"I don't know. I don't want this to mess things up with us."

"Me neither." She sighs. "So, that's it then. We both back off."

I blink. Seriously? Megan never backs off of anything. But her eyes look a little sad, and I realize she means it. Saying those words goes against everything in her nature, so even though I don't want to, I force myself to say, "Okay. I guess I can do that."

But I don't really believe either of us will be able to stay away for long.

I also don't expect to be tested in my very next class. Luke is there. In AP English. On top of everything else, he's smart too? Of course he is. I'm sure I'll uncover some sort of deal breaker if I talk to him long enough (I'm pretty picky), but for now I'm basking in the feeling you get when you're instantly attracted to someone and you haven't found anything wrong with them yet.

I take my usual desk, and as soon as he's finished talking with the teacher, he sits next to me.

"Hey, your, uh, nose looks better."

"Yeah, it pretty much is," he says. "I'm thinking of demanding a rematch, but I don't know if my face can take it."

I laugh. "I swear I'll keep my elbows to myself next time." If I'm allowed to have a next time. I'm not sure what exactly constitutes staying away.

We're silent for a minute, and Luke begins twirling his pencil around on his fingers. "So, that football game. Are you going?"

"Yeah. I always go to them."

He smiles. "I'll probably go too."

Even though I know I have to stay away from him, that smile makes me feel all floaty for the rest of the day.

Kiss #3 _xoxo_

Seventh Grade

Sometimes you have to take the flying leap. Swallow your fear. Kiss that boy you've been thinking about every night for the past month. I don't have the luxury of wading into the shallow end by degrees. Ryan Bond is moving to Wisconsin tomorrow. In less than twenty-four hours, he'll be riding away in a moving van, and I'll never know what could have been.

He's one of the only cute guys at our school who doesn't have a girlfriend. And while the girls in his grade (eighth) can flirt with impunity, there's a reason none of the girls in seventh are stepping up to fill the vacancy: Chessa. His fourteen-month-younger little sister. She's always been defensive about anyone liking him, because she's had girls use her as a way of getting close to him in the past. But when someone started a rumor that Chessa only got picked for the Crownies because the older girls liked Ryan, something inside Chessa snapped. She decreed vengeance on anyone in our grade who would dare have a crush on him, and one time, when Amanda Bell passed him a note in the hallway, Chessa ripped the note into tiny pieces and sprinkled them over Amanda's lunch. She even did the thing where she pointed two fingers at her eyes and then pointed them at Amanda.

So if Chessa ever found out I go on an imaginary date with her brother every Saturday morning, I'd probably wake up with a horse head in my bed.

I lace up my sneakers and, just like I have for the past six Saturdays, I take off running down the quarter-mile loop at the park. I wonder if he'll be here today. It *is* his last day before he moves. But it's also our last run, and I hope that means as much to him as it does to me.

I'm twitchy as I fly past crackling pine trees, hoping every sound will turn out to be his footsteps behind me on the path. That he'll pull up beside me and grin as he shoots past. That's how it happened that first Saturday, anyway. And I watched him run and I thought about it, and then I pulled up and passed him with a grin of my own. We went on like that until we were both all-out sprinting and collapsed, laughing, at the finish line. The next Saturday, I ran at 10:00 a.m. again, hopeful, but not really expecting anything. I got the biggest butterflies when Ryan fell into step behind me.

We did it the Saturday after that. And the next. And the next. And I feel like there's this connection between us, even though we've never even spoken to each other except to yell "Last lap!" before the beginning of our all-out sprint race. Every week, I would tell myself, *If he shows up today, it means he really likes me. This week I'll do something to show him how I feel.* But every week, I chickened out.

I plod through my run, feeling more dejected with each lap but still refusing to admit to myself that he isn't coming. I'm almost done and he still isn't here yet. As I'm making the curve past the parking lot, I hear what I've been waiting for—the magical thump of footsteps against packed dirt. I peek over my shoulder and start to yell "Last lap!" only to realize that the person behind me is an older woman sporting hot pink leg warmers. I slow to what is practically a stop and she gives me a dirty look as she power walks past.

He didn't come.

I walk home with my head down. I've probably been imagining this whole thing, probably—

"CJ!"

There, across the street, is Ryan Bond, holding a cardboard box and trying to wave at the same time and nearly dropping everything in the process. He is as adorable as it gets. I flit onto his front lawn, drawn to him like a moth to a bug zapper. He sets the box down and a football bounces over the side and rolls to a stop in front of the McQueens' bushes next door. He doesn't move to go get it.

"I'm sorry I didn't make our run today."

Our run. I love the way it sounds when he says it. It means he did want to be there.

"That's okay. I know you guys are really busy." I glance at the mostly full moving van in their driveway. "I can't believe you're really leaving tomorrow."

"Me neither."

He takes a step closer. I wait, hoping something will happen, like maybe he'll declare his undying love for me. But it's like every other Saturday together—neither of us makes a move, even though I feel like our shy glances at each other have to mean something. If one of us doesn't act soon, we're going to miss our moment again, and this time we won't have another. Ryan coughs and stares at the cracks in the cement. It's not going to be him.

So maybe it has to be me. I take in his sun-bleached hair and the little gap between his front teeth for what may very well be the last time and take a deep breath. I am standing at the top of the high dive, scared senseless, and I know I will regret it forever if I don't jump. So I do. Well, not literally, but I place my hand lightly on his shoulder and plant a soft kiss on his cheek. I'm struck by how warm his skin is on my lips. I mean, I'm sure he's 98.6 like any other human, but between the sun and the heavy lifting, he feels warmer. Before I can ponder the mysteries of his thermal regulation any further, I hear a voice say, "What are you doing?"

Chessa stands in the doorway, peering at us through narrowed eyes. My first instinct is to vault over the bushes and sprint until I reach the state line. She slinks closer, and I scan the perimeter for sharp objects.

"Hey, Chessa," he says.

Her features rearrange themselves so she looks almost innocent. "Hey. What are you guys talking about?"

Ryan's cheeks turn a little pink. "Nothing. Just the move and stuff."

"Yeah, I'm really gonna miss all my friends," she says with a dramatic sigh. "That reminds me. I really need to talk to CJ. Do you mind?" The smile she flashes us is all sweetness and light.

"No, that's fine." He turns back to me while Chessa shoots menacing looks over his shoulder. "Bye, CJ," he says, giving me a little wave and disappearing into the house with his box.

She waits until he's gone and then she pounces. "Why were you talking to him?"

So she didn't see me kiss him. I might actually live to see my thirteenth birthday.

"I, um, I—"

She continues to hover over me like some sort of jungle predator.

"I said, why were you talking to him?"

My brain cells fire feebly. If I don't spit out an excuse soon, she'll go all release-the-kraken on me. She reaches into her pocket, no doubt for a set of brass knuckles. Why can't I think straight right now?!

"Calm down. She was just returning a football," says a voice that turns out to belong to Megan McQueen.

Megan? Holy crap, these girls are like velociraptors; ones I didn't even know were there are swooping in from the sides.

She tosses the football to me with a surprisingly good throw for someone with a French manicure before returning to her backyard.

"Yeah. Football," I say.

Chessa gives me one last lingering glare before saying, "I'll give it to him for you." When the door closes behind her, I can finally breathe again.

"Thanks," I say, leaning against a nearby pine tree for

support. "You totally just saved my life." I can't even believe she did it. She's much closer to Chessa than she is to me. I wonder why she would—

"No problem," she says.

It's then that I realize I've never seen Megan McQueen look so sad. She's always the center of attention, and she's *always* smiling. I suspect she even Vaselines her teeth. But today she is sitting on her patio with her back to her house and her knees tucked against her chest. Her eyes are the kind of bright that means she's thinking about crying but wants to tough it out.

"How come you're sitting out here by yourself?"

She shrugs. "I just felt like it, all right?"

I sit down beside her. "You look kind of sad. Are you sure everything's okay?"

"No." She shakes her head. "My parents have friends over for brunch, and they brought their obnoxious smart kid, and they're all talking about science and art and politics, and there's so much witty banter it makes me want to throw something. They were talking about the possibility of an HIV vaccine, and I was sick of just sitting there like a slug, so I said I'd be scared to get the AIDS vaccine because I heard it had weak versions of the AIDS virus in it and I'd be worried about getting AIDS. And everyone stopped talking and they all looked at me funny like they were trying not to laugh, and finally my brother was like, 'Megan, you know all vaccines have weak and dead versions of viruses in them, right? That's how vaccines work.'" Her eyes tear up and she presses the heels of her hands against them. "I'm not stupid. I just don't know everything about everything the way they do. I'm not going back in there."

I'm trying to decide whether to pat her on the back when there's a faint beeping from inside the house.

"Crap. My soufflés!" She grimaces. "I guess I am going back in there."

She darts into the kitchen, not even bothering to close the door behind her. A minute later she's back with two spoons, a tiny pitcher, and a round white dish bulging with what looks like a very puffy chocolate cake sprinkled with powdered sugar.

"It's my best soufflé yet," she says. Her eyes are still red, but at least she's smiling now.

She sits back down beside me and places the dish between us on a pot holder. Handing one spoon to me, she breaks the top of the soufflé with another and pours on a chocolaty-looking sauce.

"Well, go on. Try it."

I start to dip my spoon in, but hesitate. "Isn't this the dessert for your parents' brunch?"

"It's okay. There are three more inside. They'll only stay puffy like that for a few more minutes, and after they fall, they don't look as cool, but people who think I'm dumb don't deserve the splendor of a perfect soufflé."

I spoon up a bite. Holy unbelievable goodness. If clouds were made out of chocolate, this is what they would taste like.

"Oh my gosh. It's amazing. Did you really make this?"

She grins. "Yep."

"Wow. I had no idea you did stuff like that." Oops. That came out harsher than it was supposed to.

"You mean stuff that's not cheerleading?"

I nod.

"It's okay. Most people don't."

Megan digs in too, and we eat until we're scraping the bottom of the ramekin.

"So, we should do stuff like this more often."

"Steal food from your parents' social events?"

"Ha-ha. I mean, hang out."

Before today, if you had told me Megan McQueen would want to hang out with me and I would want to say yes, I'd have said you were crazy. But to my surprise, I actually find myself saying, "I'd like that."

chapter
4

An image of Megan inviting Luke to the football game flickers in my head as I run at a soccer ball. *Thwack!* My foot connects with the ball, and it veers wildly toward the left, completely outside the goal. Sam watches it sail by from where he's playing goalie.

"I can't believe this is happening again. We always end up liking the same guy," I say, as I line up to kick the next ball.

Four soccer balls span out in a row across the happy green grass in front of me.

"What are the odds?!"

Thwack! This time the ball pings against the goalpost and bounces away. I'm not giving Sam much to do besides talk to me. He's pretty great at it, though, because he doesn't freak out over feelings like most boys do (i.e., he doesn't back away in fear like you're carrying the Ebola virus). And he never tries to tell you solutions to your problems when all you want to do is vent. It probably comes from growing up with a single mom and two sisters.

Sam shakes his head at me from inside the goal. "This is Megan McQueen we're talking about. Did you really expect anything less than drama? Oh, and you're a really bad shot when you're pissed off."

"Thanks." I glare at him and kick another ball.

This one goes right to him, and he catches it easily and tosses it away from the goal. Usually we're pretty evenly matched, but he's right: my mood totally affects my game.

He chuckles. "You know how I feel about the evil one." Sam has never been able to get over Megan calling him Spamlet for all of fourth grade. And I'm not saying she's all sunshine and unicorns, but she's the closest girlfriend I've ever had and probably will ever have. She's kind of like a finicky cat. Once she decides she likes you, you're in. And if she doesn't, watch out for her claws.

"I know. I know." *Thwack!* "But she's a really good friend. At least, she is when it doesn't involve a boy. Plus, she's the only girl I know who wants to get out of this miserable, little town as much as I do."

"I want to get out of Pine Bluff."

"I know. But still. It's good to have a girl I can count on too."

"But you don't trust her to stay away from Luke?"

"Hell, no. He's coming to the game tonight, and we're both

going to be there. *Something* is going to happen. But I agreed to back off, so I guess I have to."

"Why can't you both just go for him?"

"It'll put her in crazy competitive mode. I don't need any more guy drama. I don't want a repeat of sophomore year."

"True," says Sam. "Anyway, if you really think it's going to get that crazy with Megan, you could let her have him. You just met him. He's probably not even worth all this trouble."

"I know. But I haven't liked a boy in so long." I'm whining now, but I can't help it. "I haven't even kissed anyone since tenth grade. I've been keeping a low profile because I can't deal with another Screaming Lemurs debacle. Do you know how hard it is to convince people you aren't a slut?"

"Um, no. Not really."

Thwack! The last ball veers left too.

"Let's quit for today." I head over to the sideline and pick up a mesh bag for the balls. "I still have to go home and get ready for tonight."

"You really want to go watch Buck slap other guys on the ass?"

"Ew. No." I shudder. "But do you really have better plans?"

There are only four things to do in Pine Bluff on a Friday night: catch a movie at the Cineplex, go to a party at someone's house or field, hang out in the Walmart parking lot, or watch the high school football game. Sam dribbles over to me with the last ball, kicks it up to his knees, where he bounces it back and forth effortlessly, then pops it into the bag with his head.

"Show-off," I mutter.

He grins. Sam always got stuck playing goalie growing up because overweight kids can't run fast. But when you play a position for that long, you can't help but get good at it, so now he plays varsity.

On our way home, we take the shortcut, a dirt road lined with muscadines growing wild.

muscadine (*noun*)
A southeastern fruit that is kind of like a grape. Only fat-
ter. And more tart. And with a really thick skin.

We pop them in our mouths fresh off the vine—because nobody uses pesticides out here—suck out the juice, and spit out the skin and seeds.

"I guess I'll go to the game tonight," says Sam. "There are a couple of ladies I need to impress."

I roll my eyes.

"I need your advice," he says after a minute.

"On what? The ladies?"

"Kind of."

I'm surprised, but I make myself keep walking at a normal pace.

"What's up?"

He hesitates. "I need to know how to get girls to see the new me. I've lost all this weight, but it's like no one's noticed. And this girl I like, she was going on and on about Buck's abs and how abs are the hottest thing in the universe, and I'm like, 'I have abs too.'"

"Yeah, right." I know it's mean, but it slips out before I can help myself.

Sam lifts up his shirt. The Buddha belly I know has been replaced with a washboard.

"Ohmygosh. You do. I mean, I knew you lost weight, but when did that happen?"

I feel a fluttery feeling low in my tummy, even though it's Sam. I write it off as temporary ab-induced insanity.

He shrugs. "Sometime this summer. I've been working out like crazy and eating things like tilapia and lentils. So, what should I do?"

"You should show her those abs," I say. "Hey, we could paint you for tonight's football game. It's the perfect excuse to be shirtless."

"Okay. Let's do it. Can I come over in an hour and get your help with the paint? I'll drive you to the game."

"That would be great. Not having a car sucks so hard."

We get to the corner where we have to go in opposite directions.

"Later, Sam."

"Later, CJ."

He's the only one who still calls me CJ. Even my sisters call me Claire now. Sam refuses.

My little sister, Libby, is sitting in front of cartoons when I open the door.

"Hey, Libs, wanna help me order Chinese food?"

Friday is takeout night at the Jenkins house.

"I guess," she says quietly even though she usually loves picking out food.

"What's wrong?"

She turns off the TV but doesn't look at me. "I got in another fight today."

"You can't keep doing this." I rake my hands through my hair and try to remain calm. "What happened?"

"Mama said she would make cupcakes for the bake sale, but she was having a bad day. And this girl said everyone's mom baked cupcakes except mine. And then she said, 'You probably don't even have a mom.'"

"Oh, no." How can I stay mad after she tells me something like that? I pull her onto my lap. "Then what happened?"

"I poured a can of paint on her head," Libby mumbles.

I try not to giggle. "I'm sorry she said that to you. But you can't fight people every time you get angry. Try counting to ten or something."

"Okay." Libby hangs her head. "Can you sign my form for in-school suspension? I don't want Daddy to get mad again."

She pulls a crumpled piece of paper from her backpack and gives me puppy-dog eyes.

"Sure." I forge my mom's signature on the form. "But next time you have a bake sale or something, tell me. Megan and I can make you the most awesome cupcakes ever."

"I know. I just wish Mama could make them."

I know exactly how she feels. I wish I could ask Mama for advice about the Luke thing. I know none of my friends talk to their parents about stuff like that, so if Mama were more involved in my life, I probably wouldn't want to talk to her either, but I want it to be my decision. I want the option of giving her one-word answers while she racks her brain trying to figure out what's wrong with me.

I rest my chin on top of Libby's curly brown hair and squeeze her extra tight. "Me too, sweetie. Me too."

I sit at my desk, nibbling on an egg roll. I'll probably go out to dinner after the game, but I needed something to tide me over. Sam should be here any minute. Maybe he's right. What do I really know about Luke anyway? I pull out a piece of notebook paper and make a list.

He's hot.

He plays soccer.

He's taller than me. (Which is rare when you're a five-foot-ten athlete!)

He's in AP English, so he's probably smart.

He has dimples.

He's REALLY HOT.

He's the most interesting person I've met in as long as I can remember, and for a fleeting moment in front of his house I didn't feel so alone living in our town with my messed-up family.

I look over the list one more time and then I shred it into tiny pieces, because there isn't enough candy in the world to bribe Libby with if she found it.

While this is an impressive array of qualities to observe in a single specimen of boy, I'm going to back off and let Megan have him. Even though I saw him first. Even though it's obvious we have way more in common. Even though I'm bored out of my cotton-picking mind. Because my best friend likes him *a lot*, and I'm not sure I like him *enough*.

Kiss #4 xoxo

Seventh Grade

Absolutely ridiculous. That's how I look in this dress. I pull it over my head and add it to the ever-growing pile of silver, magenta, and lavender on my floor.

I grab another dress, a knee-length blue one Sarah swore would "make my eyes pop." It's no use. I look like a phony. Like when I was little and I stomped around the house in my mama's high heels. It's not that the dresses don't fit me. They're my size and everything. Maybe it's because I don't have boobs yet. I look from my ponytail to my unpainted toenails in disgust. How am I ever going to find something to wear to the Winter Wonderland Dance?

There is nothing like standing in front of a floor-length mirror and trying on dresses to make you scrutinize everything you like or don't like about yourself. I'm tall—way taller than most of the boys in seventh grade—so dances are pretty stressful for me, or would be if I actually slow-danced with boys. I have long, dark brown hair with natural auburn highlights that my sister Sarah says she would kill for and a tiny sprinkling of freckles across my nose and cheeks. I love my freckles. They're the cute, tiny, tan-colored kind. Cinnamon-sprinkle freckles. The freckles combined with my round blue eyes give me a wholesome, all-American look, like I should be in soap commercials or something.

But don't get me wrong: I'm no knockout. I have all the curves of a celery stick. That means no boobs. None. My feet are too big, and my eyebrows are like two woolly bear caterpillars, but I'm scared to do anything about it lest I end up like Amanda Bell, who showed up to school with half an eyebrow after an unfortunate experiment with her mom's waxing kit.

But the worst thing about my looks, the thing that just kills me, is that I look like a boy. I'm serious. I have entirely too many muscles for a girl. It's probably why all these dresses look awful on me. I'm just about to take off the stupid blue dress in defeat when the doorbell rings.

"Hey, girls. Megan, it's so good to see you," I hear my mother say.

Why is Megan McQueen at my house? Did she finally decide it's time to hang out? It's been a few weeks. I run downstairs. It isn't just Megan. Amberly and Britney are with her too. The entire Crown Society crew, minus Chessa. They're decked out in their dresses already with matching crown necklace charms that signify their supposed superiority over the rest of us.

"CJ, look who's here!" Lord, she's fawning all over Megan like she's the queen of England instead of the queen of seventh grade. "Can I get y'all a glass of sweet tea? Or maybe some lemonade?"

"That is so sweet of you, Miss Lily, but we really need to ask CJ about something," says Megan.

"Okay, I'll let you girls talk." She flashes one last smile over her shoulder before she manages to pull herself away from the abundance of tween-age popularity in our doorway.

"What's up?" I ask.

I narrow my eyes. The three of them are smiling at me like they're going to eat me or something.

"Can we go up to your room?" asks Megan.

"Sure." I turn, puzzled, and lead them upstairs.

They take in the kiwi-colored walls and sports paraphernalia with something between curiosity and disdain. Amberly and Britney sit on the star-patterned quilt my mom made and look at Megan like they're waiting for something. She prances over and stands in front of my desk like she's about to give a presentation at school.

"As we all know, Chessa moved away last month. It's been tough, but we've been looking for a replacement. And today we finally decided." She clasps her hands in front of her and smiles. "CJ, we want you to be a member of the Crown Society."

"What?" I fall out of my chair, I'm laughing so hard. "You're kidding. This is a joke, right?"

Britney crosses her arms over her chest. "I told you we should have picked Amanda Bell."

"Why do you have to have a fourth person anyway?" I ask. "Why can't it be just the three of you?"

"Because four is the magical number of girlfriendship," says Megan, like I was supposed to have learned this in Friendship 101.

Amberly nods fervently. "It's the trifecta."

I refrain from pointing out what *trifecta* means.

"It's like *Sex and the City*," explains Megan.

My mama would skin me alive if she caught me watching *Sex and the City*, so I've never seen it, but I nod like I get it anyway. Megan still hasn't asked me if I want to be one of them. She just assumes I do. Any girl in seventh grade would roll around in broken glass naked for the chance I've been given.

"But, why would you pick *me*?"

Megan shrugs. "You're nice and funny, and you have a good body. Being popular should be no problem for you."

"Plus you've started dressing way cuter this year. We've noticed," adds Amberly.

"But there must be dozens of other girls . . ."

Megan cuts me off with a brisk shake of her head. "Yearbook," she says, like a doctor asking for a scalpel.

I find it on my shelf, and they explain how they systematically whittled down the list of girls to me and one or two others.

Megan closes the yearbook with a snap. "So, you see. There was no one else we could have chosen."

"Well," begins Britney.

"There was no one," says Megan.

I'm still not convinced, though. "But I'm a tomboy."

"So you play soccer. Soccer is fine. We can work with soccer. As long as it's not *softball*." Megan shudders.

"Plus, we'll make you over, just like in *Clueless*." Amberly's eyes light up at the thought.

"What do you say?" asks Megan.

I can't picture myself spending time with these girls, let

alone being one of them, but the image of Megan hiding out on her patio pops into my head. I really do want to get to know her better. And if they could make me look as confident in dresses as they do, that wouldn't suck either. Before I can stop myself, I say, "I'm in."

"Awesome!" says Megan. "You're coming to my house to get ready for the dance with us."

With that, they kidnap me. Well, they drag me across the street to Megan's house while my mom waves good-bye with tears of joy shining on her cheeks. We gallop up the stairs to Megan's room, and because all the houses in our neighborhood have almost the same layout, her room is in exactly the same place as mine, with the same window seat and everything. That's where the similarities end. Her walls are painted bubble-gum pink, and there are butterflies on her curtains. A huge poster of a boy-band lead singer smiles down at us from above her bed, and I cringe. I'm not the kind of girl who tapes boys to my wall.

"Let's get started."

Megan pushes me down by my shoulders onto the seat in front of her vanity. Amberly grabs a stack of *Teen Vogue*s to use as a reference. While it's clear Megan is the unofficial leader of the Crown Society, Amberly is the unofficial leader of this makeover. Even Megan defers to her vast knowledge of all things gloss and glitter. I can't really see what they're doing to me because Megan is flat-ironing my already-straight hair, Amberly is doing my eye shadow, and Britney is painting my nails. I just try to keep up with their commands. Tilt your head forward. Close your eyes. Relax your fingers.

Partway through, it occurs to me this could be a sick joke. Maybe they're making me look ridiculous. But when Amberly finally shows me my reflection in the mirror, I gasp. It's hard for me to point out all the things they did, all the little pieces that make me look the way I do now. I no longer look like a boy in a dress. I'm beautiful.

Amberly sighs. "It's some of my best work," she pronounces before we leave for the dance.

Except for the eighth-grade dance, which is like a mini prom, you don't have to have a date to go to our school dances (all of which are held in the gym). Girls and guys show up in clusters, dance in clusters, and leave in clusters. The exceptions are the people currently going out. The couples are interspersed between the clusters, wrapped up in each other's arms, gazing into each other's eyes like they wish the Winter Wonderland Dance would just go on forever, even though you know they'll be broken up by next month.

The coolest girl cluster by far is the Crownies, and that's where I am now, even though it's hard to believe. I shouldn't be wearing makeup and standing with these girls. I should be hanging out with Sam and making fun of the crappy decorations. I hope he's not worried. I didn't have a chance to text him or anything. I search the crowd for Sam and find so many eyes peering back at me.

"Everyone's staring," I say. I fiddle with the hem of my knee-length blue dress. The one that looked awful on me at my house, but now, after their makeover, seems to fit just right. "They'll never believe I belong."

"They'll believe whatever I tell them," says Megan.

"Tool alert," says Amberly. "Steven Lippert is walking this way."

Steven makes terrible puns and tries to flirt with me in English class, and right now he's headed straight for us. He picks me out of the group like the weakest animal, his eyes going from my shoes to my headband and back again. Ew.

"What's up, CJ?"

Megan steps between us. "Claire's busy right now. She's going to go dance with us."

I'm so used to being called CJ it takes me a second to realize she's talking about me. Steven mouths the word *Claire* and slinks away with a backward glance at my legs.

We work our way to the center of the dance floor, right underneath the gargantuan papier-mâché snowflake. Before I was one of them, I thought they all danced the same way: cooler than everyone else. But now I realize they each dance differently. Britney alternates her little dance moves with a glare that is either self-conscious or angry. Hip shake. Glare. Shimmy. Glare. Amberly dances with so much hip action I'm worried a teacher will come over. Megan looks beyond cool. She flings her long blond hair around, and throws her hands in the air, and laughs with her head thrown back as she sings along to the music. I just stand there like a moron.

"Why aren't you dancing?" asks Amberly.

"I don't dance."

Britney snickers. "You can't *dance*?"

Megan doesn't laugh.

"B, can you find a boy and make him get us some punch?" she says sweetly.

When Britney exits, she turns back to me. "Dancing is an important life skill. Amberly and I can teach you."

"Yeah!" Amberly nods like a bobblehead. Oh, Lord.

"What about Britney?" I ask, stalling.

A smile forms on Megan's lips. "Do you really want to dance like Britney?"

"No." I look down at my overly large feet. "I've never really tried to dance," I mumble.

"Wait, wait, wait. You've never practiced in front of your mirror?" asks Megan.

"No."

"You don't try to copy the girls in the music videos?" asks Amberly.

"No."

Megan acts like I just told her I have a third eye growing out of the back of my kneecap. "We are totally having a sleepover. Tonight. At my house."

Britney is back with the punch. Well, she's back, and Sam and Glenn are trailing behind her with punch.

"Thanks, boys." Amberly winks at them.

"I can't believe that's you," Sam whispers to me. "No one recognized you at first. All the guys were trying to figure out who the new girl was."

I grin in spite of myself. "You will not believe what happened. I'll call you later," I whisper back.

Glenn hands me a cup of punch. "You look different. I mean, pretty. You look really pretty."

I'm shocked. Glenn Baker, who has up until now treated me pretty much like I'm a boy (despite the fact that we kissed in sixth grade), is red-faced and tongue-tied around me. And he thinks I'm *really pretty*.

"You're right," I say to Megan in disbelief after they leave to rejoin their boy cluster. "Everyone does believe I'm one of you."

"Well, you're not in yet," says Britney.

"But you said . . ."

She shakes her head. "Do you see a necklace around your neck? You have to be initiated first."

"What do I have to do?"

"Whatever we tell you to do."

I am about to say "screw this," and Megan can tell. She pulls me aside.

"Look, we all had to do a dare to get in. It's not that bad. Just do it and get it over with. Please. I really want you to be a Crownie." Megan has the biggest, bluest eyes you've ever seen. It's impossible to say no to them, and she knows it, which is why she's got them trained on me right now. She lowers her voice. "I know I acted like we only picked you because there was no one else, but that isn't true."

"It isn't?"

"Nope. Two weeks ago I saw you fighting with your mom in your driveway. She was trying to make you take dance lessons and you said you wouldn't do it." She hesitates. "I would give anything to be able to stand up to my parents like that. That's when I decided I wanted you to be my best friend."

The girl I saw on the patio is back. This is the Megan I want to be friends with. The real one.

"Okay. I'll do it." We rejoin the other girls. "So, I just have to do a dare?"

Britney opens her mouth, but Megan cuts her off.

"Yes. Just one dare. Give us a second to decide what it is."

The three of them form a huddle, and I stand there in my dress feeling stupid and trying to imagine what sort of public humiliation they're concocting. They're giggling when they turn back to me.

"You have to kiss a boy," says Amberly.

"And you have to say, 'I feel like a snowflake because I've fallen for you,'" says Megan.

I start to feel nauseous. "Who do I have to kiss?"

"We're still working on that part," says Megan.

"What about Eric Masters?" asks Amberly.

Britney gives her an *Are you crazy?* look. "Pass. You know he was Megan's boyfriend in sixth grade."

"Oh, right, I forgot. Sorry."

"What about Michael Shaw?" asks Britney.

"Pass. He has coat-hanger shoulders. It needs to be somebody really good," says Megan. "What about Buck?"

"Pass," I say, and everyone stares at me. "He kissed me in, like, second grade. I want someone new." I shrug like it's no big deal, even though I'd rather gnaw off my own arm than kiss Buck again.

The girls look impressed.

"I knew we picked the right girl," says Megan. "Hey, who's that guy over there?"

She points toward the snack table, which is really just a lunch table with a glittery paper tablecloth.

"Amanda Bell's cousin," replies Amberly. "He's totally yummy. That is such a good call."

Amanda wears a smug smile while her friends vie for the attention of her oh-so-cute cousin.

"If you kiss him, her friends are going to be so pissed," says Megan. She smiles. "He's perfect."

I watch him for a few seconds longer.

"Done."

I take off across the gym floor in long, sure strides that make it pretty obvious to anyone watching me where I'm going. Ordinarily I would be terrified of rejection, but I don't feel like me tonight. I feel like Megan McQueen's new friend. Buoyed by that feeling, I walk straight up to Amanda's cousin, parting the sea of adoring girls who surround him.

"Hi. I'm Claire."

If he thinks it's weird for a girl to walk up and introduce

herself, he doesn't show it.

"I'm Evan."

Amanda and her friends shoot daggers at me with their stares. Evan's buttoned-up-all-the-way-to-the-top shirt and slicked-over hair make me think he might be a goody-goody at his school, but at our school he is fresh meat. He's even cuter up close. He has dark brown hair like Amanda's, but thankfully no snaggleteeth. Now that I'm close enough to count his inch-long eyelashes, I am suddenly shy.

"I feel like a snowflake tonight." I can barely bring myself to say the words. "Because I've fallen for you."

It takes him a minute to process this.

"Wow. That's a pretty bad one."

He laughs, and I join in.

"I know. But I kind of had to say it."

I jerk my chin toward the girls. He sees them watching us and gives me a friendly nod to show he understands.

"I kind of have to do this too."

I wrap one hand behind his neck and give him a quick peck-on-the-lips, blink-and-you'll-miss-it kiss. Actually, I barely remember the kiss at all. What happened after was more important. I remember the half-shocked, half-happy look on his face when I pulled away. I remember the incredulous gasps from Amanda and her friends. But most of all I remember what happened when I waltzed back over to the Crownies.

"That was amazing! So totally hot!" yells Amberly.

"Did you see their faces?" laughs Britney. She squeezes my

shoulder. Now that I've done the dare, all the negativity I was getting from her before has vanished.

"It *was* pretty amazing." Megan gives me a hug. "You're officially one of us now!"

We spend the rest of the night in Megan's basement eating turkey-Brie-raspberry-jam croissants (Megan made them herself—including the raspberry jam—from scratch!) and rehashing the dance. Whose outfits were cute and whose needed help, Steven Lippert's attempt to do the worm, and, of course, The Kiss are the major topics. Then we dance around in our pj's and sing "I Will Survive" into our hairbrushes. (Well, they dance. I mostly hover on the sideline and try not to trip over myself while I mimic them.)

After Britney and Amberly fall asleep, Megan drags her sleeping bag over to mine and tells me how jealous she is of how her college professor parents treat her genius older brother. So I tell her about how my mom focuses all her attention on my perfect big sister. We talk until it's light outside about the places we want to go and things we want to do and the glamorous lives we'll have when we're old enough to leave Pine Bluff. And I finally realize what I was missing in all those years without girlfriends.

chapter
5

The body paint oozes thick and gooey against my fingers. Sam stands in front of me, shirtless, and once again I'm struck by how different he looks. Man boobs—gone. Love handles—gone. Abs—present.

"So, what am I painting?" I ask.

"Paint me orange with a navy E."

"An E?"

"Yeah. I called some guys from the soccer team. We're gonna spell TIGERS," he says. "Oh, and if you want to get creative and paint some black tiger stripes on my arms, that'd be cool too."

I wipe a nickel-sized glob of tangerine-colored paint on Sam's stomach and start smearing it around. When my fingers reach the contours of his abs, I get that fluttery feeling again. I step away abruptly.

"I've got an idea," I say.

"What?"

"You should get the girl you're crushing on to do this at the game. That way she's touching you."

"You think?"

"Definitely." I don't explain to Sam why I'm positive this will work. "Who is she, anyway?"

His eyes are on the floor when he answers. "Amanda Bell."

"Amanda Bell?! You have a crush on Amanda Bell?"

I repeat these words about fifty-seven times on the way to the game. Amanda Bell has fought to become queen of the B group since sophomore year, and she's one of those dying-to-be-popular people who act way meaner than the actual popular people. It's like that with monkeys too. The beta females are always the most aggressive. As soon as I hop out of Sam's truck, he places a firm hand on each of my shoulders.

"No more talking about it now that we're at the game, okay?"

"Done." I pretend to button my lips.

After we get inside, I stop at the concession stand so I can watch Sam in action—I mean, buy cotton candy. Poor guy. Amanda is surrounded by three other girls. He bravely approaches the pack and singles out their snaggletoothed leader. I can't hear what they're saying, but the girls are giggling, and not in a good way.

Then Sam plays his trump card: he whips off his T-shirt.

Amanda is as stunned as I was. She casts covert glances at her friends, and when she sees they too are smiling carnivorous smiles at Sam's abs, she nods in agreement. By the time I pass by with my cotton candy, she's happily rubbing paint all over his stomach. I flash him a hidden thumbs-up, and he grins.

Then I hurry to find a seat before kickoff because, despite how much I make fun of Buck and our football team, I freaking love football. The intensity of the players. The excitement in the stands. Moms clanging cowbells. Old men reliving their glory days as they holler at the boys running around under the stadium lights. It's intoxicating.

The first quarter is pretty uneventful—it's our defense against theirs, and they're both good. But then I see Glenn, our star receiver, tear off down the field. He completely blows past the poor guy who is supposed to be covering him. Buck throws a wobbly rainbow of a pass, and the crowd collectively sucks in their breath. But there's no way. Buck overthrew. Glenn won't be able to . . .

He catches it! He jumps into the air like there's a hidden springboard on the field and, with every muscle in his arm stretching and straining, plucks the ball one-handed and curls it into his gut as he falls back to the ground.

The crowd explodes. I whistle through my fingers and yell, "Yeah, Glenn!" People are screaming for Buck too, which just pisses me off. He threw a crappy pass. He is so lucky he has Glenn to make him look good. Sometimes Buck even throws the ball at the guy on the other team, but Glenn jumps in front of him just in time to intercept it. My dad calls him an offensive cornerback.

The head coach, a skinny, wrinkly, white-haired man who looks exactly like an old rooster (hence his nickname: The Rooster), claps Glenn on the back. The assistant coach, who is fresh out of college and the target of many schoolgirl crushes, stops jumping up and down just long enough to do the same.

We score shortly after Glenn's magical catch, and the game calms down again. I bounce from clique to clique since my three closest friends are busy with pom-poms and herkies.

> **herkie** (noun)
> 1: *One of those jump thingies cheerleaders do when they're
>   excited.*
> 2: *Kicking one leg out to the side so it's parallel with the
>   ground, while simultaneously trying to kick your own
>   ass with your other leg, while simultaneously jumping
>   as high as you can. So it's kind of like a toe touch,
>   except hilarious, and the best part is they have no
>   idea how goofy it looks.*

I squeeze past my ex, Tanner Walsh (Kiss #9), as he bangs away on his drums. For a band guy, he is kind of a player. In the next section over I say hey to Sam and the rest of the T-I-G-E-R-S. Amanda Bell and her friends have taken up roost behind him, and Sam is smiling the goofiest smile. I let Seth Wong, who is the T in TIGERS and also Kiss #13 and Tanner's ex–best friend (not a coincidence), spray my hair with glittery blue hair paint.

A couple minutes later, I get a tap on the shoulder.

"Hey, Claire." Luke has magically appeared by my elbow.

"Hey! I'm glad you made it."

I sneak a glance at the sideline where Megan is cheering to see if she's noticed him yet, but she hasn't. I try not to think about what it means that he sought me out. Try to keep the bubbly feelings scrunched down inside. I've already made up my mind. She can have him. I'll just ignore his lean, muscular, soccer-player body.

"How's the game going?" he asks.

"We're winning! Go Tigers."

He leans close so I can hear him over the noise of the game. "This place is packed. I had to elbow people to get to you in the front row." His deep voice rumbles in my ear, sending a small shiver down my right side. This is going to be harder than I thought.

"Yeah, this town pretty much closes down for football."

I try to concentrate on the game instead of on Luke, filling him in on what he missed so far. We're half watching the game and half making small talk, when Glenn catches a short pass and darts down the field with it. The boy is fast. He sprints past the forty, the thirty. He thinks he's beaten everyone on the other team, but then a defender the size of a wildebeest bulldozes into him. It's one of those hits you can hear from the stands. Everyone cringes and gasps as Glenn goes down and one of his feet bends in a funny direction.

He doesn't get up.

The Rooster and a medic run onto the field. The crowd waits in tense silence. Glenn clutches at his ankle, his face contorting in pain when they prod him. He's able to stand and limp off the field with help, though. The crowd gives him a standing ovation. Everyone remains pretty subdued for the rest of the half, which means Luke and I can actually hear ourselves talk.

"I can't believe I'm finally a senior," he says.

"I know. I can't wait to get away from this place." I notice Buck on the sideline, putting a finger to the side of his nose and blowing a snot rocket onto the ground. "And these people. Well, maybe not everyone. I love my friends. But a lot of people in this town suck."

"I have noticed that some of the people here are . . . different. I'm excited to be done with high school too, though."

"Do you know what you're going to do next year?" I ask. I word the question carefully, because in my family the question isn't "Are you going to college?" it's "Which college are you going to?"—but not everyone is like that.

A dark cloud passes over his face. "I know what my parents want me to do."

"What's that?"

"My dad's been in the military his whole life. He started out as a grunt and worked his way up. With my grades, he's always, 'You have to go to the Academy. Do you know how many advantages you have that I didn't have? Do you know how far ahead that would have put me?' But I don't want to go."

"What do you want to do?"

"That's the thing. I don't know," he says. "Which makes it really hard to argue."

I nod sympathetically.

"I know I don't want to be just like him. I guess I want to go to a school with a lot of different options so I can figure it out."

"I know how that goes," I say.

He looks relieved. "Really?"

"Yeah. I want to do something big to help people medically, like find an early biomarker for cancer or design a prosthetic retina or something. Which means majoring in biomedical engineering. Which means going to Georgia Tech."

"Those all sound like great things. Why would your parents care?"

"Because everyone in my family goes to the University of Georgia. As in the archnemesis of Georgia Tech. If you're not from here, it's hard to explain how big a deal it is."

"No, I get it," he says.

"I still haven't told my family I'm applying." I think about how little my parents seem to notice these days. "Maybe they wouldn't care as much as I think. Things with my family are complicated. My parents—well, my mom—" I'm interrupted by a roar from the stands.

Whoa. I can't believe how close I just came to spilling my family secrets to him. I never talk about my family anymore. When I used to, people would always give me these looks that clearly meant *Don't you know you're supposed to pretend that never happened to you?* so I learned not to.

But he doesn't notice, and we keep up the conversation easily, moving on to much happier subjects. Megan spots us talking mid–toe touch and nearly suffers a cheer-related injury as a result. For the rest of the half, she alternates between shooting Luke sexy glances and me suspicious ones. The result is she looks like one of those women who has been over-Botoxed.

I shake my head at her and shrug my shoulders, trying to get her to understand that I didn't plan for him to come over here. I'm completely innocent in all this. But then a buzzer signals the end of the half, and Luke asks if I want to go to the concession stand. I check the sideline.

Megan is watching.

But he's looking at me with question marks in his eyes, and it seems so silly to say no, so I find myself nodding my head and following him up the stairs. Megan's mouth falls open.

I'm dead.

I mean, I am seriously going to catch hell for this later. I sneak a sideways glance at Luke's dimples. It's worth it.

The line for the concession stand is long because it's half-time. "What was it like living in Germany?" I ask while we wait.

His eyes light up. "One of the best experiences of my life. I got to see all these things I'd read about in books. And I learned how to speak German." He brushes his coppery hair away from his face. "But the best part of living in Europe was we got to visit all the other countries on weekends and holidays because they're all right there. Russia is a train ride away. France is right next door."

I contemplate how wonderful it would be to have France next door instead of Alabama. "That sounds amazing. I would kill to travel to Europe." *Or anywhere that's not here, really.*

"Then we should go."

"Yeah?" *Ohmygosh, he said "we." Wait. Didn't he?*

"Yeah. We could do a backpacking trip. This summer or something. I know how to plan one pretty cheap."

That's an affirmative. He is definitely talking about doing this together, and it isn't just my over-romantic imagination.

"Okay, let's pretend we live in the kind of world where my parents would agree to that. What would we do on this backpacking trip?"

"We'll start off in Germany because I know every place to go there. And in Capri, we'll charter a motorboat so we can go swimming in the Blue Grotto, even though you're not supposed to. And then we'll go to the southern coast of Spain, where we'll drink sangria and stay up all night dancing. And we'll end in Paris, because you have to end in Paris, and I'll take you to the best *macaron* shop, and we'll have a *macaron* feast for breakfast while we sit on the Pont des Arcs and watch the sunrise."

Luke. Wants to go to Europe. With me. And do all that romantic stuff he just said. This whole staying-away-from-him plan? Not going to work. I realize Luke is looking at me and waiting for a response.

"Yes. Yes to all of it. I'm in."

He gives me a wink that sends my heart soaring into the atmosphere. "Assuming we live in the right kind of world?"

"Yeah. Assuming that."

I'm not thinking about my parents, though. I'm thinking

about Megan. I am so totally screwed. Because I am really, *really,* REALLY starting to like this guy. And the more time I spend with him, the more I realize I won't be able to let her have him.

The rest of the game passes in a blur, and Sam finds me when it's over. "Hey, we're going to get pizza at Shorty's now," he says, even though I already know about the pizza plans. He looks pointedly at Luke. "Do you want to come?"

"Sure. Hey, thanks, man."

Sam smiles at me, probably thinking he is paying me back for helping him with Amanda. He probably forgot Megan will be there too. He probably didn't see her glaring at me for the duration of the second half. So he doesn't realize we're headed for an extra-large disaster.

Kiss #5 xoxo

The Summer After Seventh Grade

It never occurred to me how much time and energy girls like the Crownies spend on things like color-coordinated accessories and hair maintenance. It's exhausting. The summer after seventh grade, I get a vacation from being girly in the form of Oak Hills Soccer Camp. For four glorious weeks I can play soccer, hang out with Sam, and not worry about clothes and makeup. When I get to camp, I realize it's swarming with cute soccer-playing boys, but I've taken a stand. I will not break out my makeup until the end-of-camp dance.

My resilience is tested the very first week when I meet Alex Martinez. It's a match made in soccer heaven. He's the best boy at camp. I'm the best girl. Is he the cutest boy? Maybe not. But being good at soccer makes him seem so to a bunch of soccer-obsessed girls. We show off on the field if we spot him on the sideline, take circuitous routes to the dessert station so we can squeeze by his table in the dining hall, and talk about him in our bunk beds after lights-out. So far, all this talking and effort has amounted to absolutely squat. Alex has shown zero interest in any of the girls at camp (although we dissect his every word and gesture for hidden meaning).

Three weeks into camp, I'm having one of those days where you feel like the luckiest person on the planet. To top it off, I score the game-winning goal at the end of the scrimmage.

Could today get any better? I collapse in the warm grass on the sideline and roll around like a puppy. It is the perfect day! I yank off my cleats and grab my flip-flops from my bag.

Underneath them is a small, folded-up piece of notebook paper that I know wasn't in there before. Alex smiles at me from across the field, and chill bumps pop up all over my forearms even though I'm still soaked with sweat from the game. I open the note.

Meet me at your cabin after everyone else goes to dinner.

I read the words again and again to make sure they're real. Then I tear off down the path to the girls' cabins so I can make first shower. Alex Martinez! I have so much to do. The other girls will just die when I tell them. But I'll have to save the news until after. I can't risk one of them giving me away.

I bound up the rickety wooden steps and drag my suitcase out from under my bed. The bottom is littered with all the things I didn't think I would need until the end-of-camp dance: mascara, a blow-dryer, pear-scented body lotion, the one dress and one skirt I brought. But if I use any of this stuff, my bunkmates will know something is up. Girls' voices start funneling in through the screen door, so I run to the shower and yank the plastic curtain closed.

By the time I finish showering, the room is a frenzy of getting ready. No one cares when I pull on soccer shorts and a T-shirt.

No one notices when I wad the makeup and lotion into my towel and step outside. I hop the porch railing and tiptoe behind the bushes lining the side of the cabin. The girls inside jabber on about everything from today's scrimmages to boys to whether we'll get ice-cream sandwiches at dinner tonight. I crouch underneath the window and apply my lotion and makeup. The tiniest bit of mascara and lip gloss is all I'm brave enough to use without a real mirror and Amberly's help.

Even at soccer camp, girls make getting ready a huge ordeal. My muscles ache from being curled up like this. It's Lindsey who's taking forever. If I pull a hammy two days before the tournament because she's taking an hour trying to make her pores look smaller, I'm going to punch her in the face tomorrow. After what seems like an eternity, I hear the last girls leave. I count to one hundred and then hobble around to the front door, rubbing my legs as I go.

I try on my dress. Then my skirt. Then my cutest pair of shorts. Then the skirt again. The dress. Shorts. Skirt. Shorts. I finally settle on the shorts because I don't want to seem like I'm trying too hard, even though I am totally trying my absolute hardest. I'm just shoving everything else back in my suitcase when the door creaks. I nudge my suitcase under the bed with my foot.

Alex stands in my doorway looking cute as ever in a T-shirt and shorts. He's nice and bronzed from playing soccer in the sun, and his eyes are the color of chocolate.

"Hey," I say.

"Hey."

He walks over to the bunk bed and settles beside me on my sleeping bag.

"Nice shot today."

"Thanks."

I think he wants me to do something, but I realize I've never had a boy kiss me before, unless you count that time in second grade. I've been doing all the kissing. So I sit back and wait to see what Alex will do. He watches me for a little while, his black hair falling into his eyes. He pushes it back over and over again, a move that frequently sends girls at camp into fits. But he doesn't speak or move any closer. Hey! I think Alex Martinez is nervous about kissing *me*! Finally, he gulps like a cartoon character and says, "You look pretty."

"Thanks."

He goes from zero to kiss before I know what's happened. One second, he's sitting a foot away from me on my bed telling me I look pretty. The next, we're kissing. And we keep kissing. For a really long time. Longer than I've ever kissed anyone else, anyway. FYI, the world's longest kiss happened at a kissing contest on Pattaya Beach, where this Thai couple kissed for fifty-eight hours and thirty-five minutes. Which sounds wildly romantic until you realize there is no way they went fifty-eight hours and thirty-five minutes without peeing.

After a few seconds, I remember what Megan said about how much cooler it is with your eyes open. So I open them. I see Alex's eyes squeezed tight shut. I see a wrinkle of concentration between his eyebrows. And just past his left ear, I see Sam standing on the porch and staring at me through the screen door, looking like someone ran over his puppy. My eyes open wider. Alex's tongue continues to poke around in my mouth.

"I was coming to get you for dinner," Sam says.

At the sound of his voice, Alex and I jump back from each other like two magnets pushed together at the wrong end. Sam clomps off down the stairs and into the woods. I look at Alex, then to the door.

"I gotta go."

I take off after Sam, leaving Alex sitting on my bed, still shiny and dazed from our kiss. Sam has a head start, but he's got at least seventy pounds on me, and he's lumbering through the trees with all the grace of a seasick rhinoceros. I catch up quickly.

"Sam!"

He ignores me.

"Sam, stop!"

He keeps running.

"We can keep this up as long as you want, but we both know I can run faster and longer than you."

He finally barrels to a stop and slumps with his back against a pine tree. His cheeks are bright red, and there are rings of wetness spreading at the neck and armpits of his green T-shirt.

"What?" he pants.

"What's the matter with you? Why are you acting so weird?"

"Nothing. Just cause I didn't want to stick around and watch you suck face with that pretty boy."

Sam wipes at his sweaty cheeks. It hits me how red and veiny his eyes are, and that pitiful expression from earlier flashes in my head, and I realize he's not just wiping away sweat.

"I—I don't understand." And I don't want to. Because there's only one logical explanation for him crying over me and Alex, and it means the end of me and Sam.

"I ran away because—"

"Sam," I whisper.

"I couldn't stand to see him kiss you because—"

"Don't."

"Because I like you, okay."

And there it is.

"And not just as a friend. And not just as this awesome chick I play soccer with and tell jokes to. I really like you. I want to be the one sitting on your bed kissing you."

I can't even look at him. Why did he have to ruin everything?

He picks at the bark of the tree behind him. "But you'll never feel the same way about me, will you?"

"No," I say sadly.

There's no coming back from this. We'll never be able to act the same, like this never happened. We'll never have our easy comfortable friendship again. I've lost my best friend.

chapter
6

I have never cared so much about a chair. A battered wooden chair with red poppies on the cushion. It is right beside me, and it is empty. And nothing would make me happier than to see Luke sit in it. He said he'd meet up with us for the post-game victory dinner, but he still isn't here.

The seats at our small-tables-pushed-together-to-form-one-long-table at Shorty's pizza joint are filling up fast, and while it may seem like people are sitting at random, don't be fooled. A strategic move for love or popularity is being made with each set of cheeks that hits the cheap plastic cushions. On my left, the empty chair, with my purse on the seat. On my right, Megan, guarding an empty chair of her own.

I grabbed her the second I got to Shorty's, so I could explain what happened with Luke. But then a bunch of other people showed up, and neither one of us wanted to have that conversation in front of half the football team. Megan hissed, "It's fine, Claire. Game on." And we've been covertly guarding our chairs ever since.

"Hey, girl." Britney moves toward Megan's seat.

"Hey." Megan puts her hand on Britney's shoulder and whispers, "There's an empty seat by Buck."

Britney smiles. She sits across from us instead, with her chair angled in Buck's direction. A bell jingles, and Megan and I both glance at the front door to find that this time, it actually is Luke. I move my purse as he approaches the table. Our eyes meet for a second. That's when Megan makes her move.

"Luke! Come sit by me." She pats the chair beside her.

Luke falters midstep. "Uh, sure."

He takes the seat by Megan, and I have to give my empty chair to Amberly. We're waiting for our food when Britney throws a fat envelope onto the table.

"I got my senior pictures back from Palmer's Photography today. They're awful."

I pull the pictures from the package and flip through them one by one. They *are* awful. The poses and everything are overdone and unnatural, almost like those horrible glamour shots that were popular when Sarah was in high school.

"They *are* a little cheesy." I pass them around.

"I think you look great," says Buck.

Britney turns the color of marinara sauce.

"Mine are really bad too," says Megan. "I cannot send pictures like that to my family and friends. I've got to get new ones."

Britney nods. "Yeah, but where? Palmer's is the only place in town."

"I don't know." Megan rests her chin on her hand. "What about Claire's mom?"

My breath catches in my lungs. I would be ecstatic if Mama wanted to take pictures again. After much deliberation over the years, Megan and I have determined that my mom is the key to fixing my family and that photography is the key to fixing my mom. We've had several fruitless plotting sessions on the subject, but this senior-pictures thing could really work. Leave it to Megan to come up with a life-changing idea while we're this close to having a throwdown over a boy.

Of course, taking pictures would involve Mama leaving our house for something other than her support group. Only a few people at the table know about my mom, so I have to answer carefully.

"It's been a while, and she never did senior pictures before, but I could ask her."

"Maybe it could be good," says Megan with equal care.

She means it could be good for my mom, but everyone else thinks she's just talking about pictures. We have an entire conversation with our eyes before I nod and say, "Yeah. Maybe it could."

Then the pizza and pasta come and break up the serious moment no one knew we were having, and the table is back to chattering about tonight's football game and how Buck is the most amazing quarterback ever—blah, blah, blah. The amazing quarterback struts over to the drink machine to refill his Mr. Pibb. On his way back he "accidentally" knocks into Sam's chair.

"Whoops. Sorry, lard-ass."

Sam rolls his eyes. "Yeah, thanks. Not fat anymore."

"Ha-ha. Whatever you say, lard-ass."

Sam sneaks a sideways glance at Amanda to see how she's taking all this. To her credit, she actually ignores Buck. My opinion of her goes up a smidge.

"Be right back. Gotta hit the little girls' room." Megan squeezes Luke's shoulder as she gets up.

I stab at my slice of chicken and artichoke, which is pretty delicious. Shorty's has the kind of pizza that necessitates the use of a knife and fork. Luke slides over into Megan's empty chair, causing me to inhale his scent of soap and something else I can't place but I'm going to call *hot boy*.

"That looks good. Mind if I try a bite?"

I'm startled, but I manage to choke out, "Yeah, sure."

Is it bad that I feel like I've had a lobotomy whenever I look at his eyes? Or his dimples? Or his biceps?

While I'm cutting off a bite, I debate on whether I dare feed it to him. I look over my shoulder and see that Megan is still in the bathroom. I dare. I spear a bite with my fork. With a hand much steadier than the rush of hormones I'm feeling, I bridge the gap between my plate and Luke's mouth. Feeding someone a bite of food can be totally platonic or totally sexy, and Luke makes this a type-two bite exchange. He keeps his eyes locked on mine the entire time, while I slide the fork from his mouth, while he chews his bite of pizza, while he says with a mischievous smile, "That *is* good."

Maintain eye contact. Do not blush. Do *not* blush. I can only hold out for so long, so I'm almost relieved when Glenn comes limping through the door and I can look away.

"Hey, sorry I'm late," he says. "Had to get this ankle checked out after the game. Don't worry, it's just a sprain."

Everyone at the table visibly relaxes, especially the coach—the young one, Coach Davis, not the Rooster. The Rooster would never go out for pizza with us. He's probably at home trimming his ear hair. Glenn plops down in Luke's old chair just as Megan emerges from the bathroom with freshly glossed lips.

"Where'd my seat go?"

"Sorry, girl, this ankle is killing me." He moves to get up.

"It's okay. Maybe I can pull up a chair."

She points a chair toward the six inches of space separating Luke and me.

"Oh, here. Let me make room for you." I scoot toward Luke, leaving a bigger space on my other side.

Megan smiles sweetly. "You know, I don't think there is room." She squeezes between Luke and Glenn and hops on Luke's knee. "You don't mind, do you, Luke?"

Luke tenses and his eyes get big. "No, it's fine."

I can't even compete with that. I think I'm being bold when I hold a fork in front of his mouth, and she goes and sits in his lap.

Coach Davis stands up and clinks his knife against his glass.

"Hey, everyone. We played a *great* game tonight." At this point I stop listening because all I can think about is Megan's hand on the back of Luke's neck (for balance, allegedly), but insert the lame-ass inspirational speech of your choice here. "If we keep this up, I think we've got a real good shot at state this year," he says before sitting back down.

Amberly blinks at him like she's got something in her eyes and flips a sheet of blond hair with pink highlights over her shoulder. Two months ago she had chestnut hair, and before that it was Jessica Rabbit red. "I really liked your speech."

"Thanks," he says. He smiles just a little too big at the compliment.

Ew. I mean, he's in great shape and has a manly jaw, so he's technically good-looking in a grown-man kind of way, but he's twenty-three! I'll have to remember to talk to her about that later, but for now I'm still stuck on the lovebirds snuggled up next to me. Luke's hand has drifted to the small of Megan's back. He looks at me over her shoulder, and I try to pretend I wasn't staring. *Sorry,* he mouths. I smile and shrug like it doesn't matter, but seriously, why does he have his hand there and why isn't he moving it? Thankfully, the dinner is almost over, so Megan only gets to spend about ten minutes in his lap before people start trickling out the door and Luke needs his leg back. I find Sam at the end of the table, canoodling with Amanda Bell. Guess she and Cowboy Hat never worked out their differences.

"Are you about ready to go?"

"Um . . ." He turns red. "Is there any way you could get a ride home with someone else? Amanda and I wanted to go for a drive."

Amanda giggles and squeezes his leg. Oh. That kind of drive.

"Yeah. Of course. You two have fun."

What is the world coming to? Sam isn't supposed to do stuff like go for drives. He's supposed to be asexual like aphids or those lizards we learned about in bio. Luke taps me, and I jump because I didn't realize he was at my elbow.

"If Claire needs a ride home, I can take her."

He's barely gotten the words out before Megan (who has also materialized out of nowhere) says, rapid-fire, "No-it's-okay-I-can-drive-her."

"It's no trouble—"

"Claire lives right across the street from me. It'd be silly for anyone else to drive her."

And with that she's dragging me out the door by the wrist while I look helplessly back at Luke. Minutes later we're alone in her car, snailing along down the poorly lit back roads because out here you never know when a deer might leap in front of your headlights. Megan hunches grandma-style over the steering wheel like she always does on our nighttime rides home.

"So, the stay-away-from-him plan worked out great," she says with a hint of sharpness in her voice.

I hate how it looked like I went for Luke first after agreeing not to. "I'm really sorry. He just showed up and sat by me at the game. I didn't ask him to."

"Where did y'all go at halftime?"

"He asked if I wanted to go to the concession stand with him.

It would have looked weird to say no. Nothing happened," I add. Yet.

Megan seems satisfied with this answer. She shrugs. "It's fine. I wasn't going to be able to stay away from him either."

I'm relieved that she isn't mad at me, but it still doesn't solve our problem.

"This almost wrecked our friendship last time," I say softly. I stare out the window at the skinny pine trees spiked into little cliffs of red Georgia clay. "I know it would be better if we both backed off. But I don't think I can."

"Me neither."

For a while, the only sound is the hum of Megan's engine and the scrape of her tires on the less-than-recently paved road.

"What if we let Luke decide?" I ask.

"Luke?" she says, like we've just discovered he actually has a say in all this.

"Yeah. We can flirt all we want, but he has to initiate the first date or kiss or whatever, and no matter who he picks, we'll both be okay with it."

"I can live with those rules."

"Then it's a deal."

I'm happy. Because I know Luke will pick me. And because (stupid me) it never occurs to me Megan will fight dirty.

Kiss #6 _{xoxo}

Eighth Grade

When you're in eighth grade, kissing is fraught with peril. First of all, you have to hide your emotions, because the earth would fly off its axis if anyone figured out who you have a crush on. Acting logically, say by walking up to the boy you like and telling him you like him, is a big no-no. So you have to resort to the most infinitesimal of hints and hope that in some sort of dating butterfly effect, you'll land a boyfriend and have a regular kissing partner.

And second, even if you do have a boyfriend (like me!), you're in eighth grade, which means you have absolutely no privacy. Seriously. Eric Masters has been my boyfriend for one month, two days, and four hours, and we still haven't kissed! (We had one nanosecond alone, and I totally choked.) But that's all about to change.

Amberly and I talk kiss strategy while we sit in mismatched lawn chairs on the back porch of her trailer. She has to babysit, so we watch her little brother and his best friend play a redneck version of clay shooting with a BB gun and some empty beer cans.

"My parents won't let me go on a real date until I'm *six*teen," I whine.

"Lame."

"I know. And it's not like we can drive, so that eliminates

most of the normal places and situations where you might have a first kiss."

"There are lots of places you can kiss," says Amberly. "You just have to get creative."

"Like where?"

She twirls a strand of espresso-colored hair around her finger. That girl is always dyeing her hair. "Like . . . behind the equipment shed near the football field. Under the stage in the assembly room—Glenn loves that one. In the girls' bathroom on the back hallway—just use the handicapped stall; no one will ever see you."

"Amberly!" My face flushes even though hers doesn't.

"What? I like kissing."

"I'm sure the handicapped stall is a great place to kiss. But I really wanted my first kiss with my first real boyfriend to be special. I don't want it to feel like we're sneaking around or doing something dirty."

"Why not?" Amberly giggles when I make a face. "Kidding."

We go back to watching "clay shooting." Every few minutes one of the kids yells "Pull!" even though they're just throwing the cans in the air for each other.

"Hey." Amberly's eyes light up. "What do you mean by 'real date'?"

"I can't go anywhere alone with a boy. Until I'm an old maid. Ugh."

"But what about if other people are there?"

I frown. "I think that's okay. We went to the football game

with his parents last Friday. They were watching us the *whole time*, though," I say like it was an atrocious invasion of privacy because, you know, IT WAS.

Amberly shrugs. "Course if it was me, I'd just have Glenn come home from school with me and make out. My mom drops him off at his house when she gets back from work."

"I can't believe your mom doesn't care if you have a boy over when she's not home."

The look on Amberly's face makes me wish I'd just shut up. "Not everyone's parents are like yours," she says quietly.

For a few minutes, we listen to the ping of steel pellets meeting aluminum.

"Oh! I have the perfect plan." Amberly sits up straight in her lawn chair. The wild grin on her face makes me nervous, but I need to get kissed already.

"Tell me."

"Glenn lives up the street from you, right?"

"Yeah . . ."

"So, I'll spend the night at your house this Friday, and Eric will spend the night at Glenn's."

"And how does this translate to me kissing Eric?"

"We sneak out."

"Are you crazy?! My parents are like ninjas. We'll totally get caught. The stairs are super creaky, and the alarm system will beep if we open the door."

"Okaaay. So, we tell your parents we want to have a campout, and we pitch a tent in your backyard. We've done it before. Then Glenn and Eric will do the same thing."

I'm totally panicked, but I blurt out, "That could work. That's genius."

Amberly smiles. "I know. But the key is you don't tell your parents the boys are camping out too. Otherwise they'll know something's up."

So far, the plan is working. Our campout sleepover is set. So is the boys'. Amberly and I can't look at each other on Friday without giggling. It's all we can talk about at lunch, and we rattle on and on until Megan and Britney look seriously annoyed.

After school, Amberly and I walk to the turnaround to meet my dad, staggering under the weight of our book bags. The teachers at our school give so much homework you'd think they were part of a worldwide conspiracy to give eighth graders scoliosis.

"Ohmygosh," I say. "Guess what Eric just said to me."

"What?"

"He said, 'See you *tonight*,' and he winked at me."

Amberly grabs my hands, and we jump up and down screaming.

"This is going to be the best night ever!" she yells.

I see my dad's green SUV and shush her.

"Hey, Daddy."

We climb into the middle seats that make me feel like an airplane pilot.

"Hey, Claire-Bear. Look in the bag."

I rustle around in the canvas grocery bag at my feet. "Bananas and guacamole?"

He laughs. "That's for your mom. The other bag."

The other bag contains hot dogs and everything you need to make the perfect s'more.

"Thanks, Mr. Jenkins," says Amberly. "I am sooo excited about the campout."

She bursts into a fit of giggles, and I kick her.

"What are the bananas and guacamole for?" she asks.

"Mama has *cravings*."

"They get weirder every month," says Daddy. "But as long as she doesn't dip the bananas in the guacamole, I'm okay with it."

We pitch the tent as soon as we get home. We borrow Sarah's because it's purple and has a ceiling fan (she refused to go on family camping trips until my parents bought it). My dad sets up the fire pit and repeats fire-pit safety instructions I've heard, like, a hundred and fifty times. Roasting things on sticks only keeps us occupied for so long, though.

"Is it midnight yet?" whines Amberly.

"Um, no. It's still daylight."

"Ugh. I cannot wait to make out with Glenn."

The boys are under strict instructions not to come within ten feet of my house until midnight, when we're pretty sure my parents and Glenn's will both be asleep. We change into our pj's, me into a fitted tee and soccer shorts, Amberly into a low-cut tank top and Soffes rolled over at the waistband until they barely cover her butt. We take magazine quizzes to find out which

Hollywood starlet we would be BFFs with and whether Glenn and Eric are our soul mates. Libby storms the tent and tries to join our sleepover, but I banish her to the house, and then my parents make me apologize for making her cry.

"Little brothers and sisters are *so* annoying."

"Tell me about it," says Amberly.

"I can't believe my mom is having another one. And she's forty-one! I don't want a smelly little brother to babysit."

"It's the worst. All I ever do is babysit." Amberly flips her magazine shut and tosses it back in the pile. "What time is it now?"

"Nine forty-five," I reply. "Hey, we could write notes to them while we wait."

"Yeah. Let's do that," she says, so I run to my room to get stationery and markers.

"'Dear Glenn,'" Amberly reads aloud as she writes in blue marker with her bubbly handwriting. "'I can't wait to make out with you in two hours and fifteen minutes. XOXO, Amberly. P.S. I think you're hot.'"

My letter to Eric is not so bold:

Dear Eric,
What's up? NMH. Amberly and I just finished making s'mores, and now we're counting down the hours till we get to see you.

♥

Claire

After we finish writing, we spend huge amounts of time putting on lipstick and making kiss marks. We practice on a blank piece of paper to make sure we get them just right. Amberly has Angelina Jolie lips, so her kisses look like they could eat mine.

"Ew. Don't open your mouth so big on your kisses."

"Why?" She looks at me slyly.

"I don't know. It looks slutty or something."

"Because it looks like a blow job?"

"Amberly!" I pretend to be scandalized, even though I secretly want to know anything she has to tell me.

"Have you ever given one?" she asks.

"No. And I never would!"

"I would. I'm going to let Glenn touch my boobs tonight."

I gasp. "Over the shirt or under?" The nuances are very important here.

She shrugs. "We'll see."

We can't bear to wait until midnight, so we tiptoe out of our tent around eleven, hop the fence in my backyard, then sneak along the other fences until we get to Glenn's. Leaves and twigs crackle and snap under our feet as we creep up to the boys' tent. I can see Glenn's brown curls and Eric's copper-colored shag through the triangle of light that makes up the tent's doorway. They sit hunched over handheld video games with their backs toward us. All that zapping and beeping covers the sound of our approach. At the last second, Amberly and I rush the sides of the tent and pound against them with our fists.

Swearing fills the tent and the boys stumble out. We

exchange awkward hi's all around.

"So, we just wanted to give you these," says Amberly.

"We better go in case my parents check on us."

We hand them the notes before scurrying back into the woods.

Ten minutes later, the boys are at the door of our tent with notes of their own. We grow braver and braver with every note swap. We stray farther, stay longer. We don't know this is practice for the nights we'll sneak out Amberly's window and steal her mom's beat-up Volkswagen for a joyride. Amberly gets bored with writing and wants action. So at the bottom of the next note she scrawls, *P.S.—Meet us behind Claire's dad's shed at 12:07.*

"But it's twelve o'clock right now," I say.

"Exactly. We better hurry."

We tear through the woods to the boys' campout, hopping fences and tripping over tree roots in the moonlight. When we reach their tent, we chuck the notes inside, giggling, and run away. We don't stop until we're back in my yard, where we lean against the shed and wait, panting and whispering.

My heart races—from the run and because of what I hope will happen next. After a few minutes, we hear leaves rustling by the fence. Amberly squeezes my wrist and grins.

"Claire?" Eric's whisper winds through the trees.

"We're over here," I say back.

Eric and Glenn start to take shape in front of us.

"Hey, girls," says Glenn. "What's the urgent meeting about?"

"Come inside the shed with me, and I'll show you," Amberly says in the low, sexy voice she uses in front of boys. "See you guys."

She winks at Eric and me and drags Glenn through the door into the shed. I'm glad it's dark tonight, because I can feel my cheeks turning bright pink, partly because of Amberly and partly because I am alone with Eric for the first time.

"Hey." I kick at the dirt with my Pumas.

"Hey," he says.

A giggle echoes inside the shed, so we walk farther into the backyard, and I lean against my pear tree. My parents do this thing where they plant a fruit tree each time they have a kid. A Shenandoah pear for me. A Belle of Georgia peach for Sarah. A Hollywood purple-leaf plum for Libby. I like to think our trees mean something. Peaches are fussy trees that require lots of care. Pears are easy to grow. Strong and resilient.

Eric takes a step closer. So close I can see his green eyes have a gold ring around the edges. This is it! I must look scared, because he says, "I won't kiss you if you don't want me to."

Isn't he the sweetest? "I don't mind," I say.

I know, I know, I'm *dying* for him to kiss me, but I'm trying to play it cool, okay? Apparently that was all the encouragement he needed, because before I can blink, we're kissing. And it is. The. Best. Kiss. Ever. It's my first kiss with any feelings behind it. And now all the anticipation leading up to this moment and all my feelings for Eric flow through our open mouths like it's some kind of emotional energy transfer. It's a rush that spreads to the tips of my toes. After that first kiss, we kiss again and again, each time creating another jolt of magical energy. They say people in France call French kisses *soul kisses*. I am certain by the way he is kissing me that Eric is kissing me with his whole soul.

Later, when the boys are gone and we're tucked into our sleeping bags, Amberly pounces on me. "How was it?"

"Amazing."

"It was so hot making out in the shed. I mean, the saws and drills and axes hanging from the walls kind of made me feel like I was in a horror movie, but when Glenn pushed me on top of your dad's workbench, it was awesome. For a second I thought he was gonna screw me, and then my life would be over—"

"*What?*" I'm not ready to even think about doing anything but kissing. Okay, maybe I sometimes *think* about things, but I would never, ever do them. Plus, it sounds like she doesn't think she has a choice in the matter. "Do you *want* to have sex with him?"

"No."

"Well. Then, why would you? I mean, you don't have to."

"I don't know. I guess I'm worried he'll break up with me if I don't. I feel like I have to do stuff with boys or they'll leave me . . . but they always end up leaving me anyway."

She doesn't add *like my dad*, but I know we're both thinking it.

Amberly shrugs. "So, how were things with Eric?"

I lie back against my pillow and gaze dreamily at the purple ceiling fan.

"I think I might love him."

I'm addicted to kissing. It's all I want to do—every second I'm with him. And when I'm not, it's all I can think about until the next time we're together. The average person spends 20,160 minutes of their lifetime kissing, and I swear Eric and I are trying to squeeze all those minutes into a few weeks. We try lots of Amberly's suggestions. Now that the first kiss is out of the way, I'm not particular. We even find a few places of our own.

"Amberly, you have to try the stairs that lead down to the gym," I say, as soon as I squeeze into a chair beside her at lunch. "No one is ever there if you get a hall pass at the same time and meet up."

"Score. Maybe I'll take Glenn there this afternoon."

Megan rolls her eyes when she thinks I can't see. She and Britney don't have boyfriends right now.

"Can we puh-lease talk about something else besides kissing?" she asks.

Jealous.

"Isn't he your first boyfriend?" Britney looks sideways at Megan. They've been thick as thieves since I started going out with Eric.

I pretend not to notice her tone. She's been nice to me ever since I officially became a Crownie, but every now and then a sharpness slips into her voice. "Yeah. He's great. I'm so lucky we found each other. He's, like, the perfect guy."

Megan sighs and pokes at her salad.

"Are you okay?" I ask.

"Yeah. I'm fine."

She doesn't look fine. Maybe she's really bummed about not having a boyfriend right now. I hope it doesn't have anything to do with Eric—she's always seemed so okay with him being my boyfriend. Or maybe she's been fighting with her parents about school again. Bs are unacceptable in the McQueen family. Toward the end of lunch, Eric stops by our table and gives me a back rub. My chewing slows until I'm holding a Tater Tot almost stationary between my back molars. I totally can't eat while he's touching me.

"How's it going?" he asks Megan.

"Good. Everything is really awesome."

She smiles at him, and they talk about how his big brother went to the carnival last night.

After school, Britney and I hang out at Megan's house because Britney is spending the night with her. Megan is back to normal—for a while.

"We have to ride the Ferris wheel when we go to the carnival tonight," says Britney.

"Oh! You guys are going to the carnival. That's so cool. I want to go."

Megan raises her eyebrows at Britney.

"Do you want to go all four of us?" I ask.

Megan picks nonexistent lint off her lavender bedspread. "Um. Let me go ask my mom."

She shuffles to the door and leaves the room as slowly as humanly possible.

"I'm sure she'll say yes," I tell Britney. "This'll be awesome."

The carnival is one of those caravan ones that come to town every year with dilapidated rides held together by paper clips and a prayer. Everyone knows someone whose cousin's friend's nephew died in a tragic accident on one. And there are weird things like pig races and stands selling cotton candy and funnel cakes. I can almost taste the powdered sugar and fried batter.

Megan's door opens again, but she just stands there like she doesn't want to enter the room. "Um. My mom says I can only have one friend come to the carnival with me and spend the night. So, I guess it'll just be me and B."

She says all this with her eyes fixed somewhere around my chin. A tense and awkward silence follows.

"Oh. Um, okay."

I think it's weird for her mom to make such an arbitrary decision—plus, I thought she liked me. I think it's weird that Megan is sitting on her bed looking guilty and uncomfortable instead of storming around the room calling her mom a controlling witch. I think it's weird that this all feels very personal in a way I can't pinpoint.

"Well, see you guys later," I say. "Have fun tonight."

Megan still can't seem to look me in the eye. "We will," she says quietly.

I trudge home with the nagging feeling I've missed something important.

chapter
7

I wake up the Saturday after the football game with my stomach in knots because I know I should ask my mom about senior pictures today. It really is a great idea. Quite possibly *The* Idea. Our only shot. I pad down the hallway to her bedroom. She's probably not awake yet, though. I should eat breakfast first. Yeah, I'll cook pancakes for Libby and me. Then I'll talk to Mama.

Libby and I spend most of the morning making chocolate-chip pancakes, flipping them on the griddle as soon as bubbles pop up around the edges and drawing happy faces with whipped cream and extra chocolate chips. We make way too many and give my dad the rejects. Afterward, I clean the kitchen from floor to ceiling. And then, of course, I have to tidy up my room as well, and paint my toenails, and finish a paper that isn't due until next week.

I finally enter my mom's bedroom at 2:00 p.m. She's still in bed. Not promising. I tie open the thick curtains, and light floods the room like an unwelcome intruder, highlighting Mama's tangled brown hair and the half moons dark as bruises under each eye.

"What are you doing?" She throws an arm over her face.

"I, um, I wanted to spend some time with you."

"Today is a bad day. I'm not feeling well."

"Oh."

Talking to my mom is not going to happen today. On bad days, food goes uneaten, clothes go unchanged, and promises go unkept. I hover by her bed for a few more seconds, but then I chicken out and creep down to the basement, where her studio used to be. Still is, I guess. Her equipment is still there—set up, untouched, and covered in a thick layer of dust.

When I give everything an initial wiping with a rag, dust particles fill the air in nose-tickling, sneeze-producing puffs. I sweep the painted cement floor of its dirt, fuzz, and the occasional desiccated insect carcass. Then I start in on the walls. They're covered in photographs of other people's babies: chubby babies, teeny babies, babies that are smiling and jolly, and babies that are crying and red-faced. It's no wonder she could never come back down here. I wipe down each one, wrap it in newspaper, hide them by the stack in cardboard boxes, and then hide the boxes.

On Sunday, I know I have to try again. I lean against the wall outside my parents' bedroom with my palms pressed against my eyes. "You can do this. You can do this. You can do this," I whisper to myself. I try not to think about how the next few minutes could change our lives, because if I do I'll completely lose it. One day. One goal. Get Mama to take pictures.

It's 10:00 a.m. The covers are still pulled tight around her head, but that's normal. My dad's side of the bed is smooth and pristine—he usually ends up falling asleep on the couch in his office. When my eyes adjust to the darkness, I weave through the room and peel back the comforter.

"Mama?"

"Mmm-hmm . . ." She tries to pull the comforter back over her head, so I sit on it.

"It's ten o'clock. How about you get up and have some breakfast? I'll make you something."

"Not right now, sweetie. Maybe in a little while."

She rolls away from me, but I don't move.

"Everyone's getting their senior pictures made at Palmer's. But they look terrible. And Megan and I, we were thinking, maybe you could take some pictures."

"Take pictures?" She turns to me, surprised. "But I haven't done that in years. And I never took senior pictures anyway."

"That's okay," I say quickly. "Megan could come over, and you could just try it. This afternoon?"

"I don't think so."

I can see her slipping away. But I won't let it happen again. I grip the comforter in clenched fists and take a deep breath. In a house where people don't talk about things, I am about to drop a bomb. "Please, Mama, we . . . we need you. I know losing Baby

Timothy was the most horrible thing that's ever happened to you, but Libby and I are still here, and we need you to be our mom. I want you to be you again. I thought if you took pictures, it would help."

Mama's eyes grow wide. She hugs her arms across her chest as if she's trying to protect herself.

"Claire, I—"

"Please." My voice shakes with my desperation. It shuts down whatever excuse was forming in her mind.

"I guess I could think about it," she says slowly. But I feel like she's just saying it to make me feel better. Or so I'll stop talking about it. "Not today, though. I'm too tired."

I know what that means. That means never. I have to make this happen now.

"You can't back out. She's already coming over."

"She is?" Mama always did feel the need to impress Megan, and I can see her wavering.

"Yes." It's a lie, but I can make it true with a thirty-second phone call.

She gets in the shower, and I call Megan (that is, I squeal into the phone about how excited I am that my mom is going to take pictures again). Megan squeals back and promises to come over in a couple hours. I help my mom put on her makeup. Then we head down to her studio, where I help her get her equipment ready. Her cheeks turn pink from the exertion, and I can't remember the last time I saw her look so healthy.

We're just setting up an area with a backdrop for formal

pictures when Megan appears with several outfit choices draped over her arm. She thrusts an envelope at my mother.

"Look how awful these are, Miss Lily. You have to help me."

As my mom flips through the pictures, her nostrils flare the tiniest bit, and I start to hope. She shifts from foot to foot, hesitating, but the bad pictures are taunting her, and she can't not fix them. She can't say no. I am in love with those bad pictures.

Mama takes the formal pictures of Megan first. I act as her assistant, making minute changes to the lighting, adjusting the binder clips on the black drape wrapped around Megan's midsection. I can't believe the metamorphosis taking place in my mom. With each passing minute, she becomes more sure of herself. The intensity seeps back into her eyes.

It's working! I can't even process all the emotions I'm feeling, and as a result I teeter somewhere between happy tears and giddy laughter. On the inside, that is. On the outside I am calm and serene, because the last thing I want is to ruin today with some stupid emotional outburst. But everything goes fine.

Over the next few days, I find Mama at her computer every now and then, editing the photos with a small smile on her face. Then she spends two days in a row in bed, and I'm certain that's it. Our photography rehabilitation plan was a failure, and she's lost for good. But the very next day, when I mention doing some casual shots with Megan, a sigh in my voice, she actually wants to. Just like that.

We try some pictures of Megan at school, posed in her cheerleading uniform on the bleachers and by the goalpost. We try some on the swing set in Megan's backyard. The pictures are all obnoxiously beautiful because they're of Megan, but something is missing. Mama sees it too, and she's fired up by the challenge.

"What's your favorite thing to do in the whole world?" she asks Megan.

"Cook," Megan answers instantly.

"Can I take some pictures of you cooking?"

"Sure. I have to make cupcakes for the cheerleading squad's bake sale tomorrow. Would that work?"

Fifteen minutes later we're in Megan's kitchen, Mama snapping photo after photo while Megan whips up cupcake batter and icing—from scratch, of course. No Duncan Hines for this girl. Mrs. McQueen enters the kitchen as Megan eases a rack of cupcakes from the oven. As usual, Megan's mom has on zero makeup, and her unruly blond hair is held in place with a pencil.

"Mmm. What is that smell?"

"Cupcakes. You want one?"

"Oh, yes."

Megan ices a cupcake and hands it over. "You have to eat it fast, though. They're still warm enough to melt the icing."

Her mom peels back the paper and takes a big bite. "This is delicious." She finally notices my mom and the camera. "What are you guys doing?"

"Miss Lily's taking my senior pictures. Because, you know, the first batch was so bad."

"Oh, right. That's great."

I breathe a sigh of relief when she doesn't make a big deal about it.

"Hey, that reminds me. We need to work on your college applications this weekend. Come find me in a couple hours so I can read your essays, okay?"

"Um, yeah. Sure."

Mrs. McQueen flicks her cupcake wrapper into the trash and walks out of the room.

"You still haven't told them about culinary school, have you?" I whisper after she's gone.

"Are you kidding? They're having a hard enough time dealing with the fact that my reach schools were David's safety schools. I figured I could apply to them both at the same time and work it out later."

"When are you—?"

"Have you finished sending in all your applications?" Her eyes flick toward my mom.

Touché. I still haven't told my parents I want to go to Tech and not Georgia.

"Yeah, pretty much."

There's an awkward silence.

"Do you girls want to keep taking pictures?" Mama asks.

"Yes!" we answer at the same time. And that concludes our conversation about colleges and life plans. Whew.

Megan plucks an apple-cider cupcake from the first rack.

"They're finally cool enough to ice."

She dips her spatula into a bowl of cinnamon buttercream

and slathers it on, getting some on her fingers in the process. Mama snaps a picture of her face as she licks the icing off the end of her index finger. I peek over her shoulder at the camera screen. The look on Megan's face is a mixture of satisfaction, joy, and pride at her accomplishment. It's a look that's mirrored on my mom's face.

Kiss #7 xoxo

Eighth Grade

I check my cell phone for the nineteenth time this morning. Eric hasn't called me all weekend. We usually spend every night on the phone, talking until we can't think of anything else to say and then listening to each other breathe. But I haven't gotten so much as a text or IM since school on Friday, even though I called him Saturday night at half-hour intervals.

I run upstairs to tell Mama I'm going over to Megan's. I haven't seen her since her sleepover with Britney. I kind of figured she would have come over to hang out by now. My parents' bedroom is empty, but the shower water taps out a beat against the bottom of the tub and steam slips through the crack in the bathroom door.

"Mama?"

No answer. I step toward the bathroom and push the door open a little more, averting my eyes because my naked six-months-pregnant mother is not something I want to see, now or ever.

"Mama?"

"Claire."

The pitiful rasping sound of her voice makes me feel like someone dumped a bucket of ice water on my soul. Her body is hunched against the side of the shower. More blood than I've ever seen in my life puddles beneath her before it mixes with the shower water and swirls down the drain. Her hair sticks to her face and neck in wet clumps, and she is pale, so pale.

"Claire, go get your dad."

I tear down the stairs. When I throw open the front door, the buzzing sound of my father's lawn mower fills the air. I sprint toward the noise, yelling and waving my arms, and he releases the mower handle at the sight of me. The blades sputter to a stop.

"Something's wrong with Mama!" I shout. "She's in your bathroom."

He takes off toward the door without answering.

"I'll call 911."

I whip out my cell phone and dial. 9-1-1. It's ringing. And ringing. *Don't you know my mom could be dying?* I almost yell. Finally a click.

"Hel—"

"My name is Claire Jenkins. I live on 605 Turncrest Lane. I need an ambulance. Now. It's my mom. She's six months pregnant and something happened. There's a lot of blood." I manage to choke it all out, but my voice cracks on the word *blood*.

My legs buckle. I'm sitting on the grass. I somehow stay on the line, but everything after goes by in a blur. I know an ambulance comes to take away my parents. I know a second later Sam's mom pulls up, scoops Libby and me into a bear hug, and brings us to her house.

Sam knows just what to do. When I crawl across the bedroom floor and lay my head on his chest, he stiffens, but only for a second. Then he puts a hand on my shoulder and listens. As I pour out the whole terrifying experience of finding my mom. As I confess how guilty I feel because I said I didn't want a little brother. After a minute, I feel the lightest feathery feeling against my hair. So light at first I can't tell if I'm imagining it. But with each stroke of my hair, his hand is steadier. I realize I can hear his heartbeat, and it sounds like it might beat right through his T-shirt.

"Your heart's beating so fast."

"Is it?" he asks, and I feel it go even faster. "I guess I'm thinking about a lot of serious stuff right now."

I nod. "Me too."

I say prayer after silent prayer while I'm curled up against Sam. I'm so glad we were able to work our way back to our normal friendship after soccer camp (Gradually. Painstakingly. Over many months.), because I don't know what I'd do without him right now. After what seems like hours, my dad calls, and I take the phone with shaking hands.

"Your mama will be okay" is the first thing he says. I let out a deep breath. "You'll be able to visit her after school tomorrow. But . . . I don't know about Baby Timothy. Pray for him, Claire-Bear. Pray very hard."

My dad crying is the scariest thing I've ever heard. It means the world as I know it is spinning out of control. But even so, I can't cry. I've never had to cope with something this big, so I keep it swallowed down inside.

* * *

When I walk into school the next morning with Sam, I try to avoid everyone I know on the way to my locker.

"Hey, Claire. I am so sorry," says Amanda Bell, who has the locker next to mine.

She gives me a pity smile and pats me on the shoulder while I shove some books onto my locker shelf.

"For what?" How could she know?

"You mean you don't know yet?"

She smiles again, but this time it's more smile, less pity. I seriously doubt she knows anything life-shattering.

"Amanda, I have no idea what you're talking about."

I slam my locker shut. I am so tired of girl drama. I have real things to worry about. I couldn't give a crap if someone called me a bitch or bought the same shoes as me or whatever Amanda is going on about.

"Well," says Amanda, who seems determined to milk this moment. "I just can't believe Megan would do that to you," she calls over my shoulder.

A bolt of fear shoots down my spine, but I keep walking. What did Megan do?

When I round the main hallway, I know exactly why Amanda was pretending to feel sorry for me. The first thing I see is their hands. His hand. Her hand. Their fingers wound up together like laces on a shoe. I almost don't believe it, but there they are, prancing down the hall together like he isn't my boyfriend. And holding hands!

Everyone else in the hallway stares, first at their hands, then at my face. Like they're waiting for us to have a Wild West showdown.

I take two steps in their direction before veering into the girls' bathroom. All I can think is, *But that's* my *boyfriend.* Amberly and Britney burst through the door behind me.

"OMG! Are you okay?" asks Amberly.

"I don't understand. Why is he holding hands with her?" It is almost a relief to let this drama consume me. To let it be the only thing I think about at school today.

"She's his girlfriend," says Britney.

"This is cuh-razy," says Amberly. She puts her arm around me.

"Since when?" I try to think of the last time Eric and I were together. "He was my boyfriend at lunch on Friday."

Britney winces. "Since Friday night. When I spent the night at her house, we went to the carnival with him and his friend. Eric and Megan got stuck at the top of the Ferris wheel, and she told him how much she missed being his girlfriend, and then she kissed him."

My jaw hits the floor. "She stole my boyfriend?"

"Technically, you stole hers," replies Britney. "They went out in sixth grade. So you can't be mad at her."

I don't know if I will ever understand how girl code works. I wait for Megan to come into the bathroom and apologize, but it doesn't happen. When I work up the nerve to venture into the hallway, Megan and Eric are talking by his locker, and all of eighth grade is still watching. Their eyes burn into me as I walk up to Megan, still in a handhold with *my* boyfriend, and ask, "Did you really do what B said?"

Megan's lips purse. She gets a hurt look in her eyes like *I've* done something to *her* by confronting her about it.

"Yes. Eric and I still have feelings for each other."

"Oh."

Eric, of the feelings, is looking everywhere except at me. I don't know what I expected from them, but this isn't it. I feel like such an idiot. Whispers rustle like insect wings in every corner. Everyone is laughing at me, or worse, pitying me. Anger and hurt well up inside me like competing storm fronts. I rush to the nearest exit and shove the door open. How could he do this to me? How could *she* do this to me? I wander to the bleachers in front of the football field and plop down. A few minutes later, Steven Lippert appears. Normally I would tell him and his stupid tuba to get lost, but today I'm too upset to care.

"This always happens," I say, half to myself, half to Steven.

"What does?"

"Boys always choose her over me. They always like her better."

I cover my face with my hands and cry through my fingers. My life is so much more screwed up than that, but this pain is a manageable pain. If I give in to the other kind, it might be stronger than I know how to handle. He pries my hands away and holds them over my lap.

"I like you *much* better. And I think you're prettier than her too."

"You do?" My voice comes out pathetic and squeaky. I gaze up at him like he's the sole source of hope left in the world.

"Much."

Steven scoots closer and kisses me, his hands still holding mine in between our stomachs. He leans me against the bleachers like he knows what he's doing. And I let him. His words and his confidence make me forget what he looks like and what I think about him—before and during the kiss. But as soon as our lips pull apart and my eyelids flutter open, it hits me.

I have kissed Steven Lippert.

I take in Steven's greasy brown hair, the constellation of acne covering his forehead, and the orange chunks stuck in his braces. I remember reading somewhere that a kiss transfers from ten million to one billion bacteria, and it occurs to me that my mouth tastes faintly of Cheetos. It is all I can do not to projectile vomit.

I make the face girls make in horror movies when they expect to see their one true love but instead see a flesh-eating monster. Then I run away from the bleachers like a legion of zombies is chasing me. When I reach the edge of the field, I cut through the woods to avoid the rent-a-cop, and even when I hit the main road, I keep running. All four miles home. I fling open the front door, my hair sticking out every which way, my face red and tear-stained, to find my big sister Sarah playing Candyland with Libby on the living room floor.

"Hey. I drove home from Athens this morning and checked Libby out of school. I'm staying the whole week," Sarah says.

I sink onto the rug in front of her. I love that Sarah doesn't mention that I'm not supposed to be home from school yet or that I look like I've had a run-in with a leaf blower.

The next day, my dad takes us to the hospital to see Mama and Timothy. At the entrance to the Neonatal Intensive Care Unit (I learn pretty quickly it's called the NICU), Daddy pauses.

"Are you ready?" he asks.

I nod.

He nods back and kisses me on the top of my head. "You're my one, Claire-Bear."

Then we stand over the sink and scrub scrub scrub our hands with soapy water until they're pink and shiny. I put on a yellow hospital gown, gloves, and a mask and follow my dad inside. Sarah and Libby are staying with Mama because Libby isn't allowed to see Timothy yet. They can't risk exposing a micro preemie to her little-kid germs, and also it might be too much for her.

Now that I'm inside, I'm glad Libby stayed back. The NICU gives me the same uneasy feeling I get when we sing Christmas carols at the nursing home. All the bodies, hooked up to the machines, fighting to stay alive. That scares me. But if it's scary to me, I can't even imagine what it's like for Timothy. I have to be brave for him.

I take a deep breath and hold my dad's gloved hand for courage—as long as he's here, I can handle this—and we weave past beeping monitors and nurses with clipboards. They talk about things like "surfactant" and "bilirubin," and I file away the words to be googled later. I peer into Timothy's incubator. Everywhere there are tubes. A tube that carries food through his nose and into his stomach. A tube that disappears into a hole in his throat and pumps his lungs for him. The spaces on his fragile body that are covered with tubes and monitors outnumber the spaces where skin peeks through.

He doesn't even look like a real baby. More like a doll. A two-pound doll with waxy red skin, arms and legs no thicker than my fingers, a fine coating of hair, and eyes that are still fused shut.

He's beautiful.

I pull out the smiling pictures of our family Dad asked me to bring and tape them to the sides of his incubator so he won't feel so alone. Then I reach my hand through one of the holes and rest a few fingers on top of his head.

"Hi, Timmy. I'm Claire. I'm your sister," I say. And after my dad walks away to talk to a nurse, I whisper, "Fight hard, because we love you."

chapter
8

I throw my arm around Sam's shoulder and in the process practically clobber him with the coffee cups I'm holding. "Guess what!"

He ducks, and some of the coffee spills through the little spout in the lid onto the pavement next to his car. "You're not coordinated enough to hug someone while holding hot beverages?"

"Ha-ha. No. My mom's feeling better. It was just a slump. She took more pictures of Megan yesterday. You should have seen her—she looked so different." I sigh a happy, contented sigh, and grin until it feels like my face is going to fall off.

Sam's face matches mine. "Hey, that's awesome."

"Right? Oh, here, I brought you a latte."

"Thanks." I hand him one of the cups and he starts to take a sip but then pauses. "Is this the skinny kind? Because you know I—"

"Yes, Sam. I know you're a stud now." I pinch at the nonexistent fat on his waist, and he sucks in his breath and twists away from my fingers with a sheepish expression. Oh. Maybe he's still self-conscious about his body and it's not okay for me to joke.

"So, how's everything with Amanda?" I ask.

"Good." He practically blushes, and it is kind of adorable. "We went to the movies this weekend. I really want to ask her to be my girlfriend, but I don't know if it's too soon."

I shrug. "You could ask her on a couple more dates first. If she says she's busy without suggesting another day for a date, that might mean she's not interested. If she says yes, she probably wants to be your girlfriend."

I can't even believe I'm giving Sam tips on how to prolong his relationship with that drink thrower, but she's different around him. She's so nice it's hard to believe she's the same person.

"Cool." He blushes again, and the first bell rings and we hurry inside before we're late to homeroom.

A few weeks later, Mama asks me to go to Walmart with her after school. That's right. She is voluntarily leaving the house to go somewhere other than group and she wants me to go with her. She still isn't back to her old self—her old self would have required a full face of makeup and a flatiron before a Walmart outing—but I'm ecstatic.

We grab a cart and pick up some laundry detergent and

vitamins before heading to the school-supplies aisle. On the way, I see Amberly restocking scented candles in her blue Walmart vest, and I wave. Mama is picking out some things for Libby, and I'm telling her about Sam's new girlfriend, when I see two women from church—Mrs. Tate, who has blue hair and not in the cool way, and Mrs. Dorland, who has wrapped her cart handle in tissues and still looks uncomfortable touching it. Both of them cooked dinner for us a couple times after Timothy. I try to herd Mama toward the Crayola markers, but before we can get much farther down the aisle, I hear, "Yoo-hoo. Lily?"

I close my eyes. Here we go. There are two kinds of southern church ladies who come to your house in times of crisis. The first are kind-hearted saints, angels bearing casseroles. The second are like Mrs. Dorland and Mrs. Tate.

They bustle over wearing bobcat smiles. "I thought that was you, Lily," says Mrs. Dorland. "I was just telling Arnette here, 'I think that's Lily Jenkins.'"

"She sure was," says Mrs. Tate. "How are you doing, Lily?"

My mother's smile in return is fragile. "I'm good."

She was barely ready to come out in public. She certainly isn't ready for *Them*.

"Lord, Lily, I can't remember the last time I saw you out and about," says Mrs. Tate.

"I know. We hardly even see y'all at church, since, well, *you know*," says Mrs. Dorland.

Yes. That's right. Throw it in her face that her son died and she hasn't been handling it well. Heartless hag.

"Well, I guess that's right. We, uh, we—"

I glance at Mama. Her chin quivers and she is blinking furiously.

Mrs. Tate attempts to pull her face into a look of concern, but her eyes are bright, and I can see exactly what she's thinking. *Lily Jenkins. Out in public. And crying. Isn't this a juicy piece of gossip!* I am this close to ripping out her blue hair.

I step in between her and Mama so I'm right inside Mrs. Tate's personal bubble and then I glare at her, and at Mrs. Dorland too for good measure, for two long, uncomfortable seconds, because I want them to know that I know. With any luck they'll spend their afternoons telling their friends about that angry Claire Jenkins instead of about Mama.

"We're really very busy. We better get going," I practically spit.

Mrs. Dorland puts a hand over her heart. "Oh, *well*, we'll see y'all later then."

I spot the door to the restrooms at the end of the aisle, and I somehow manage to get Mama inside before she breaks down. She retreats into a stall and locks the door behind her, but I can hear her sobs. She's shut me out. All my hard work, the days of watching and hoping when she started taking pictures, when she started becoming herself again, all of it is about to unravel in the bathroom at Walmart. The door opens, and I turn, ready for a fight.

"What?" I say through clenched teeth.

Amberly looks at me with wide eyes.

"Oh. Sorry. I thought you were someone else," I mumble.

She moves closer so we can whisper without Mama hearing. "They're still out there."

"What? What are they doing?"

"Pretending to be interested in SpongeBob lunch boxes so they can look at the bathroom door every two seconds."

I shake my head. *Vultures.* "I need to get her to the car."

Amberly eyes the stall where Mama is still weeping. "I think I can create a distraction. Count to twenty and then leave?"

"That would be amazing," I say.

She heads outside, a determined look on her face. I turn back to the stall. What if I can't get her out of there?

"Mama? Mama, let's just go to the car, okay? I'll drive home." I hold my breath. She doesn't answer, but the lock clicks open, and her tear-stained face appears. I put my arm around her and usher her to the door—I hope it's been twenty seconds by now. Mrs. Tate and Mrs. Dorland and their carts are still there, but they're turned in the other direction, staring slack-jawed at Amberly, who doesn't appear to be doing anything more interesting than talking on her cell phone.

I get Mama out a back exit and into the passenger seat of our car without anyone else we know seeing us.

"Are you okay?" I ask. "It was horrible what they said to you."

She nods. "I know. I don't want to talk about it, sweetie." She curls over and buries her face in her lap, and I put the key in the ignition because I don't know what else to do.

There's a tap at my window, and my breath catches in my

throat, but it's just Amberly. I get out of the car and close the door behind me. She holds out a bag.

"I didn't know if you needed the stuff in your cart or not."

"Thanks," I say, checking the receipt so I can pay her back. "For everything. How'd you get their attention, anyway?"

She blushes. "Oh. I just made a fake phone call detailing my favorite positions for"—she makes air quotes with her fingers—"fornication."

I giggle. "I wish I could have seen that."

Amberly nods at the car. "Is she going to be okay?"

"Yeah. I mean, I hope so." I fidget with the handles of the shopping bag.

"I know what it's like," she says. "Hiding things." She hesitates. "I know you like to talk to Megan about everything, but you can talk to me too, you know. I'd understand."

She's frowning like she's in pain, and I see the question behind her eyes, but I don't have a good answer. Amberly's my friend, but she's my party friend, my talk-about-boys friend, my glittery-false-eyelashes friend. Megan is my serious friend. But then a million late-night conversations in Amberly's bedroom come flooding back, and it hits me: Amberly's serious friend is *me*. And she's always offered up her secrets without ever asking for mine in return.

She touches my shoulder and smiles before heading back inside. "It's not a big deal," she says.

But it is, to me. I can't stop thinking about it. Even in the days after, when I'm consumed with worrying about Mama, beating myself up over all the things I might have done differently to keep her from spiraling away from us again, thoughts about Amberly worm their way in. Why don't I treat Amberly the way I treat Megan? Why isn't she good enough to tell my secrets to? But I don't like the way it makes me feel about myself to think about it, so I try to push those thoughts away.

Luke is moving with the speed of a three-toed sloth. He's been flirting with both of us for weeks (weeks!) and still nothing. Last week was the homecoming game, and Megan got crowned queen, which means her half of the pact is going pretty well. Now if only I could get my half of the pact to cooperate. I mean, I get it, it's high school, and a rejection would be a complete humiliation, but man up already. I can only handle so much shameless flirting.

I'm always tempted to bring up our trip, but we're never alone, and the last thing I need is for Megan and the rest of the school to hear about it. Luke never mentions it either. Maybe it didn't mean anything. I can't help but wonder if he's forgotten.

When I slide into my desk in AP English, Luke's already there, bent over last night's calc homework.

"Hey, what are you doing this weekend?" I ask, busying myself with rearranging the insides of my book bag so I stay casual.

"I'll probably stop by Buck's party tonight. You going?"

"Yeah. I'll probably get dragged to that. I really want to see that new zombie movie, though." *Hint. Hint.*

"Oh, yeah? I'm not big into horror movies, but let me know if it's any good."

"Okay, sure."

Ugh. It's been like this for weeks. I keep clubbing Luke over the head with hints, and he keeps missing them. Or maybe he isn't missing them. Maybe he doesn't like me. But he hasn't asked Megan out either. He can't not like either of us. Can he? I'm still pondering this when the bell rings almost an hour later. Whoops. Good thing I've already read *Fahrenheit 451*.

"I'll see you at soccer on Sunday," Luke says. "And, uh, I hope someone does end up dragging you to the party tonight." He smiles at me for way longer than you're supposed to if you just want to be friends.

Every time I think about giving up, something like this happens. Every freaking time.

Kiss #8 xoxo

Ninth Grade

"Elizabeth Jenkins, you come down here right now. You are way too little to be climbing trees that big."

Libby doesn't reply. She just grins at me from her branch at the top of Sarah's peach tree, chirping and chattering like the squirrel she's pretending to be. My parents get freaked out by the amount of time she spends in the fruit trees (well, they would if they were home more), but I understand. It's a magical place. Not magical enough to keep me from getting irritated at her right now, though.

"C'mon, Lib, please. Dinner's almost ready and . . . if you come down now, we can have a special dessert after."

I regret my promise even as I'm making it, because I know there is no such dessert. It works, though. Libby's ears perk up at the mention of sweets, and she shimmies down the tree like a little monkey. Her skinny legs wrap around my waist. Her arms hug my neck.

"Hungry," she says.

"Me too."

I wobble to the house with my five-year-old sister balanced on my hip. Something is wrong, and I can smell it even before I open the back door. Thick gray-green smoke billows from the kitchen. Libby and I hack and cough as we take in the disaster that is—*was*—tonight's dinner. It is a split-pea-soup explosion.

Green slop shimmers in puddles on the floor, drips like tiny stalactites from the ceiling. The pressure cooker spews angry bubbles—its lid has been catapulted to a patch of linoleum by the trash can. The counter underneath it and the wall behind it look like a Pollock painting.

I am in over my head.

I call Megan. After the whole boyfriend-stealing incident in eighth grade, she and I became friends again pretty quickly. For forty-eight hours, she and Britney and Amberly and I paired off on opposite sides of the lunch table like there was an invisible line between us. Amberly sided with me because she can't stand "home wreckers" (when she was seven years old, her dad ran off with the Piggly Wiggly checkout girl). Britney sided with Megan, but then she'd always been closer with Megan, so it wasn't a big surprise.

Then Megan heard about what happened with my mom and Timothy. She was the best friend I could have had. Sam came to my house every day for the four months Timothy was in the NICU and tried to distract me with soccer and video games, but sometimes you just need to talk to a girl about stuff. And while Amberly is great with boy drama, Megan is better with problems of the life-shattering variety. She just showed up in my room two days after Timothy was born and said, "I heard," and those two words opened a floodgate within me, and I told her everything while she hugged me tight. Eventually we got around to talking about Eric too, and she told me how sorry she was. Amberly told me I didn't have to forgive her yet, that it was crazy for Megan to do what she did, and if I wanted to keep on ignoring her, Amberly would give her the silent treatment right along with me. But it suddenly didn't seem as important as having my best friend propping me up while I tried to stand strong for everyone else.

When the casserole parade ended and my parents still practically lived at the hospital, cooking fell to me. Oh, sure, I could microwave Hot Pockets and do things like grate cheese and chop vegetables when my mom cooked, but I had no idea how to cook an entire meal by myself. I called Megan for advice, and sometimes she came over when things went seriously wrong. Like today.

When she arrives, she takes in the kitchen with a mixture of horror and amusement.

"What'd you do?"

"I just wanted to make split-pea soup. Something went wrong with the pressure cooker."

"You think?" She only laughs at me a little before pulling out ingredients for chicken and pasta while I grab a mop.

"Is it just you and Libby or am I making enough for everyone?" she asks.

"Everyone, please," I say as I scrub the mop against the ceiling while simultaneously trying to dodge falling globs of soup. "Mama and Daddy are on their way back from another doctor's appointment at Children's, but they got stuck in traffic."

Megan frowns. "How's he doing?"

"He has another cold." I check to make sure Libby isn't

listening. "It's pretty bad this time."

"Poor little guy."

Megan pops the chicken into the oven and boils tortellini on the stove.

"What about my dessert?" asks Libby.

Crap. I totally forgot about that. How come little kids have such good memories when it comes to promises? Megan raises her eyebrows at me.

"I promised her dessert so she'd come down from Sarah's tree and eat dinner," I whisper. "But we don't have anything."

Megan's eyes spark. She smells a challenge, or maybe that's just the lingering odor of pea soup. "Do you have sugar and eggs?"

I nod.

"Then we can make meringue. Libs, you can be my meringue girl."

"Okay!" Libby bounces with excitement while Megan sets her up on a stool with a mixer she has to hold with both hands.

"You have peanut butter," Megan calls from where she's rustling around in the pantry. "I'll use that to make the filling. Now we just need a crust."

This actually does present a problem. We're out of flour. But Megan manages to overcome even that hurdle, whipping up a crust out of some butter and a half-empty box of chocolate-chip cookies. I'm telling you, that girl is the MacGyver of cooking.

Megan and I make plans for my birthday next week and then she goes home, and Libby and I are just eating our last bites of dinner at the dining room table when I hear the front door open.

"We're back," calls my mom from the foyer.

"We're in the dining room," I call back.

I put together a couple of plates for my parents as they make their way to the table, my mother holding Timothy and my father trailing close behind with Timothy's oxygen tank and apnea monitor. The monitor connects to a band around his chest with sensors to alert us if he stops breathing. A spaghetti-thin tube passes oxygen into the prongs under his nose, held into place by a stripe of adhesive tape on either cheek. That's all people can see the first time they meet Timothy.

When I look at him, I see round, blue eyes like mine, Sarah's contagious smile, and a shock of jet-black hair. He's the only one of us who got my dad's hair.

"Thank you for making dinner." Mama looks around at the food. "I thought you were making soup."

"Oh, we decided chicken and pasta sounded much better." I smile at Libby, and she lets out a burst of giggles.

"Here, let me hold him so you can eat," I say, trading her a plate for my baby brother.

"Tim Tam!" I squeal. That's right. I nicknamed my brother after an Australian chocolate cookie. Grammy special orders them for us because she has a crush on Hugh Jackman. "How's my boy? How's my boy?" I touch my nose to his and make silly faces until he laughs his beautiful baby laugh. His chest catches in the middle of his next peal of laughter. His little upturned nose wrinkles, and he forces out a cough. A horrible, wet sound that makes me feel like I can hear things inside his lungs ripping.

"What did the doctors say?" I ask my parents.

Libby stops attacking her second piece of peanut-butter pie and waits for their answer.

"We have to keep him on the oxygen and the monitor all day while he beats this infection," says my dad. "As soon as he's in the clear, they'll move him back to nights and feedings only."

Libby and I sigh in unison. We've been dreaming of the day when we can pick him up without any equipment attached to him. When he can join us for our picnics in the fruit grove and help us spread the blanket so a corner points at each tree. Although you could hardly call Timothy's a tree. We planted a Rainier cherry because Rainiers are Mama's favorite fruit. They're the sweetest, rarest, most delicate cherries, but if the temperature goes too high, or the wind blows too hard, or the rain rains too hard, they don't make it. Their chances at survival can change by the hour. My parents think none of this matters, but I feel like I have to look after that tree. Like their fates are connected, like in *E.T.* or something.

"Well, that's okay. You'll be off the oxygen soon," I tell Timothy. "Say 'I'm tough. I'm tough.'"

He can't say real words yet, but his grin shoots arrows through my heart.

"It's time for his medicine now," says Mama. She takes her empty plate to the kitchen. There's a rustling sound as she searches for the right bottle.

I have a new level of respect for my mom. In the eleven

months since he was born, she's become an expert on his condition—he has bronchopulmonary dysplasia, which means his baby lungs look like they've got emphysema. She keeps the house hospital-grade clean so he won't get sick. She keeps track of *everything*. His diet. His schedule of medication. His physical therapy. The never-ending string of doctors and specialists. She has dedicated her entire being to taking care of my baby brother.

Sometimes one thing can happen that makes everything else you think about someone shift. Timothy was that one thing for Mama and me. He made me see that she's more than just some beautiful southern flower that Daddy picked. She's tough and smart and she cares so much. And now, when she looks at me, I feel like she sees the things I am instead of the things I'm not. We've never been closer.

My mom comes back with the medicine, and I hand Timothy over so I can start on the dishes. With Sarah away at school most of the time, and Mama and Daddy always at the hospital, I have to be another grown-up in my house. I don't mind. I would do anything for that kid.

"If I marry Chase, and you marry Corey, we'll be sisters!"

Megan emits a high-pitched squeal and practically pulls my arm out of its socket to get me over to the seats Amberly and Britney have saved. Her other hand points toward second base, where the boy I'm supposed to marry is leading off.

"There's just one flaw in your plan," I say. "I've never even talked to him."

"Like it matters. We'll fix that after the game."

We take our seats on the butt-numbingly hard bleachers, and Megan cheers for her boyfriend, a senior and one half of The Collins Twins. By dating one of them she has cemented her position as the most popular girl in the freshman class, and probably for the rest of high school. Corey is still single, and prom is approaching, which is why I'm watching a baseball game in a sundress instead of jeans. I feel like such a phony. But I'm not the only one. Girls in makeup, big hair, and what passes for trendy dresses in this town pack the stands so they can stalk, er, watch the team. They probably don't even know what a shortstop is.

"I still can't believe you're dating Chase Collins," gushes Britney.

Megan grins. "I told you. I can get any guy in this school."

Chase Collins isn't just any guy. He's six feet, two inches of blond-haired, green-eyed daydream material. So is his brother Corey. Although, even though they're identical twins, Chase is the hotter one. I think it has something to do with the semi-vacant look constantly plastered on Corey's face. Chase slides into home and, after he slaps the red dust off his thighs, turns toward the stands and blows a kiss to Megan.

"He's so romantic," she says. Her voice is flippant like it always is, like Chase is a new handbag she's showing off, but her eyes give her away. She watches Chase Collins walk to the dugout like her heart is straining with every step he takes away from her. I've never felt that way about anyone.

"So, what do you think of Corey?" Megan says, as if I'm supposed to be able to tell if someone is my soul mate by watching him play baseball.

"He's all right." I think back to earlier today, when this guy Tanner who sits across from me in math was tapping out a drumbeat on his desk. He winked when he caught me looking. "I kinda like this guy in my geometry class. Tanner Walsh."

Megan taps on the side of my head with her knuckles. "Hello. He's a band nerd. And besides, he's a freshman. Freshmen can't take you to prom. And I really, really want you to go."

Band nerd or no, Tanner is hot. She's right about prom, though. I don't want to be the only one of my friends not going.

So a month later, here I am. In a pastel prom dress. Eating dinner at the Melting Pot with my two best friends (Britney didn't get a date) and a guy I've only spoken to once before today. Corey, my date, sees a basketball hoop in every fondue pot. He lobs a strawberry across the table.

"He shoots . . ." Plunk goes the strawberry into a vat of chocolate. "He scores!"

He leaves his shooting hand hanging in the air, wrist bent, the way people do after sinking a ball. No one notices. Amberly tries to talk to her date, a baseball-player friend of The Collins Twins, but he seems more interested in checking his phone for sports updates. Chase and Megan feed each other bites of cheese- and chocolate-dipped food from the ends of their skewers. Corey is annoyed with the lack of spectators.

He beans his brother in the face with a brownie bite. "Dude. Stop being such a fag." I wince at his word choice.

"What the hell, dude? I have a girlfriend," says Chase.

Megan glares at Corey, then raises her eyebrows at me as if to ask, *Is your date seriously throwing food in a nice restaurant?*

I roll my eyes to say, *Yes, I can't believe he is so immature.*

Amberly and her date miss the entire exchange because she finally manages to get his attention by licking chocolate off the end of a banana. As soon as dinner ends, we catch a limo to the hotel room (a suite, actually: two separate bedrooms), where Corey pops open the cooler to reveal Bud Light and Boone's Farm. He tosses beers to the guys.

"We've still got an hour before prom. Drink up. Okay, ladies, who wants some . . ." He glances at the label. "Blue Hawaiian?"

"Me!" Amberly already has a plastic cup from the bathroom, unwrapped and ready.

"All right, Amberly! Way to be first to step up to the plate. Who's next? Megan? What about you, Claire?"

I shrug and accept a cup of Boone's Farm, my first real alcoholic drink. It's electric blue and tastes like candy. Just before it's time to go down for prom pictures, Amberly, Megan, and I realize we have tongues the color of Smurfs, so we cram into the bathroom to de-blue ourselves, while Amberly fusses with our already-perfect hair and makeup.

The boys booked the suite at the same hotel as prom, so all

we have to do is walk downstairs with our mouths full of Life Savers mints. In the darkened ballroom, a DJ presides over the floor while dancers get blasted with strobe lights and rap music. Megan walks in with her shoulders thrown back and her hand on Chase's arm like it's a freaking Hollywood movie premiere. The rest of us are close behind them, and we find a table for our clutches and jackets before making our way toward the sounds of DJ Beat Blizzard.

The actual prom part of prom is much more fun than I thought it would be, probably because Corey and I spend it dancing and not talking. It passes by in a blur, until I'm dizzy from the Boone's Farm and the dancing. Then the official part is over. It's time to go upstairs to our hotel rooms and hang out until Megan and I have to be at her house for curfew.

"Hey, we should do something next weekend," says Corey. "We could go muddin'."

"Mmm," I say, nodding so it kind of seems like I'm saying yes.

muddin' *(noun)*
> 1: *The driving of a truck through fields, swamps, etc., generally by a person of hillbilly descent, until said truck is covered in mud (truck is usually falling apart and often sports a rebel flag and/or gun rack and/or camouflage bug guard).*
> 2: *Something Claire Jenkins will never do.*

"Here, have another Boone's." Corey tries to push a full cup on me.

"Oh, um, no thanks, I don't want to get sick off all the sweetness."

"C'mon, Claire, get in the game."

"I'll take it!" Amberly grabs the cup and chugs like she spent prom in a desert.

Shrugging, Corey guzzles another few beers. I don't know when it happened, but we're all alone now, sitting side by side on the queen-size bed. At some point, Megan and Chase went to the other bedroom and locked the door. Amberly and her boy never came back from the bathroom.

"You look hot," Corey says.

He lays a ham-like hand against my cheek and smushes his face against mine. The kiss is all wrong. His lips cover mine, stretching over my whole mouth and leaving a ring of saliva. His mouth tastes like beer. I know I should be ecstatic. I got to go to prom with a senior. I am currently making out with one half of The Collins Twins. Any other freshman girl would be memorizing every detail so she could tell her jealous friends at school next week.

Corey's hands start to wander. Ewww. Don't get me wrong. I totally want to do more than just kiss. But not in a hotel room at prom with a guy I barely know who has beer breath and hairy knuckles and speaks almost entirely in bad sports metaphors. I want to do all that stuff with someone special. Someone I'm head-over-heels in love with.

He shoves a clumsy, sweaty hand down the front of my dress, and it is my cue to get out of this situation. Now. I try to push his hand away, but he doesn't let me.

I giggle uncomfortably. "Stop it."

But he doesn't.

"You know you want to. Stop teasing me." His other hand slides down to my butt.

Ugh. What a jackass. This guy is seriously starting to piss me off. But then noises that sound suspiciously like sex drift toward me from the bathroom, and my annoyance shifts to panic. Is he expecting me to have sex with him?! I thought the whole sex-at-prom thing was only on TV. I don't, I mean, I can't, I mean, I'm not ready for this. Especially not with him.

"Corey, stop it! Seriously."

He keeps grinding all over me. He's really not listening. But he wouldn't do *that*, would he? He'll stop. He has to. But he hasn't stopped yet. What if he . . . ? This could get ugly. My right leg is about the only part of me not pinned underneath his hulking body. I slide it outward and upward, my heel scratching against his hip.

"Oh, yeah," he moans.

He probably thinks I'm trying to wrap my leg around him. I'm not. I rest the spike of my heel on his thigh. And then I give him one more chance.

"Please. Stop. Now," I say through gritted teeth.

He responds by trying to wedge his hand farther between my dress and my boob.

"Huh!"

I kick into his thigh, concentrating on projecting every ounce of soccer strength down my leg and into that spike heel. Success! I feel cloth rip, his soft skin and hard muscle. Most importantly, I feel him retract his offending body parts. He scrambles off me with a howl and lands on the hotel floor, where he curls into the fetal position with one hand holding his thigh.

"You fucking bitch. I'm bleeding."

I stand over him with my hands on my hips. "I told you to stop. Asshole."

I need to get out of here. Fast. The anger is fading, and once it's gone, crying is inevitable.

"What's going on?" Megan and her date appear in the doorway, and Corey's face changes. He realizes he's about to be exposed for the Neanderthal he is.

"I can't believe you guys set me up with this *baby*. She doesn't even go to second base." He runs a hand through his hair and stalks to the door. "I'm gonna see if Kirsten's still pissed at her date. At least she puts out." He turns back to me. "Call me when you're ready for the big leagues, Claire."

Then he slams the door. Megan's at my side in a second.

"Are you okay?"

"I'm fine. Can we just go?"

"Of course. David's supposed to pick us up soon anyway. It's almost midnight."

"What about Amberly?" I jerk my head toward the moans coming from the bathroom.

Megan frowns. "She told me she might spend the night here."

So we go downstairs and we wait outside for her brother. I rub my hands up and down my arms and wonder if that's what it's always going to be like. If guys are always going to want more than I'm willing to give them.

David finally pulls up in his old Accord. He and Megan have the same golden hair and wide blue eyes, but the waif look isn't as attractive on a boy. Since he's a senior, he should be at prom instead of chauffeuring his little sister, but he wasn't feeling up to asking any girls.

Once we're both sitting in the backseat, it's safe for me to bawl my heart out. I cry so hard I get the hiccups. I don't bother holding back in front of David. We've been spilling everything in front of him for years now. He studies me with a mixture of curiosity and trepidation.

"Is she going to be okay?"

Megan nods and hugs me close. David cruises down the highway in silence. He's as quiet as she is outgoing. And quiet is a really polite way to say he's socially awkward to the point that people wonder if he's autistic. People can never believe he's Megan's brother. And make no mistake, he is Megan McQueen's big brother, not the other way around. She's the girl every guy dreams about dating and every girl dreams about being (or tripping in the hallway), and he's the nerdy genius kid who never talks. He's much better when he's around us, though.

I finally stop crying enough to speak. "I'm so stupid. I didn't realize prom meant sex."

"No, it doesn't," she says. "I didn't have sex with Chase."

"You didn't?" Hiccup.

"I don't wanna know," says David. "Especially not while I'm driving. La-la-la-la-la."

Megan cups her hands over his ears like earmuffs. "No. I just gave him a blow job."

"Ah! I still heard that. I'm scarred for life."

She rolls her eyes. "So, that's it?" she asks me. "He wanted to have sex and you said no?"

"Not exactly. He wouldn't stop, so I had to kick him off the bed."

"What! I can't believe I set you up with that clown. I had no idea. Chase is so sweet."

When I tell them the whole story, David is shocked and Megan is seething. "That *asshole*. I hope it leaves a scar," she says.

"I hope you know you did the right thing, Claire," David says gently.

His words make me cry all over again.

When we were in the hotel room, all I could think about was getting Corey off me. I reacted on pure adrenaline. But now, in the quiet safety of David's car, I wonder if I overreacted. I mean, I did want to kiss him. Well, I thought I did.

"I don't know," I say. "I keep thinking, did I really need to kick him? I could have told him I would tell my parents. I could have screamed for help. I know you guys would have heard me and everything, so I guess I was safe the whole time, really, but it didn't feel that way. For a second there, it felt like he was going to do anything he wanted and no one and nothing was going to stop him and it didn't matter that I didn't want him to. And I panicked. He's probably telling everyone I'm crazy right now."

"Hey." Megan grabs my hand and makes sure I'm looking her right in the eye. "David's right. You did exactly the right thing. He's the one that's wrong for even putting you in that position."

I nod, and even though I'm still second-guessing my actions, I keep coming back to the same point. No matter what I did, no matter how I handled it or how many alternate scenarios would have worked out better, I didn't let him do it. *I* chose what happened to me. Not him. Nothing else is as important as that.

As soon as we pull into Megan's driveway, a rap on the window startles me. It's Sarah.

"Where have you been? I've been texting you for forty minutes."

"Sorry, I—" I don't really want to talk to Sarah about what happened with Corey. "But it's not even one yet." My first thought is I've been busted for drinking at prom. But I can tell from Sarah's face it's something much worse. "What happened?"

"It's Timothy," she says. "He stopped breathing a little while ago, and they had to rush him to the hospital. I'm supposed to bring you and Libby now that you're back."

"Do you want us to come too?" Megan gestures to herself and David.

"It's probably best if it's just family right now," Sarah says. "But in the morning?"

Megan nods. "We'll be there. Call me as soon as you know anything."

"I will," I tell her. Then I bolt toward the house in my bare feet and sequined dress. "What's wrong? Is he going to be okay?" I ask as Sarah runs alongside me.

I picture Timothy, his apnea monitor going off, his tiny chest still. We've had scares like this before. Everything always turns out fine.

"It's too soon. They haven't told Mama and Daddy anything yet. But. Daddy had to do CPR."

"What? No." I cup my hand over my mouth. He never had to do that any of the other times.

I change clothes as quickly as I can.

"I already put Libby in the car," Sarah calls from the bottom of the stairs.

She drives like a woman possessed, but it still feels like an eternity before we get to that hospital waiting room. We find my parents holed up in a couple of garish purple-and-yellow patterned chairs. Coffee cups in their hands. Stricken expressions on their faces.

"How's he doing?" I ask.

Mama shakes her head.

"We haven't gotten an update yet," says my dad. "They're doing everything they can."

It's the most frustrating answer you can get. I feel powerless. I wish I could be doing something. Anything. When I was in that hotel room with Corey, at least there was something to fight against. My sisters and I squeeze onto a couch that has no business holding three people. There's nothing to do now but wait and hope and pray. Sarah holds me, and I hold Libby, and we cry salty tears into each other's hair.

Finally, a man in a white coat approaches my parents. I don't like the look on his tired face.

"Stay here," Daddy says quietly.

He and Mama follow the doctor to an alcove off the main waiting room, while Sarah and I watch anxiously. Libby doesn't notice because she's fallen asleep in Sarah's lap. I can't hear them from where I am, but I concentrate on the doctor's lips, and the first words he says are "I'm sorry."

Mama lets out a wail that makes people stare. Daddy has to wrap an arm around her to keep her standing.

"No." I shake my head and repeat it over and over as the tears fall fierce and fast down my cheeks. Sarah sobs so hard her whole body lurches. This isn't what was supposed to happen.

My parents come back to us as different people. Broken people. Mama can't speak, so Daddy does his best to tell us why we'll never get to see Timothy smile again.

"His lungs just gave out," he explains. "With the

infection . . . they were just too tired to breathe anymore."

It's like someone sucked all the air out of the room. It can't be true. Timothy can't be dead. But I know by the way the light has gone out of my parents' eyes that he is.

chapter
9

Someone is making turnip greens. It's the first thing I notice when I get home from school—the smell is unmistakable, kind of like body odor but in a strangely appetizing way. I follow the scent into the kitchen, where I find my mom wearing a cherry-print apron and stirring a huge pot of greens. There's a ham bone inside for flavor and a single whole pecan because she swears it neutralizes the bitterness or some crazy thing. Mmm. I can't wait to pile hot sauce on them.

"Hey, Mama. Those look delicious."

"Thanks, sweetie."

We completely sidestep the fact that this is the first meal she's made in two years that didn't come from a cardboard box. I'm just relieved the Walmart incident is in the past and the good days outnumber the bad ones now.

"Take a look at the table. I printed out some proofs from when I photographed your friend Glenn."

I flip through portrait shots of Glenn on his front porch and action shots of him at a football game.

"They're amazing."

"You think?"

"Yeah. Why else do you think everyone at school is tripping over themselves to get an appointment with you?"

Ever since my mom's photos of Megan hit the school, Lily Jenkins senior pictures have become the must-have senior accessory. She's taken almost a dozen now. Mama turns back to the stove to check the beeping oven and eases out a heaping dish of gooey homemade macaroni and cheese.

"You made mac 'n' cheese too?"

"Mmm-hmm."

"I better put these pictures away so we can eat." I start to clear the table.

"I thought we could eat in the dining room, all four of us. Can you and Libby set the table? And maybe slice up some tomatoes too?"

"Sure." I race upstairs to Libby's room with the goofiest grin on my face. *She's okay again!*

"Libs." I throw open the door. "You won't believe this."

She's sitting cross-legged on her bed with her stuffed elephant, Mr. Heffalump, wrapped in a stranglehold of a hug.

"Is everything okay?"

She nods.

I lower my voice to a whisper. "Guess what. Mama's making dinner."

"I know." Libby squeezes Mr. Heffalump tighter.

I scoot onto the comforter beside her. "You do? Then why do you look so sad?"

"What if I said the wrong thing or did the wrong thing and it ruined everything? I was scared to break the spell. So I hid."

"Ah. I know how you feel." Those weeks after Walmart tore me to pieces on the inside, and with every high comes the fear of the next low. I give her and Mr. Heffalump a bear hug. "But we have to enjoy every second of this like it might not happen again. Because it might not. We have to hope for the best. Now come on. We're setting the table."

We hop up. Just as we reach the door, I see my mom coming upstairs, so I stop Libby and put a finger to my lips. From where I'm peeking through the hinges, I can see her knock on Dad's office door, see her open it when he says, "Come in." He turns in his desk chair and almost drops the papers he's holding when he sees it's Mama, and in an apron, no less.

She looks at him almost shyly. "Can you come down for dinner in a few minutes? We're having turnip greens and macaroni and cheese."

"Yeah. Yeah, of course. I'll be right down."

The smile on my dad's face when my mom asks him to come down for dinner breaks my heart.

* * *

I drive us to Buck's Hawaiian party in Britney's 4Runner. It's my night to DD. My friends and I spent the last hour decking ourselves out in various combinations of luau gear from the Party City in the next town over. Megan has unleashed the big guns, aka her boobs. She's wearing seashells over them. I am at a serious disadvantage tonight.

Amberly lets out another melodramatic sigh from the backseat. "I don't know if there's anyone out there for me. Y'all all get to see guys you like at the party tonight. You're so lucky."

"Lucky? Megan and I like the same guy, and the last time that happened, it about wrecked our friendship."

The car goes silent. We don't usually mention how things are going with Luke. He's the dimpled, dreamy-eyed elephant in the room.

Megan saves us by changing the subject. "How are things going with Buck?"

"So good," replies Britney. "We've been on a few dates, but they've all been amazing."

"Have you had the DTR talk yet?" I ask.

DTR talk *(noun)*

    1: abbreviation for "Define the Relationship talk"

    2: A talk, usually initiated by a girl, that involves the
       dissecting and classification of a relationship, e.g.,
       friends with benefits (the optimal outcome of the
       DTR talk for a male) or exclusively dating (the opti-
       mal outcome of the DTR talk for a female).

The fact that Megan and I are acting so interested in Britney's fledgling relationship with a guy we think could be the missing link is a testament to how much we don't want to talk about Luke.

"Not yet. But maybe tonight. Neither of us have been seeing anyone else. I think it could be the night he asks me to be his girlfriend."

The party is already pretty packed when we get there. Everyone clusters around Buck's pool and the keg. I scan the crowd, waiting for my Lukedar to ping, but he isn't here yet. Megan heads straight for the table of mai tais. I think she's nervous about seeing Luke, and, let's be honest, I'd be anxious too if seashells were the only thing separating my boobs from the rest of the world.

"Hey, Buck," she calls as she garnishes her Solo cup with a pink umbrella. "Awesome party. I love the theme."

"Hey, thanks!"

Megan smiles back at him, but she's already launched into a discussion with a girl from the cheerleading squad on which type of waterproof eyeliner is best for pool parties. How does she do that? She can make anyone feel important or special. I can't talk to people I don't like without my face giving me away, so I sidestep Buck when I grab a Coke from the mai tai table. Unfortunately, he notices.

"What? No mai tais for Yoko?"

I roll my eyes and keep walking. "That hasn't been funny since tenth grade."

Buck goes back to macking on Britney, while his best friend

and sidekick, Jimmy Marcus, creeper extraordinaire, weasels around yanking at girls' bikini straps. If Jimmy is within a two-mile radius, double knotting is a must.

I spot Sam sitting in the hot tub with Amanda Bell, one arm flung around her shoulders, and I feel like a proud mama for helping him get his first girlfriend. A pack of guys jostles me to the side so they can set up a flip-cup table. After what happened at my house this evening, I'm not in a wild party kind of mood (I'd rather enjoy my natural high), so I weave through the crowd by the pool to get back inside.

The inside of the house is just as packed, though, with people and animals. Not live ones—Buck's dad is one of the most prominent taxidermists in the Southeast. And since Buck lives in one of the nicest neighborhoods in town, stuffing dead animals is more lucrative than I ever would have guessed. I squeeze past a couple of raccoons and an ungodly long line for the bathroom before finally making it to the front porch.

I sprawl out on the porch swing and relax. It's good to be alone for a minute. I rock back and forth and watch my pointed toes pass more planks of wood each time the swing soars outward. My mom cooked an unbelievable dinner tonight. And I saw my dad squeeze her hand when he helped her wash the dishes. I smile so hard my face hurts.

"Claire?"

I almost spill my Coke all over myself. Luke makes his way through the logjam of cars in Buck's driveway.

"Hey."

"What are you doing out here by yourself?"

"Oh, um, I had kind of a strange night at home."

He sits next to me on the swing. "What happened?"

For an instant, I panic. Almost no one knows the whole story about what my home life is like. I've tried to hide it from everyone except my closest friends. But Luke fixes me with kind blue eyes, and I feel my resolve melting.

"My mom has some problems. With depression." I bite my lip, wondering if I should keep going. "I used to have this perfect family, but for the past few years, everything's been a big mess."

"I'm sorry."

"It's okay. I think things might finally be getting better. Tonight, she made dinner, and for the first time in a long time, we sat in our dining room and had dinner as a family." I take a nervous gulp of Coke. "I know that must sound like no big deal."

"No, I know what you mean," he says. "My parents get in these really intense fights sometimes because my dad's such a jerk. I guess you might have figured that. Anyway, it can get scary, so I know what it's like to want things to be normal. Your dinner sounds great."

I smile. "It was. We were stiff and awkward, like we weren't exactly sure what to do or what to say, and it wasn't like it used to be, but I'm so happy. To me, it was perfect."

He puts his arm around me. His hand moves up and down my shoulder, giving me chill bumps and making me forget what I was going to say next. Our eyes lock like they're passing electricity back and forth. I am acutely aware of the mere eight inches hovering between our lips. Luke leans closer, closing the gap. If he kisses me . . .

And at that precise moment, the front door creaks open and Megan steps onto the porch with a panic-stricken look on her face.

"Claire! You will not believe . . . Oh. Hi, Luke." Her face shifts into a smile so quickly I almost wonder if I imagined the look I saw before.

"Hey."

Her eyes rake over us. "What are y'all doing out here?"

"Just talking," I say.

"Oh." I can see her gears turning. She takes a step toward us and trips. "I need to go home. I feel really drunk. I think that Creepy Creeperson Jimmy Marcus might have spiked my drink with Everclear." She looks at Luke. "Have you had anything to drink yet? Do you think you could drive me home?"

She teeters again and grabs the porch railing for support. Her boobs strain against their seashells. Was she stumbling before?

"Sure. I haven't had anything yet."

"I'll do it," I say. "Just let me get the keys from Britney."

"She and Buck disappeared to his bedroom and shut the door." She shudders. "I am so not walking in on that. And besides, her car's blocked in."

Luke stands. "It's okay. I can do it. I just got here, so I'm parked on the street."

"Do you need me to go with you?" I ask.

"No, we'll be fine." She fumbles down the stairs and falls

against Luke, accidentally, I'm sure. "Oops. I'm sorry."

"It's okay. Here." He puts an arm around her waist, his head bent toward her. I can't tell where he's looking, but I'm praying it's not at her seashells, and do his fingers really need to be skimming the top of her sarong?

"Thanks." Megan gazes up at him with the look princesses wear in Disney movies.

This isn't going to end well.

Kiss #9 xoxo

Tenth Grade

The most painful breakup in the history of the universe started with a flyer. A four-by-six neon-green sheet of paper slipped in front of me before bio.

Screaming Lemurs Premiere Concert
Opening for the Mangled Guardrails
9:00 p.m. at the Maverick

"Check it out," Tanner says. "We're a legit band now."

He leans over my desk while I read it, so he's way inside my personal bubble—close enough for me to smell the shampoo in his hair, which has recently been dyed rock-star black. The skin around my neck gets hot.

"Dude. That's awesome," I say.

"Thanks. So. You think you can make it?" He tugs at the earring in his left ear while he waits for me to reply.

I would give *anything* to go to this concert, but . . .

"I don't know. My parents are super strict. They'd never let me go to a bar."

"No. It's okay. It's teen night," he says quickly.

"Yeah . . . they'll still say no."

Tanner is crestfallen.

"I really want to hear you play, though." I look at him with big, flirty eyes and hope he gets the subtext, which is *I really want to make out with you, though.* "I'll try to work something out."

He smiles. He gets it. "Cool."

When I get home from school, I carefully remove the flyer from the front zipper pocket of my book bag. Then I race over to Megan's. I let myself in and run upstairs. Her door is shut, but there's light and music coming from inside. When I twist the knob, I hear several thumps, and Megan scrambles to pull on her robe.

"I'm chan-ging. Do you mind?" She turns around. "Oh, it's you. I thought my parents were home."

"What's going on?"

She glances from side to side even though we both know we're alone. Then she opens the robe.

"Um. Are you planning to be a prostitute for Halloween?" I ask.

She rolls her eyes. "No. I'm planning to lose my virginity tomorrow."

"Seriously?"

Every excruciating detail of their physical relationship has dominated our lunchtime discussion for Lord knows how long. I shouldn't be surprised. They've been stuck on third for months. And with Chase in college now, she's probably feeling more pressure.

"Yep. It's our seven-month anniversary. He doesn't have class on Fridays, and I'm going to stay home with the stomach flu. It's like fate." She stares into the distance with bright eyes. "Now help me figure out what to wear!"

She jerks open her robe again like a flasher. It's all black lace and pink ribbons crisscrossed in ways that don't make sense to me. Garter belts hold up her thigh-high stockings.

"Do you like this one better?" She gestures to the one she has on, then leaps over to her closet and pulls out a hanger. "Or this one?".

It's white and sheer. Significantly less complicated and significantly less trashy.

"The white one," I say immediately.

She turns to appraise the white one. "Is it cliché to wear white when you lose your virginity?"

"I don't think so. I thought you were supposed to."

She shrugs. "Okay. Let me try it on for you."

She strips right in front of me. None of my friends have any modesty. But then, if my body looked like any of theirs, I guess I wouldn't either. I still have more muscles than curves.

"I think I do like this one."

She examines her butt in the mirror from eighty billion different angles.

"If I put candles and rose petals around the room, d'you think it'll be too much?"

My jaw hits the floor. "You're doing it here?"

"Yeah." Megan looks at me like I'm an idiot. "He has a roommate. Plus if my mom calls, I need to be home."

"Aren't you worried about getting caught?"

The thought of sneaking a guy into my bed is enough to make me feel like I'm having a panic attack.

"Nah. He'll be gone way before my parents get home. And he's going to park a few streets away and walk over so your mom doesn't narc on me. No offense."

"I doubt she'd even notice anymore," I mumble. Then I remember why I'm here and I perk up. "I have to tell you something too. We *have* to go to this concert on Saturday. Amberly just texted me that B's parents will be out of town, so we can stay at her place. It'll be awesome."

I whip the flyer out of my back pocket, but Megan doesn't seem interested.

"I'll see," she says. "I mean, I might be hanging out with Chase, and I doubt he'll want to go to a high school concert."

"Oh. I'm Megan." I prance around the room in an exaggerated impression of her. "I'm having sex with my college boyfriend tomorrow, and I'm waaay too cool to hang out with high schoolers."

She flings a pillow at me, and we burst into giggles. I leave her to her lingerie because I need to get back to my house and start dinner.

I'm shocked to find my dad's car in the driveway. Ever since Timothy, he's been staying late at work, sometimes sneaking in after we're asleep. He's always liked working and he's always been on the quieter side, but I guess tragedy sometimes turns people into more extreme versions of themselves. Today he's home early, though. Maybe he'll even eat dinner with us. I pop a Stouffer's lasagna in the oven and head straight to his office, where I find him bent over some drawings. Shocks of gray have sprung up around his temples in the past couple of years. When I was little, I used to wish I had black hair just like him.

"Hey, Dad. We're having lasagna in half an hour."

He lets out an exhausted sigh. "Can you just leave my plate in the microwave? I've got a lot of work to do."

"Okay, sure. Well, guess what. I got a ninety-eight on my bio test."

"That's nice." He doesn't even look up from his desk.

My shoulders slump. It's like nothing I do matters anymore. The meals I cook, the babysitting I do, the grades I make. None of it. I narrow my eyes at the back of his head.

"I'm going to a sleepover at B's house Saturday night. I won't be home until Sunday morning."

"Okay."

He doesn't ask about parental supervision. I stomp out of the room in disgust. I expected my mom to crumble after we lost Timothy. But not my dad. He's supposed to be the breadwinner, the genius architect, the overly involved father. He's supposed to know what to do—no matter what. We're supposed to be in this together. I put him on a pedestal and dismissed her as a housewife who dabbled in photography, and I never realized she was the glue that held him together.

Libby and I eat dinner at the kitchen table alone. We tried eating in the dining room right after, but it was too depressing with just the two of us. Afterward, I wrap one plate in plastic wrap and put it in the microwave for my dad. I place another on a tray with some garlic bread and a mason jar of sweet tea. I tiptoe up the stairs, past the closed door that still hides an empty nursery, and push open the door of my parents' bedroom.

It's dark, but I can see the outline of my mother's body under the covers. Her skin is lifeless. Her hair is brittle. She's lost tons of weight—I barely recognize her. I don't usually notice how different she is. Maybe if my dad hadn't come home early tonight and gotten my hopes up, I wouldn't have. I shove the tray on the nightstand and try not to look at her, but it's too late. The sobs start deep in my chest, clawing their way out by the time I get to my room and shut the door. I sink into the carpet. Curl into a ball under the doorknob.

Why am I the only one trying in this family?

I miss Timothy too. I miss him so hard it feels like my heart might keel over from the strain, and I dream about him at night and wake up with tear-stained pillows. Every once in a while I'll dream about that day at the hospital, but most of my Timothy dreams are painfully normal. I'll have one about a time when we played peek-a-boo while I was babysitting or one about a memory that didn't happen where he's four years old and I'm teaching him to kick a soccer ball. The waking up is what really guts me. Realizing he'll never be four years old and I'll never teach him to play soccer. After his funeral, I spent days in bed with Sarah and Libby in a pile of arms and legs and tears, talking about what Timothy would look like if he grew up, what he'd be like if he lived, and how Grandma takes care of him in heaven.

But after all that, I got out of bed. And yes, it's hard, and some days, most days, I don't want to, but I force myself to do it anyway. And I feel like I'm doing it all by myself, and it is killing me.

Timothy died.

And now neither of my parents is interested in living.

At lunch the next day, Britney and Amberly and I work out all the details for the concert and sleepover. My eyes are drawn to Megan's empty seat. I hope today is going well for her.

I don't get to ask her about it until Saturday when we're at Britney's getting ready for the concert.

"How was it?" I pounce on her the moment she walks in the door.

"Perfect. I had everything set up, and it was so romantic. Chase was sweet as can be." She sighs deeply. "It was amazing."

Amberly picks at her fingernails. That night after prom, the night when I stabbed Corey with my heel and we lost my little brother, Amberly lost her virginity in the hotel bathroom. She was depressed for weeks after.

"I just feel like this was one step toward starting the rest of our lives together. He's been talking a lot about our future. He really wants to buy a house here and raise a family. And I know that's not exactly what I had planned, but we love each other so much, you guys. I know we'll be able to figure something out."

Not exactly what she had planned? It is the antithesis of what she had planned. It is the sledgehammer-wielding thug that annihilates what she had planned. I shiver. If this is what sex does to people, I don't know if I ever want to have it.

We talk about Megan and Chase ad nauseam until Britney stands up and pulls a bottle of wine from under her bed.

"I thought we'd make tonight interesting. Drink up, *chicas*," she says, pouring us each a glass.

Amberly's mom and Britney's mom both drink too much. The difference is that Britney's mom can put away entire bottles of white wine and sleep off her hangovers in a four-poster bed with a cold compress over her eyes and still be called a lady. When Amberly's mom drinks cheap rum by the handle and ends up barefoot and screaming in the 7-Eleven, people call her white trash. We steal their alcohol all the time, but they never notice. Britney can take a whole bottle of wine and leave it empty in the recycling bin and her mom will assume she drank it. We sleep over at their houses whenever we want to do anything—Amberly's if we're sneaking out, because the trailer doesn't have an alarm.

I haven't had a drink since last spring at prom, but then I think about how my dad acted and gulp down half a glass.

"Easy there, champ," Megan giggles.

"Don't you want a glass?" I ask Britney.

"Can't. I'm driving," she says. She's the only one of us to get her license so far, so she pretty much always drives. "I'll drink some when we come back for the sleepover."

I try to forget about how bleak things are and have fun for one night. I borrow the shortest skirt Britney owns. At the

Maverick, I go to the bathroom with Amberly and take shots out of her flask. I dance with my friends until people stare. I'm tired of being good.

Finally, the hip-hop music playing over the speakers stops, and Screaming Lemurs takes the stage. Every girl in school nearly has a seizure. In middle school, these guys were some dorks in *the* band. Now they are heartthrobs in *a* band. Each song is greeted with a new wave of squeals. Some are covers—everything from Nirvana to My Chemical Romance to Aerosmith. Some are Screaming Lemurs originals. They are damn good.

Their lead singer croons into his microphone, wearing guyliner and, I suspect, women's pants. He's hot, but it's the obnoxious kind of hot where he thinks every girl wants to make out with him. And to be fair, lots of them do, Amberly included.

"I know he's an ass," she yells. "But I want to kiss him anyway. I don't care if we never call each other."

The guys at bass and rhythm guitar are brothers, but they couldn't be more different. Bass is shy and a little nerdy and spends most of each set peeking through his long, diagonal-cut bangs like they're a protective shield. Rhythm is a jock and plays on the football team. He's probably the worst guy in the band, but he ups their cool points by ensuring varsity-athlete attendance at every show.

Seth Wong plays lead guitar. He's gorgeous and sensitive and he gets the star-student award for English, like, every year because our teachers swoon over his poetry. He writes most of their songs, and when he sings backup vocals, his face contorts with angst and you can see how personally connected he is to the lyrics.

And then there's Tanner Walsh. Wailing away on drums with white-hot determination. I can't not look at him. His sinewy arms flailing the drumsticks in every direction, his bottom lip half pulled into his mouth when he gets to a difficult part. I'm mesmerized for the entire show.

"We're gonna play our last song now," Tanner says into his microphone, breaking me from my reverie. It's the first time he's spoken since the show began. "It's about love." He rubs at his nose with the back of his hand and begins tapping out a gentle beat on the cymbals.

This song is a nice, slow one with Tanner singing backup. When he gets to the word *love*, I swear he looks right at me. A thrill shoots down my spine. Did that really just happen? Did he really just look at me? While he was saying *love*? It must have been a coincidence. He couldn't have—he just did it again! I know I didn't imagine it that time. He sang *love*, and his eyes held mine while he said it and for a few seconds after. The third time he does it, we stay in a gaze lock for the rest of the song. I think I might spontaneously combust.

"Did you see that? Tell me you saw that," I say to my friends when the song ends.

"I saw it," says Megan. "And it was *hott*. With two *T*s."

The Mangled Guardrails start arranging their gear on stage, but as far as the girls from my school are concerned, they're nobodies. As soon as the Screaming Lemurs emerge from backstage, girls attack them from all sides. I don't want to be one of those girls, so I stay with my friends, but I smile at Tanner over the tops of his groupies' heads. He smiles back. He pushes through the throng, making a beeline for me, much to the annoyance of a few extra-clingy admirers.

"What did you think?" Tanner asks, scratching at the bridge of his nose. It's obvious he's asking me and not the group of us, so we work our way toward a shadowy stretch of space away from the stage lights, and I lean against the wall by a broken jukebox.

"Y'all were amazing. I'm so glad I got to see you play."

"Me too." He puts one hand against the wall on either side of my head, and I can't explain how crazy this makes me. I blurt the first thing that comes to mind.

"It felt like you were singing that last song just to me."

"I was."

I can tell he's going to kiss me. But then he pauses and stares at me with parted lips and a smile in his eyes. The way he moves toward me is tantalizingly slow, like he's trying to savor every delicious second of anticipation. I never realized before now, but usually when boys kiss you, they move in for the kill fast, like if they hesitate and give you a second to think, you might change your mind. Tanner's approach says he's confident that I want to kiss him as much as or more than he wants to kiss me. And he's right. He knows what he's doing.

His day-old stubble scratches at my cheeks. His salty lips

crush against mine. By the end of the kiss, I'm coated in a sheen of what is probably his sweat. It's okay. Rock-star sweat is like pixie dust—it makes magical things happen. I've heard the rumors about Tanner: that he's a bad boy, that he gets around. I don't care. I pull him closer and kiss him harder. Didn't I say I was tired of being good?

chapter
10

Mama's voice carries into my bathroom while I'm blow-drying my hair.

"Hey, Claire, can I drive you to school this morning on my way to run errands? I need a new lens."

My mom. Awake. At seven thirty on a Monday morning. It's all I can do not to pinch myself.

"Sure."

I text Megan that I don't need a ride today. She's been MIA this weekend (not a good sign), and my stomach is in knots with wondering what happened between her and Luke, but there's no way I'm turning down a ride from my mom. I practically skip downstairs and into the kitchen to make my scrambled eggs. Libby sits at the table with a bowl of peaches 'n' cream oatmeal and a shocked expression.

"You okay?"

She points to the counter, where two insulated lunch bags sit side by side.

"She made lunches too?" I whisper.

Libby nods.

I peek inside. The food is totally normal. A chicken-salad sandwich, some fruit, a yogurt. My mom's heels click toward the kitchen, causing me to shove the bag back into place and pretend egg scrambling is an all-consuming task. Wait a minute. Heels! I glance down. She is wearing heels. And makeup. And pearls. Before everything went wrong, I thought it was weird that she got all dolled up even to run to the grocery store. But in the years after, it was much stranger to watch her leave the house with a messy ponytail and haunted eyes.

"We're leaving in five minutes," she announces before breezing out of the room.

Libby shovels in the rest of her oatmeal, and I eat my eggs straight from the pan. Then we pile into the car, me riding shotgun, Libby in the backseat. Mama and I make awkward small talk. Libby doesn't say a word—even when we drop her off. She just leans in between the seats to give Mama a hug before running inside.

I'm still thinking about Libby when we pull up to the turn-around in front of George P. Rutherford High School.

"Have a good day at school," Mama says. She smiles a brilliant smile, like the ones she used to smile all the time before Timothy.

"Thanks." It's all I can think of. I hover by the car window, wishing I could say so much more. Her eyes search mine, still smiling, and she gives the tiniest of nods. I think she knows.

When I slide into my chair at lunch, the first thing Megan says to me is "I know you're mad."

"Huh?"

"You didn't ride with me this morning because you're mad at me about Luke?"

"No. My mom wanted to drive me."

"Oh. Well, that's great."

An awkward silence follows.

"*Should* I be mad at you about Luke?"

I start to feel queasy when she takes so long to answer.

"We're together," she finally says.

Those two words are like a punch in the gut. I knew this was going to happen. The girl gets everything she wants—and apparently Luke falls into the category of everything. But for a little while at the football game, and on the swing Friday night . . .

"How did this happen?"

"When he drove me home from the luau on Friday, I was really upset, and he was so sweet about it. And when I tried to kiss him, he didn't let me because I was drunk. He's such a gentleman. So I said I had to make it up to him, and could we go to dinner the next day—"

"Wait a minute. You broke both rules. We weren't supposed

to kiss him or ask him out. That was the deal." *A deal that apparently meant nothing to you.*

Megan waves a hand as if to swat away what I'm saying. "This is bigger than rules. Luke and I are supposed to be together. We have this *connection.* I can't explain it."

I open my lunch bag and inspect my chicken-salad sandwich, willing myself to stay calm. I will not cry. I will not get angry. Not in the middle of the cafeteria.

"And don't act like you're so innocent, Miss Wait-on-the-Porch-So-You-Can-Catch-Luke."

"That wasn't what I was doing. You're just trying to make yourself feel better about what you did."

Hurt flickers in Megan's eyes. "Okay, maybe you're right. But the thing is—"

"No. That is not how this works. You don't get to make excuses and pretend like it's all okay. You made your choice and you got what you wanted. Well, I hope you're happy with Luke. I hope he was worth our friendship."

I don't know if I mean it or not, but I sure as heck want her to think I mean it. I take my delicious homemade lunch and eat it at the soccer girls' table. I can feel Megan looking at me every five seconds. I make it a point not to look back. Let her worry.

At the end of lunch, Megan waits for Luke so she can say good-bye before she leaves for her internship. I shouldn't watch, but I can't tear myself away as she bounces up to him and throws her arms around his neck. As he leans down to kiss her with lips I've imagined kissing about a thousand times, I want to throw up.

* * *

Fortunately, we had a quiz in English today, so I was saved from having to make awkward conversation with Luke. Unfortunately, when I get to the park this afternoon, Luke is the only other person on the field. *Greaaat.* He starts a game of keep the soccer ball in the air without hands. We bounce the ball back and forth with our heads, knees, and feet.

"So. You and Megan?" I ask. I want to ask him so much more than that. Like, *What about our trip? Or do you go around promising those to every girl you meet? What did you talk about with her that could have been more special than that?* But I'm a chicken, so I don't say anything else.

The ball hits the ground with a thunk.

"Yeah. It just sort of happened."

"Why do you say it like that?"

"Like what?"

"Like you're apologizing?"

"I don't know." He stares at me until I look away. "You should know I . . ." He sighs. "You're a really cool chick."

I'm still trying to work out the hidden meaning under all the layers of vague when a bunch of other people show up. Luke gives me a sad smile before picking up the ball and running away.

After the scrimmage, Sam drives me home. A really horrible country song comes on the radio, but I don't belt out the lyrics with him like I usually would. He turns down the music.

"You okay?" he asks. "About Megan and Luke, I mean."

"Yeah."

"They suck."

"Thanks."

"Call me if you need someone to pee in his soccer cleats."

I half smile at him. "Deal."

I'm cornered. Britney and Amberly are hell-bent on facilitating a Claire-Megan make-up, even though it has only been twenty-four hours since my lunchtime explosion. I am in no mood for apologies/tearful embraces/talking about feelings of any kind. I'm in the mood for listening to angry music and punching things.

I cross my arms over my chest. "Why do I have to act like it's okay every time she steals my boyfriend?"

Britney frowns. "Luke wasn't your—"

"Because she's a really good friend when you need her," says Amberly.

It's true. But it isn't what I want to hear right now.

"She owes me a big apology."

"She's scared. You bitched her out the first time," says Britney.

"She deserved that. And 'Luke and I have an amazing connection' does not count as an apology."

"I think you really need to hear what she has to say. There's more to that night than you know," says Amberly. "If she did apologize, would you listen to her?"

This whole girl-code thing is a load of crap. It always seems to work against me. I let out an exasperated sigh.

"Maybe. But I'm not talking to her first. She has to do

something." I recross my arms in an attempt to get some of my bravado back, but now that I've caved, the gesture doesn't have the same oomph.

Amberly grins and forces a hug on me. "This is why I love you."

xoxo

Tenth Grade

Megan just got bitch-slapped via email. For the first time in her life, she's been dumped. She sits slumped over her desk, unable to tear herself away from her computer screen.

"He says we've grown apart. And, get this, he's bringing someone else home for Thanksgiving next week." Her voice is angry and raw. Tears threaten to spill down her face.

"What a jerk," I say from where I'm flopped on her bed. "I am so so sorry."

"A month ago, right after we had sex, he said he couldn't imagine his life without me. And now I have to wonder if he was with her that whole time. How could I have been so wrong about him? I thought he was the *One*. I actually tried to imagine myself staying in Pine Bluff because I know that's what he wants." That's when she really starts bawling.

This is more serious than I thought. I hop up from the bed and kneel in front of her, squeezing her hands tight in mine.

"You know he doesn't deserve you, right? He's a stupid hick who goes to a stupid college and has no life skills other than being good at baseball. And you're beautiful. And strong. And talented."

Megan sits up straight in her pink desk chair.

"You're right." She sniffs. "I'm Megan McQueen. Boys don't dump me. I dump them. And then they spend the rest of their lives trying to get over me."

"That's the spirit. Are you going to talk to him when he comes home? Try to get some closure?"

"Oh, I'll give him closure." Her fingers fly across the keyboard, googling something.

Megan's "closure" takes the form of Operation Crabs. Yes, crabs. Like the STD. Apparently, you can order them online. A week later, a cardboard box arrives in the mail. The box contains a plastic bag, and the bag contains dozens of tiny specks. *Crabs.* Just looking at them makes me itch more than a school announcement about a lice outbreak. Megan adds the plastic bag, still tightly sealed, to a box filled with pictures, a teddy bear, dried flowers, and a pair of Chase's boxer shorts. She used to sleep in them almost every night.

We drive to his house together. In his driveway she cuts open the bag and carefully sprinkles the crabs into the boxers.

"Be free," she says. I shudder.

She knocks on the front door while I wait in the car. Thirty minutes later, she's back, and I can tell she's been crying.

"You okay?"

"I need ice cream."

I've never seen Megan this upset over a breakup. When I stop by her house the night of Jimmy Marcus's field party, I find her wearing all black (black pants, black top, black pashmina draped over her head) and lighting candles. Things are worse than I feared. It's a good thing I'm armed with cupcakes.

"Megan, why are you dressed like that?" I try not to smile.

"I'm in mourning," she says solemnly. "For my relationship."

"Well, I brought you something to cheer you up." I hold up the box from The Little Cake Bakery.

"Those aren't?"

"They are your most favorite favorite cupcakes that I convinced Tanner to drive three hours round-trip so I could buy. So now you can't be sad." Not that it took much convincing. Tanner has had his license for all of three weeks and he's always looking for an excuse to use it.

"You bought me Marie Antoinette cupcakes?"

"Yep." I ease open the box so we can admire them in all their cupcakey glory.

Megan and I grab a cupcake apiece and gingerly peel back the wrappers. It is important to take the largest bite possible when eating these cupcakes so you can taste all the flavors at once. The vanilla cake with its raspberry center. The European buttercream. The homemade crushed-almond toffee on top. You have to practically unhinge your jaw in order to pull it off, but it's totally worth it. After we've polished off our cupcakes and licked our fingers and, okay, fine, the wrappers too, it's time for me to lay down the law.

"C'mon. We're getting ready for the party. And I'm not letting you wear that."

Megan crosses her arms over her chest. "I'm not going. Everyone knows I got dumped."

"No one cares. How many boys have called you since you

and Chase broke up?"

She smiles. "Eight."

"See?"

"But it isn't the boys I'm worried about," she says, her eyes scared.

"That's exactly why you have to go. You have to show them it doesn't make a damn bit of difference."

"I don't know," she says, but I can tell she's caving. I pick out a red dress that screams, *Chase who?* and Megan reluctantly puts it on.

Later, Britney and Amberly come over so we can go together. Megan drives us down to the field in Britney's 4Runner even though she still only has a learner's permit (being DD guarantees she won't be sending Chase any drunk texts). The woods are so dark you can barely see the gravel road that winds through Jimmy Marcus's property. She hunches over the steering wheel, inching the car along until the flickering lights of a bonfire and a clearing lined with cars begin to take shape.

A ton of people are already clustered around the fire by the time we get there. I look around for Tanner—I can't wait to see him! We've only been dating for five weeks, but it feels like so much longer.

I find him lounging on an overturned log, a junior girl I don't know curled up beside him. Her hair is dyed alternating stripes of dark brown and brassy blond. She giggles and touches his arm. For a second I'm jealous, but as soon as he sees me, he jumps up and weaves through the huddles of people holding

Solo cups so he can kiss me hello.

"Hey, cutie, want some apple cider?"

I take a sip. There is more to this cider than just apples. I drink up. My alcohol intake has definitely increased this year. I'm gearing up for a few hours of making out in the back of Tanner's Jeep when a tricked-out truck pulls up. A truck I can't believe I'm seeing. I pull away from Tanner and try to find Megan—stat. Chase hops out of the cab, and I'm praying Corey isn't with him. He rushes past the beams from the floodlights mounted on top of the cab to open the passenger door.

Oh no he didn't.

Out of the truck pops a girl who is obviously determined to redefine white trash.

He did.

And she is wearing tighter-than-tight cutoff denim shorts, cowboy boots, and a shirt that says, I kid you not, Dixie Pride. In rhinestones.

Megan has already spotted her. Her eyes flash. "That bastard. I can't believe he's here. And with another girl."

Her bottom lip quivers, and I cross my fingers that she'll be able to keep it together. But I've just noticed something else. "Hey, Megan—"

"How could he do this to me?"

"Megan."

"She looks like such a skank. *Everyone* is talking about it. Who comes to high school parties when they're in college anyway? He's doing it just to torture—"

"Megan!"

"What?!"

"He's scratching."

"Seriously?"

Chase glances first left, then right, then surreptitiously tugs at the crotch area of his faded Wrangler blue jeans with his middle and index fingers. We start giggling and can't stop. Megan looks like normal again.

"Let's be honest," she says. "Things were never going to work out with Chase. He doesn't even know what arugula is."

"True. Plus, he has crabs." We burst into giggles again.

Megan tries to compose herself. "I can't believe I actually thought about staying in Pine Bluff for him. I could never be happy here."

"No. You couldn't." And neither could I. I love that about her—that her dreams are as big as mine. She keeps me from feeling like an outcast for wanting something different from everybody else.

"We're making a pact, right now. That no matter what happens, we get out of this town."

"Done."

"And we do something big with our lives. We, um, we live out our dreams in the wide world beyond."

I give her a serious nod. "Pact number three: No matter what happens, we will escape from Pine Bluff and live out our dreams in the wide world beyond."

Megan repeats after me and spreads her arms wide as if

embracing the forest and the field full of cow pies. Then she frowns.

"That band chick is hitting on your man again."

It's the same junior. I shrug.

"He's with me."

"I can't believe you're not worried. Don't you know what they do on those band trips?"

"Um. Play musical instruments?"

"No. It's like a band-nerd make-out fest."

I roll my eyes. "Okay, I'll see you later. I better go keep an eye on 'my man.'"

I walk up to Tanner and tug on his belt loop.

"Hey." Then I kiss him while Junior Band-Chick Skunk-Hair girl is midsentence flirting with him. Megan should be happy. I've done everything but pee on his leg.

"Hey," he says back.

"I've hardly gotten to talk to you all night." I push out my bottom lip. "Come on."

I lead him to a nearby bale of hay.

"What did you want to talk about?" he asks.

I smile what I hope is a sexy smile. "Nothing."

We stay on our hay bale, not talking, until the bonfire dims a little and Tanner's cell phone buzzes.

"I'll be right back. I have to get this," he says.

"Okay."

While I wait, I rub my arms to keep warm. Seth Wong plops down in Tanner's place and keeps me company with jokes and marshmallows. He makes up a song on the spot about how s'mores are awesome, but they're not as sweet as me. That kid is hilarious.

"Can I talk to you about something?" he asks.

"Sure." I've never seen Seth so serious. He plucks stray pieces of straw from the hay bale while I wait for him to talk.

"Tanner's my best friend, but, you know, he has trouble staying with just one girl." He squeezes my shoulder. "I don't want you to get hurt."

"What is it with everyone tonight? This is the second time." I spear another marshmallow with too much force and shove it into the fire.

"I know it's none of my business. Just be careful. You seem really sweet and . . . maybe a little naive." He practically mumbles that last bit.

Why doesn't anyone think I can take care of myself? Taking care of people is all I do these days.

"I knew Tanner's rep before we got together," I say. "He's changed. I know what he was like with other girls, but he'd never do that to me."

"Okay. I'm just saying, you're an amazing girl. You deserve a guy who sees that and treats you like that." His gaze is so intense it's like he's trying to memorize my every pore.

"Thanks."

I can't decide whether to feel complimented or annoyed, so I add, "And Tanner is that guy. Oh, crap, my marshmallow's burning." I blow it out, but it's already a charred sticky mess.

"I'm gonna go get another cider."

Even though I blow off Megan and Seth, their words swirl around in my head for the rest of the night, so I can't concentrate later while Tanner and I make out in his Jeep. The first few times we parked on the dirt road near my house, I was so nervous. Partly because I worried we'd get caught and partly because after what happened with Corey, the idea of being alone with a guy with no one in shouting distance made my breath catch in my chest. But then I realized Tanner wasn't Corey and he'd never do anything I didn't want him to, and now I'm 100 percent comfortable with him. Usually. I'm kissing him and running my hands over his sinewy back muscles, but half of me is somewhere else. He stops fumbling with my bra strap.

"What's wrong?"

I push myself up from the seat and rearrange my shirt.

"I don't know. I just. I just wonder sometimes how much I really mean to you."

"Baby, how can you say that? You know how much I care about you."

"Some people at the party were talking about your reputation, and it freaked me out. Like, maybe I'm stupid for not worrying about it."

"Don't let them mess with your head. I know how I used to be, but it's so different with you. I don't even want to be that guy I was before." He cups my chin in his hand. "I love you."

It's the first time he's ever said it, so of course my heart practically explodes with happiness.

"I love you too."

He kisses me, a slow, sweet kiss. Then he unfolds a creased-up sheet of notebook paper from his back pocket.

"I wrote you a song."

"You did?" See what I mean? Tanner is all gooey insides, no hard shell around me. Megan and Seth have no idea what they're talking about.

"Yeah. I hope you like it." He rubs at his nose, a nervous habit that I love because it connects cool, rock-god Tanner to the shy, nerdy Tanner of the past.

He taps out a drumbeat on the seat, my legs, the Jeep bars overhead, really anything he can find.

The way I feel when you're with me,
My spirit is a bird that you've set free.
With love on its wings,
It soars through the sky,
Coming to rest somewhere in the stars.
Coming to rest inside my heart.

"That's as far as I've gotten. But I'll write more."

Isn't he a genius? FYI, if you ever want to make a girl fall for you, write her a song.

I am light as a feather when he drops me off half an hour later. He always lets me out in the driveway and never walks me to the door because even though Tanner loves me and I love him (officially! OMG!), I'm not ready to explain why my mom never leaves her bedroom and my dad barely speaks.

I breeze inside, ready to burn off some excess energy dancing around my room and then curl under my covers and dream about Tanner. Until I smell the smoke. I follow it to the living room, where Libby is perched like a gargoyle in front of the fireplace, stabbing with a heavy iron poker at what looks like papers.

"Libby, what are you doing?"

When she turns to me, her round cheeks are red and streaked with tears.

"You were gone, and Mommy's always in bed, and Daddy wouldn't play with me because he's too busy with his stupid work."

I rush over and snatch her away from the flames and the poker away from her. There's barely a fire, just enough to blacken the papers and curl them at the edges. Numbers and sketches and official-looking stuff cover the white patches between the burn marks. My eyes get big.

"Are those Dad's?"

Libby nods and sniffles. "I took them from his briefcase."

I take a deep breath and try to figure out what to do next. First, I get a jug of water from the kitchen and dump it over the fire. Then I turn to my sister. Crap. I don't know how to do parenting on this level.

"Okay, okay." I run my fingers through my hair. "Libby, you should never, *ever* play with fire or the fireplace again. It's very dangerous. Do you understand?"

"Yes," she says in a small, guilty voice.

"Okay, good. I'm going to go talk to Dad." Her tears start fresh. "Don't worry. He's in more trouble than you right now."

I set her up with *Beauty and the Beast* and a mug of hot chocolate. The fire is gone now. I scoop the charred remains into a dustpan, walk calmly to my dad's office, and fling them on his desk. Soot and blackened paper fragments and inky drops of water fly everywhere.

"What the hell, Claire!"

He kicks away from his desk in his rolling chair. His big hands swipe at the black splotches on his shirt, but he'll need Spray 'n Wash if he ever wants those marks out. His black eyebrows come together in the middle. He's mad, but I'm madder.

"Those are from your briefcase. I found Libby setting them on fire when I got home because you couldn't be bothered to watch her. Would it kill you to spend time with her? Or act like you're the least bit interested?" I spit each word at him, not knowing if I'm talking about Libby anymore. What I really want to ask is, *If I'm your one, then why do I feel like I'm in this alone?*, but that thought cuts too deep.

He frowns. "You've been drinking."

Of all the things I expected him to say, that was not one of them.

"Yeah. I have. I've been drinking for a while now. But you and Mom never noticed because you've stopped being parents."

"I don't need my intoxicated sixteen-year-old talking to me this way."

"Oh, we're not making this about me." I swallow the lump in my throat because what I have to say is too important. Someone thinks I'm worth loving, even if it isn't him, and that thought keeps me strong. "This is about our family. It isn't right that Mom still stays in bed all day."

His eyes widen, but he recovers. "You have to understand. She's been through so much."

"I *do* understand. I've been through it with you guys. But it's been seven months. You get to a point where you have to start trying to heal. And we hit that point a long time ago."

My dad takes what I'm saying as a personal attack. And I guess maybe it is. "You can't expect everyone to grieve on your timeline. What are we supposed to do? This isn't something you can snap out of. Your mother isn't going to forget he existed just because you're ready for her to move on."

"I'm not asking her to forget. Hell, I'm not even asking for her to be happy. But she *has* to get out of bed."

I don't know how to fix my mother. But I do know that lying in bed and crying all day won't fix anything. Because I've tried that.

"Your mom just needs time."

I am done with giving things time and waiting to see if they get better.

"No. Mom needs a therapist. And not just someone at church—a real therapist. She needs someone who can make her want to try. And Libby needs her parents. And I need . . . I need some help around here. I'm not a grown-up."

"Claire—" He reaches out to me, but I jerk away.

"No. If you want to hug someone, Libby's downstairs watching a movie."

I turn and slam the door on my way out, and then go to my room and slam that door too. I flop on my bed and look around. I better get comfortable, because between the drinking and the way I just talked to my dad, I'll probably be in here for the rest of high school. I replay everything I said to him and wince. At least I'll have thoughts of Tanner to keep me company.

chapter
11

Megan must have gotten the report about me maybe being ready to make up, because she comes over to my house after school that same day. She shuffles into my room with her shoulders drooping and her head hanging low—very un-Megan-like posture.

"Can I talk to you?"

I turn my desk chair to face her.

"I guess," I say, even though nothing she says will be good enough. I forgave her before, but you can only give someone so many chances.

She sits on the absolute edge of my bed, like she's poised to spring up and run at any moment. I wait and wait, but she just stays there, silent, biting her lip, looking more and more like she's about to unravel. I'm determined not to cave, though. My brain goes over the likely excuses, but there is not one, not a single reason, why it was okay for her to—

"Chase is engaged," Megan blurts out. Then she bursts into tears.

There were a lot of things I thought she might say. That was not one of them. She usually treats Chase like something mildly unpleasant she'd like to wish out of existence. Like store-bought pie crusts.

But by the way she's sobbing into my bedspread, it's obvious she feels much more strongly about him than she does about ready-made baked goods. And even though I should be really pissed at her, and am still a little pissed at her, I can't help but sit beside her on the bed and put my arm around her while she cries.

"Chase is an idiot. We hate Chase."

"I know."

"Would you really want to be engaged to him?"

"N-no. I mean, I know it's a good thing we broke up, because we want different things out of life, and I'm embarrassed that it hurts this much, but it does." The words come out all garbled by her tears. "Amanda texted me a link to his fiancée's blog while we were at the party, and I was looking at pictures of them, and they looked so happy. Like, really, truly happy. That was so close to being me. And I started freaking out, wondering if I'll ever be able to make someone else that happy."

"Hey." I pull her back into a sitting position because I need her to hear me say this. "Hey, of course you will. Someday. Just not stupid Chase Collins. He's *twenty* and getting married. You don't want that. You want out of here, remember?"

She nods like she's thinking about believing me. "After that, I drank too many mai tais. And then I found you guys on the swing." She hesitates. "Luke was such a good listener. I was crying, and he put his arm around me and started running his hand up and down my shoulder, and then he looked deep into my eyes, and I swear he was wanting to kiss me. I did try to kiss him first, but I wasn't imagining the connection. I mean, he wouldn't have done those things if he wasn't interested."

I don't say anything back. Her story sounds similar to when Luke was comforting me. But . . . she must have misinterpreted what he did. I know what it was like with Luke on that porch. I'm positive he wanted me. I don't tell Megan this, though. Because he ended up with her. He chose her. So maybe I was the one who misinterpreted things.

Megan stops crying now, suddenly serious, like she's just remembered the reason she's here.

"I know it was really crappy of me to break those rules we made about Luke." She traces the designs on my comforter with her index finger. "I guess when I was alone with him, it was like I forgot all about the rules. I just wanted him so bad."

"I get it," I say. "There were times I really wanted to kiss him too. But I didn't. And I *really* liked him." *Like* him.

"I know."

"When you told me at lunch, you didn't even seem sorry."

"I *am* sorry. I was just so nervous about telling you. I totally screwed it up."

"Yeah. You did," I say, and Megan winces.

"I'm really, really, really sorry, okay? Can't we be friends again? Please?" She peeks at my face, and I guess what she sees makes her realize I'm going to forgive her because she smiles and adds, "Don't forget Pact number one."

I roll my eyes, but I'm smiling too. "Oh. Ohhh. Well, if you're invoking Pact number one, I guess I have to forgive you, don't I?"

In my heart, I know I forgive her. I do. But that doesn't mean I would leave her alone in a room with my boyfriend. If I had one. Which I don't. Thanks to her.

Mama snaps another photo of me and adjusts her footing on the bark chips carpeting the back half of our yard. *Click. Crunch.* She's taken senior pictures of most of my friends now, and yesterday she shyly asked if she could take mine. She squats in front of me, taking another test shot, playing with the angles and the lighting until she gets it just right. I lean against my pear tree—we thought it would be a good place to start—and smile the picture smile I've been practicing in the mirror all morning. Whenever I feel my smile getting stiff, I take a deep breath and let it out in a slow, gentle sigh, smiling as I do so because Megan says Oprah says it's the secret to a natural-looking smile.

"You look beautiful, sweetie," Mama says with the camera still in front of her face.

"Thanks." *Click.* That time I know my smile was natural.

We speak in soft voices because that's what the fruit grove makes you do. Ever since Timothy died, it feels like a church.

"I can't believe how much I missed," she says.

"What are you talking about?"

I think I know, but since we don't talk about *stuff* in my family, I must be wrong. She lets the camera hang against her chest by the neck strap. Without it between us, I can see her eyes are red with tears. Maybe I'm not wrong.

"You're all grown-up now. I'm so sorry." Her voice cracks, and she clears her throat. "I should've been giving you mother-daughter advice and taking you shopping and . . ."

She sinks to the ground. After everything that's happened with my mom over the past few years, I could be upset. Or bitter. I'm not, though. Maybe I will be in a couple of years. Maybe I'll look back and be really resentful and need therapy or something. But right now I'm so relieved and so happy to have her back, I don't have room to feel anything else.

"It's okay." I leave my spot by the tree and sit next to her, the pieces of pine bark digging shapes into my palms, and put my head on her shoulder. "You're here for me now. That's all that matters."

Mama puts her arm around me and rubs my back in between my shoulder blades like she used to when I was little and I couldn't fall asleep.

"I can't change anything that happened. There are so many things I wish I could do over." She shakes her head. "All I can do is try to make it up to you."

I've dreamed of her saying these words. I've imagined exactly what she would say to me and what I'd say back and every different possibility, each more perfect and wonderful than the last. I've focused on this moment in my mind, like if I wished for it hard enough, I could will it into existence. And now here it is, and I'm terrified.

Because I want it to last and I need it to be permanent. I need her so freaking much that it hurts to breathe. And I don't know how much I can hope for, but I'm already hoping for everything. And it will be that much worse if she disappears again.

"That sounds good to me," I say, scared that I'll ruin everything if I let myself say more.

We sit there like that for a long time, my head on her shoulder, her hand on my back, both of us watching the fall breeze ripple through our little grove that is four fruit trees strong. Timothy's tree made it, even though he didn't. It's at least three feet tall now, and although we've never seen it flower, its leaves are waxy and green and alive. I guess they weren't as connected as I thought.

Sam grabs a Diet Dr Pepper from my fridge. Since we've practically grown up in each other's houses, he doesn't bother asking.

"Sam!" Libby tears across the kitchen and tackle hugs him. "I didn't know you were here."

"Hey, girl. I just got here."

She grabs for his drink. "Can I have a sip? Ewww. Never mind, it's diet."

"Yeah. Because I gotta drink the diet if I want to keep this bod. Check out these guns."

He flexes his bicep, and she laces her fingers over the top of it so he can lift her off the floor.

"Now me. Now me," Libby says. She flexes her skinny arms. "Which way to the gun show?"

Sam gives them a squeeze. "Your sister's a beast." He winks at me.

After some gratuitous flexing by both parties, Sam and I head to the living room so I can help him with his AP Calc homework. My books and notes are already spread over most of the coffee table, and I talk him through a few problems.

"Can you believe Megan and Luke have been dating a month now?" I ask.

"They have?" Sam continues to scribble away at his piece of notebook paper.

"Yeah. I was kind of hoping it wouldn't last."

Sam gets a serious look on his face. "You know, the guy's not the best boyfriend."

"What do you mean?"

"A couple of times when it was just guys hanging out, he said stuff about Megan. Like, he makes fun of the stupid stuff she does. And he called her dumb."

"Really?" I can't help smiling a little.

"Okay, I didn't say that so you'd get excited. I said it so you'd realize maybe he isn't the nicest guy."

"Well, maybe he *would* be a good boyfriend. He just needs the right girl. Luke's smart. He needs a smart girl to match him."

Sam smacks his palm against his forehead. "Ugh. You're

ridiculous. I could tell you the guy never washes his socks, and you'd be all like, 'Isn't it sweet how he's conserving water.'"

"I would not. He does wash his socks, though, right?"

"Ohmygosh."

"Okay. Okay. Sorry. We'll talk about something else. Liiiiike . . . did Amanda Bell steal your V-card yet?"

"Dude. There will be no talk of V-cards during homework time."

I poke him in the ribs. "Did she? Did she?"

"No, she didn't. And I—"

All talk of V-cards really does screech to a halt, because my mom pokes her head into the room.

"Sam, are you staying for dinner?" she asks.

"Yes, ma'am."

"We're having fajitas. I'll set an extra place." She bustles back to the kitchen.

"She looks great," Sam says.

I grin at his compliment, more so than if it had been for me. "I know. These past few weeks have been amazing."

"That's great." He squeezes my shoulder. "Now, teach me how to do derivatives."

It's these little things that keep happening. So small and seemingly insignificant that half the time I wonder if I'm making them up. But they happen so often I can't help but worry. Sometimes Megan is cold right after Luke talks to me. And she eyes us suspiciously if we so much as bump shoulders. Megan and I officially made up about the whole Luke thing weeks ago, but now she's acting like she's the one who was wronged.

It's ridiculous. I'm the one sitting here at our lunch table waiting for the bell to ring so I can watch the guy I like waltz into the cafeteria and kiss someone else. Which happens right. About. Now. I avert my eyes during the Luke-Megan daily lunchtime smooch. He always stops by our table for a second before getting food. Today he flips a plastic chair around backward and plops down.

"Hey, Claire, are you ready for that calc quiz today? Just so you know, I already took it first period and it sucks."

"I'll be ready by two fifty."

"Ugh. It is just like Mr. Carnes to give us a quiz the day before Thanksgiving break. How'd you do on the test last week?"

I smile. "I aced it."

"I knew it." He elbows Megan. "This girl is a freaking genius."

I can't help it. My smile gets bigger. Luke always has a compliment for me these days.

Megan's smile, on the other hand, is brittle. "Yeah. Claire's always been the smart girl. Hey, Luke, do you like this shirt?" She arches her back so her chest pokes out more than usual. "I can't decide . . ."

Luke is not immune. Her boobs are the equivalent of a tractor beam. "Yeah. Are you kidding? It looks really hot on you."

"Aw." Megan giggles and looks pointedly at me. "Luke says I'm the hottest girl in school, possibly the universe. Right, babe?"

"Uh-huh. Hey, I gotta get my lunch. Claire, call me if you

guys scrimmage over break." He heads to the hot-lunch line.

Megan frowns. "Actually, we're going to be hanging out with B and Buck a lot over break, so he may not be able to make it."

Did she just glare at me or did I imagine that too?

I check my watch when I get to the food court the next day. Amberly and I are meeting up for Johnny Rockets and shopping. Since Britney and Megan are so busy with Buck and Luke, we've been spending a lot more time together, especially now that we're on break. The mall nearest Pine Bluff is over half an hour away, and it's still nothing like the one Sarah took me to in Atlanta, but at least it has an American Eagle.

Now that I think about it, I realize it's been months since I talked to Sarah. I haven't even told her about Mama taking my senior picture and everything. My call goes through to her voice mail. "Hey, this is Sarah. I'm probably out with my Pi Phi Angels or cheering for my Dawgs, so leave a message!" There is laughter in the background and in her voice. I sigh. Life is easy when you're Sarah. I leave a quick message telling her I have exciting news, then stuff my phone back in my purse because I see Amberly.

"Hey, you hungry?" she asks.

"Starving."

We grab lunch and find a table near a window.

"Did your mom drop you off?" I ask.

She nods.

"Cool, well, I have Mama's car, so I can drop you off at your house after so she doesn't have to come back and pick you up."

"Can we swing by Coach Davis's house on the way?" asks Amberly. She picks a piece of lint off her shirt while she says it, like it's no big deal.

I am on her like a bloodhound. "*What?* Why?"

She rolls her eyes. "Chill out. He won't even be there. I'm just dog sitting for him."

"Oh. How did that happen?"

She shrugs. "I saw him at the park with his German shepherd, and CoCo liked me *so* much, and Mike needed someone to watch her while he was away for Thanksgiving . . ."

"Wait. Mike? You call him by his first name now?"

"Calling him Mr. Davis makes him sound so *old*. He's only a few years older than us, you know." Amberly is suddenly very interested in getting just the right amount of ketchup on her french fry. "So will you go with me or not?"

I'm not fooled for a second. As calm as she's pretending to be, the skin near her collarbones is turning red.

"Okay, fine. We can go. But you can't do anything creepy like roll around in his sheets or sniff his T-shirts."

"Shut up." She throws a fry at me.

"Seriously, though, is it weird having a crush on someone so old?"

"I don't think so," she says. "I think that's why I'm attracted to him. Because he could really take care of me. I've never had someone do that before."

I don't know what to say, so we eat in silence for a while. The way Megan acted at lunch the other day pops into my head.

"Hey, can I talk to you about something?"

"Sure. What's up?"

"Do you think Megan's been acting a little . . . weird about me and Luke?"

I expect her to act all surprised and ask *What do you mean?* Instead, she says, "Yeah. I do."

"Oh. Really?"

"Yeah. She gets jealous whenever he talks to you or anything. Plus, it sounds like he doesn't treat her all that well."

"He doesn't?" That sounds eerily similar to what Sam said, but I *know* Luke is a good guy.

"Yeah, he was really sweet at first, but then it's like he got bored or something."

"She never told me that."

"I think she never told you because she's worried he might like you." She stirs her milk shake with her straw. "And you know what else I think?"

I shake my head.

"I think Luke has a thing for you."

"Oh." It isn't my imagination. Amberly sees it too. Not that it matters, because he's with Megan. I fight to maintain control of my facial features, but I must be failing, because she looks at me with a sad smile.

"And you still have a thing for him too."

"But I haven't done anything. And I wouldn't. I mean, Megan is my best friend."

"I know," says Amberly softly. "Just make sure you don't forget that. Because if you were the one dating him and she was the one who couldn't stop thinking about him, you'd want her to stay away, right?"

I wince. "Yeah. Yeah, I would." *But Luke and I are supposed to be together,* I want to say. *So it's different. Isn't it?*

xoxo

Tenth Grade

I'm leaving the house for something other than school, soccer, or church for the first time in two months (it was supposed to be three, but my dad let me off early for good behavior). It's okay. Two months of hard time is totally worth all the changes taking place since my drunken harangue. Dad promised to spend more time with Libby and me—he actually ventures down from his office twice a week for dinner. And he tries to ask us about school and stuff too. But even though he's making an effort, I can tell he's forcing himself. Without Mama, he's just going through the motions of living, and it hurts to watch.

Mama has been seeing a therapist. Getting her to that first appointment was damn near impossible, but now she goes twice a month, and she attends a support group with other women who are dealing with similar stuff.

It's weird because she seems happy to go to group, but she still seems tired and depressed around us. It's like she's divided people into two categories, Before Timothy and After Timothy, and unfortunately, everyone in my family falls into the BT category. But at least the days she spends out of bed outnumber the days in bed now. So that has to be a good thing. I was hoping to get my mom back, though, and instead of a ghost who stays in bed crying, she's a zombie who watches soap opera after soap opera.

I get why it's so hard. Her life was amazing. I mean, sprinkled-with-fairy-dust perfect. She wasn't equipped to deal with what happened. Timothy's death made me realize the world can be a bad, dark, out-of-control place. Before something like that happens to you, it's like you're in this happy bubble. And with each good thing that happens and every year that passes, the bubble gets bigger and bigger. His death obliterated my happy bubble, and it must have been so much worse for my mom because her bubble had had time to grow so much bigger.

Tonight, though, I'm putting family stuff aside and enjoying my freedom because Tanner and I have a date (his parents are out of town, so he's making me dinner!), and I'm coming over a couple hours early because I have a surprise for him.

I text Tanner while I put on my makeup.

> what are you doing?

> sittin around the house, u?

Oh, good. He's there.

> getting ready. can't wait to see u!!

> me too

When I'm ready, I call Megan because she got her license last month and I don't turn sixteen until March. I'm quiet and distracted on the way over, barely able to give directions at the appropriate times. Megan slows as she approaches an intersection.

"Is this where I turn?"

"Yeah. Turn right." I smooth my dress to keep it from getting those sitting-in-the-car wrinkles. "And thanks for driving me."

"No problem. My fee is that you have to tell me every last detail of the meal. I'm judging him by how he cooks."

"Sure."

I flip down the sun visor to make sure I don't have mascara flecks on my cheeks.

Megan gives me a funny look. "What's with you? You look fine. Better than fine. You look totally hot. It's just a date with Tanner—nothing new."

Oh, but you're wrong. I take a deep breath. "How did you know you were ready to lose your virginity?"

"OMG. Are you thinking about it? Because if you are, there's something I've got to tell you."

"What?"

I'm so glad I asked her after all. I thought she had told me everything already, but if she has insider information, I need it. I've been so freaked this week I even searched for tips on Google in a moment of extreme desperation.

"It wasn't as perfect as I made it out to be," she says.

My eyebrows rise practically into my hairline. "But you said it was the most amazingly romantic moment of your whole life."

"Yeah. That's because I'm Megan McQueen, which means

I have to have perfect sex on the first try. But really, parts of it hurt, and parts of it were pretty awkward. It was still romantic and wonderful, or it would have been if Chase hadn't turned out to be such a d-bag, but don't expect it to be perfect."

"Okay. Good to know." I hear myself say the words so calmly, but on the inside I am in panic mode, my brain frantically running through scenarios where things go wrong. I took every precaution I could think of: I'm showing up early because the idea of losing my virginity after I'm full of food seemed problematic; I bought condoms in three different sizes; I shaved my legs.

"Hey, I didn't think you and Tanner had done, you know, other stuff yet. Have you been holding out on me?"

"No, you're right. We haven't."

"Then isn't having sex kind of like . . . I don't know . . ."

"Like going from double-dog dare to triple-dog dare?"

"Yes."

triple-dog dare (*noun*)
1. *The most extreme of all dares in the following dare hierarchy: dare, double dare, double-dog dare, triple dare, triple-dog dare. By skipping from double-dog dare to triple-dog dare, one creates a "slight breach of etiquette" and "goes right for the throat."*
2. *Popular culture: The scene in A Christmas Story where Schwartz triple-dog dares Flick to stick his tongue to a frozen telephone pole.*

I shrug. "We haven't been able to be alone together for two whole months. So everything physical has been on hold, but we've been getting so much closer. You wouldn't believe the phone conversations we have. Now I just want our physical relationship to catch up to our emotional one. Oh, turn left. This is his street."

Megan eases her car up to the front of a blue house with a wraparound porch.

"Well, don't forget, you don't have to do *everything* tonight. If you feel like it's too much, just stop. If Tanner hasn't gotten any play for two months, he'll probably be ecstatic just to make out with you. And call me later!" she yells as I get out of the car.

I clomp up the driveway in my wobbly high heels. A cold January breeze whips at my bare legs, sending me into convulsion-like shivers. Oh, well. Today, looking hot is more important than being warm. Tanner's Jeep is in the garage. So is a red Civic that doesn't belong to either of his parents. Maybe one of the guys in the band got a new car. I weave between lawn tools and paint cans in the garage, thinking a jam session might throw a temporary kink in my plans.

I open the door to the narrow basement hallway connecting his room to the family room. Tanner's bedroom looks like someone exploded a laundry basket filled with dark jeans and band T-shirts. It's empty. And sure enough, I hear music playing behind the family-room door. The music sounds kind of girly, though. I'm totally going to harass them for listening to it.

I turn the knob. Tanner is slouched on the leather sofa with his head tilted back against the cushion, eyes shut, mouth open, legs slung wide. A girl kneels on the carpet in front of him, a blond-and-brunette-striped head of hair positioned over the zipper of his jeans. It's pretty obvious what's happening, but it still takes me a few seconds to convince myself I'm seeing what I think I'm seeing.

"Tanner?"

His face morphs from bliss to fear in a nanosecond. His head snaps up. His eyes shoot open. The junior band girl jerks her head away, causing him to squeal in pain. She rakes a hand across her mouth and skitters away from him in a backward crab walk.

"Claire?" he asks like he's hoping he's imagining all this. "What are you doing here?"

I look at him holding his hands over his junk and her wiping her red face.

"I'm leaving."

I turn and try to storm out with some shred of dignity. This plan fails spectacularly when my heel gets caught on an orange extension cord in the garage, and I fall with a splat against the window of the red Civic. Seeing my smudged lipstick on the glass gives me an idea. I scrawl the word KARMA in Coral Crush before continuing down the driveway.

"Claire, wait."

He's finally managed to zip his pants and chase after me. I ignore him and keep dialing. Pick up. Please, pick up.

"Hello?"

"Megan, can you come get me? I'll explain when you're here."

I hang up the phone as soon as she says "sure" and stand at the end of the driveway with my arms crossed.

"Baby, can't we talk about this?" Tanner tries to touch my shoulder, but I shake him off.

"There's nothing to talk about." I glare at him though my tears. "You cheated on me. You've probably been cheating on me this whole time." I can tell by his guilty expression I've guessed correctly. "Ugh. I can't believe I almost lost my virginity to you tonight."

All the color drains from Tanner's face. Few things can terrify a teenage boy more completely than the realization that he has missed an opportunity at sex.

"Claire, w-wait. I know we can work this out." He's desperate as Megan's car whips around the cul-de-sac to pick me up.

"You blew it." I slam the door in his face, then roll down the window because I think of something else. "And your song lyrics suck!"

chapter
12

The whole world is making out. All night I've been watching couples go at it. Megan and Luke. Britney and Buck. Even Sam has Amanda Bell.

Amberly and I hole up in the kitchen and sip our wine coolers in silence. Our feet dangle from the granite countertops where we're sitting. Amberly slouches against a cabinet. She blows listlessly at a stray wisp of honey-colored hair that has broken free from the loose bun piled on top of her head. She looks just how I feel. Britney planned this party so we could celebrate the end of the semester while her parents are away at their lake house. But I don't feel much like celebrating.

"So, not having someone to kiss right now pretty much sucks," Amberly says.

"Yeah. You know I haven't kissed anyone since tenth grade? It's been almost *two years*."

"Aw. You win. We need to get you some action tonight."

A hand slithers around my waist.

"Ladies. Ladies. Ladies." It's Jimmy, twining his creepy arms around both of us. "I hear you're in need of my services."

I peel away his fingers. "I don't think I'll ever be in need of your services."

"Me neither." Amberly shrugs off his other arm. "I'm not nearly that desperate. Or that drunk."

"But when you are, I'll be there." He stands there with his patchy goatee and his red-rimmed eyes, looking us up and down. It makes me feel like there are worms crawling all over me.

"Creepasaurus Rex," Amberly mutters under her breath. "Let's go," she says in a louder voice. "I need the bathroom."

We check our hair and makeup, intentionally taking as long as humanly possible. But when we come out, Jimmy's still there. Waiting.

"Let's split up and lose him," I whisper to Amberly.

"Meet in B's room in twenty minutes?"

I nod. We take off in opposite directions. It seems like she's heading outside to the hot tub, so I weave through the house toward the staircase leading to the second floor. Jimmy sticks to me like a flesh-eating bacteria. Crap. I have got to ditch Count Creepula. I leap up the stairs two at a time, duck inside the nearest door, and close it fast. Footsteps thud down the hall, and I watch the doorknob like it's a bomb.

"Hi," says a voice behind me. I nearly jump out of my skin.

Luke sits on the lumpy couch in Britney's dad's office with his elbows propped on the knees of his ultra-dark-wash blue jeans.

"Hi," I say breathlessly.

"Whatcha doing?"

"Escaping. From Jimmy."

"I'm hiding out too," Luke says.

"Why are *you* hiding?"

As my sympathetic nervous system recovers from Luke scaring the bejesus out of me, I notice his mouth is pulled down so far at the corners his dimples have all but disappeared.

"I'm having a crappy day. I wanted to talk about it, but Megan is drunk and just wants to hook up. I really need a friend who can listen right now."

Poor guy. I remember the talks we used to have before he started dating Megan. I sink into the cushion next to him, releasing a puff of cigar-scented air. "I can be that friend."

Luke's eyes dart around the room like he's searching for a way out. Like he'd do anything to not think about what he has to tell me. But also like he'll explode if he doesn't.

"You can't tell anyone," he finally says.

"I promise I won't." My wide eyes open even wider, something that always happens whenever I say the words *I promise*.

"You know how my parents get in those horrible fights?"

I nod.

"Sometimes . . . he hits her."

Luke's face tenses as he watches for my reaction. I've never had a friend with an abusive parent before. For all the problems they have, my parents almost never get angry. Everything I know about domestic violence I learned from watching Lifetime movies when I stayed home sick from school, so I don't know what the proper reaction is.

"I'm so sorry," I say as a reflex. "Is that what happened tonight?"

"Yeah. They were fighting because a furnace repairman came over today. Everything seemed fine, but as soon as the guy left, my dad accused her of flirting with him. It got bad. She threw a glass against the wall. And then she called him stupid." Luke winces. "So he backhanded her."

His hand is just a few inches away. Without thinking, I put my hand on top of it. You can't listen to something like that and do nothing. The hand-holding is completely platonic. Mostly.

"I don't know what to do. I have the same temper. I don't want to be a monster like him."

"You aren't. You could never be like that," I tell him—because it's true and because his eyes are begging me for some kind of confirmation that he is not a monster.

We're so wrapped up in each other we don't even hear the door open.

"What the hell is this?"

Luke and I jump back from each other, startled. It is an act that makes us look guilty as sin. If I were Megan, I'd be pissed too.

"I knew it. You've been after him this whole time."

"We weren't doing anything. We were just talking," I say.

Megan narrows her eyes. "You can leave now. I need to talk to my boyfriend."

I slink out to the hallway, but I can't help lingering on the stairs. Their voices echo from the office.

"Nothing happened. I just needed someone to talk to."

"Oh. And you can't talk to me? I'm only your girlfriend."

"I tried to talk to you before, but you wouldn't listen. You were more interested in getting my pants off."

"Well, I'm listening now."

"No, you're not. You're being a bitch."

There's a pause. I lean closer to the door. I shouldn't be listening, but I can't move. I have to hear this.

"I'm sorry, okay? You can talk to me about whatever it is. I can be a good listener too."

He sighs. "It's different with her. She gets me. Claire and I don't have perfect cookie-cutter families like yours. You don't know what it's like for people like us."

The thought of Luke and me as an *us* sends Megan over the edge. "I am so sick of hearing about how Claire is so smart and so funny and so freaking perfect. If you don't want me for anything else but the way I look, we're done."

"Well, good, because I'm tired of your bullshit anyway." I hear something slam, maybe Luke's hand against the desk, and take it as my cue to leave.

As I slip downstairs I feel shocked and sad for my best friend like I'm supposed to, but buried underneath that, I feel the tiniest flicker of hope.

Kisses #10, #11, #12, and #13 ₓₒₓₒ

Tenth Grade

Megan grabs me by the shoulders.

"Are you sure you're ready to do this?"

Our four-girl powwow occupies one of three bathrooms in Screaming Lemurs's lead singer's parents' house. Outside, a party rages, and the knocking and doorknob jangling grow more insistent.

"Yes." Well, maybe. Every time I think of Tanner hooking up with that chick on his couch, I think our plan is awesome. Every time I imagine myself enacting the plan, I feel a little queasy and my face turns red.

Amberly balances on the side of the tub so she can adjust the straps on her stripper heels.

"You know people are going to talk, right? You have to be prepared for that."

She would know. No girl in school has a reputation worse than hers. But it's just because of the way she dresses. And arches her back. And eats certain foods. She can't walk out of a room with a boy without people assuming they hooked up.

"I can handle it. Gossip never bothers me. Plus, I'm sure it'll all blow over in a week or two."

"And he deserves it," says Megan. "So everyone will totally be on your side."

Britney looks up from her lip gloss. "Seriously. Who cheats

right before a date anyway? Like, could he not wait the two hours for you to—" Megan's elbow catches her in the ribs. "Ow, what?"

Megan rolls her eyes. "Nothing. Are you ready? Because Mission: Humiliate Tanner Walsh starts now."

We put our hands in a pile and say "break" before we open the door, because we're cheesy like that. We have hatched a diabolical plan of epic proportions: I will make out with all four of Tanner's best friends and bandmates. Not the most creative plan, but it's every girl's revenge fantasy, and crabs was already taken.

Megan leaves the bathroom first so she can distract Tanner under the pretense of talking about my feelings. The winding line of people doing the I-have-to-pee dance glares until they see who it is. Amberly leaves next. Her job is to keep tabs on the whereabouts of the four guys I need to kiss. And Britney is making sure that if that junior girl comes within ten feet of this party, she'll leave in mascara-stained tears.

I take a lap around the party. A few guys check out various parts of my body as I pass. I can't blame them—my sexiness factor is dialed up to one notch below prostitute. Megan picked my outfit (a micro micro mini and a tank top that doesn't go past my belly button), and Amberly did my makeup (my eyelids weigh about two pounds each). I subjected myself to their skankover because any time you embark on a revenge mission against your ex, you have to look eat-your-heart-out sexy, but I can't help tugging at the bottom of my tank top and the hem of my skirt. This so isn't me.

I don't see Tanner, which means Megan is doing her job, so I search for Lead Singer. I find him in the living room, chest puffed out, one arm slung across the mantel, flirting with no less than four adoring fangirls.

"Come with me to get a beer," I say, grabbing his arm and causing a flurry of vicious scowls. *Oh, chill. I'll only take him for a second and then you can go back to discussing what combination of product makes his hair so dreamy.*

I drag him into a bedroom and shut the door behind us.

His eyebrows wrinkle in confusion. "The keg's in the kitchen."

Step 1: Get him alone. Done. I can do this. I can totally do this.

"I know." I take a step toward him, so we're just inches apart and I can smell his metro cologne. "I broke up with Tanner."

"I heard. You think you guys'll get back together?"

"Nope. But that isn't what I wanted to talk to you about."

I inch a little closer, thankful he can't see my racing heartbeat. His eyes widen. "What *did* you want to talk to me about?"

"I think you're hot. And even when I was dating Tanner, I always wondered what it would be like to make out with you."

I hold my breath. Will he buy it? Everything hinges on him believing me.

Lead Singer is the most vain guy in the universe, and he thinks every girl is secretly in love with him, regardless of their relationship status, so of course he swallows my lie hook, line, and sinker. A cocky smile settles over his face, and he pulls me toward him by the small of my back and kisses me like the world is ending. I start to enjoy it—even though I'm on a revenge mission, even though I have no feelings for him whatsoever—because the boy is just so darn good at kissing.

When we pull away, my smug smile matches his. *Step 2: Kiss him.* Done. I did it! And it worked. And it was even kind of fun.

"So, what'd you think?" he asks with a look that says he already knows the answer.

"That was fun. We better get back to the party."

"Okay. Come find me if you start wondering about anything else."

Tool, I think, even though I'm still practically panting from the kiss. I step out of the bedroom with shaky knees and tingling lips. Time to find my next target.

Rhythm Guitar lounges in a recliner chair sipping beer and watching ESPN Classic. Why guys like to watch ten-year-old football games is beyond me. I walk right over and sit in his lap like it's the most normal thing in the world.

"Hey. Tanner and I just broke up."

He tears himself away from the game for a second. "I'm sorry."

"Thanks."

I touch his arm, and his bicep flexes in response. This is so going to work. He's a simple creature.

"I'm going to kiss you now."

He stares at me with equal parts interest and confusion.

"'Kay."

I lean into his chest and plant my lips on his. He kisses like a jock. His lips crush too hard against mine, and his tongue plunges around in my mouth aggressively. I need to put a stop to this before I chip a tooth, so I break the suction on our slurp fest of a kiss. I hop out of the recliner and ruffle his hair.

"See you around."

"'Kay." He goes right back to his beer and football like nothing happened.

Two down. Two to go. This might be easier than I thought. Amberly gives me a high five. I wipe the slobber from my mouth with the back of my wrist.

She giggles. "Hot. Who's next?"

I think for a second. "Bass."

"He's in the basement playing pool."

"Awesome."

I note Tanner is still nowhere in sight before heading downstairs to the basement, where Bass is playing pool with three other guys. There aren't any girls around. A guy in a Halo shirt sinks the eight ball just as I walk up. I touch Bass on the shoulder.

"Hey, can you sit the next one out? I need to talk to you about something."

"Uh, okay. Sure." He follows me to a leather couch, twisting the hem of his T-shirt in his hands as he walks.

We sit there for a few awkward seconds.

"So, like, are you okay?" he asks.

"Yeah. I guess," I say. And then, because he seems so genuine: "I can't believe he cheated on me."

He nods. "My last girlfriend cheated on me too. If it makes you feel any better, I think he's pretty miserable right now."

"It does." I smile. "A little."

He tells me about finding his ex sucking face with some other guy in the back of the band bus after an away game, and I tell him about walking in on Tanner. He's not at all like his brother. This is actually difficult. Bass may be kind of nerdy, but he's a sweet nerd who cares about my feelings, so should I really be revenge kissing him? I think of Tanner. Cheating on me. And then I put my hand on his chest.

"Thanks for being such a good friend," I say.

I lean forward, like I'm getting up, but when I do, I kiss him. His eyes open big and he makes a choking sound. It's too much of a shock for him. OMG, what if I kiss him into a coma or something? But then he recovers and kisses me back, and when I finally pull away, he looks happy and dopey, and maybe a little in shock still. He just sits and stares when I leave.

Three down. Which means I currently have saliva from three different guys sloshing around in my mouth. It's a mono outbreak waiting to happen. I kind of thought kissing Tanner's friends would make me feel, I don't know, empowered or something, but instead I feel a little empty. It's probably because Tanner still has no idea.

Amberly waits for me in the living room.

"One more to go," I say.

"You need to hurry," she replies. "I don't think Megan will be able to keep Tanner occupied for much longer, and I have no idea where Seth is. I know I saw him earlier, but I swear I've searched the whole house. Maybe he's outside?"

I head out the back door and, as soon as I shut it, realize Megan and Tanner are sitting in chairs by the fire pit not five yards away. Uh-oh. Megan sees me and her eyes get big, but luckily I'm able to dash around to the side of the house before Tanner turns his head. I lean against the wall and close my eyes in relief. A tap on my shoulder almost sends me into a frenzy. I whirl around.

"Seth!"

His shiny black hair is gelled into a faux-hawk. "What are you doing?"

"Oh, um. Avoiding Tanner."

Seth glances in the direction of the fire pit. He gets this little frown like he's going to try to talk to me about serious things. But I don't want to talk. I'm tired of planning kiss-segue conversations, plus I'm super nervous, so this time I go right for the kiss. For a second nothing happens, and I worry I'm about to be seriously embarrassed, but then his lips open and his tongue finds mine. One hand winds itself into my hair. The other splays across my back, pulling me closer. I can feel the tension in each of Seth's fingertips as they press against my ribs. There's a passion in his kissing that frightens me. He grabs my hand when I end the kiss.

"I knew you felt the same way," he says.

"What?"

"This whole time you've been with Tanner, and even before, I've liked you."

All I can do is stand there with my mouth hanging open. I didn't know he liked me. I didn't want to hurt anyone. Well, anyone except Tanner. I feel guiltier by the second about making him the fallout of my kiss warfare.

"And now I know you feel the same way." His grin falters. "Because, why else would you kiss me?"

"He cheated on me," I say to Seth's Converse.

I expect him to be annoyed. Or sad, maybe. I don't expect him to wrap me in his arms and hold me.

"I know." He kisses my temple. "And I'm so sorry. But you're with me now. I'd never do that to you."

Could this get any worse? I wiggle out of his embrace. "No." This time I look him right in his kind brown eyes. "I mean, that's why I kissed you. I kissed all four of you guys to get back at him."

His face looks like it's having a fight with itself.

"'All *four* of you'? So, this was just . . . And you don't . . . Damn it!" He slams his hand against the wall of the house.

"I'm sorry." I feel like the worst person in the world.

"It isn't your fault," he says firmly. And with that he stalks toward the fire pit, leaving me standing by myself.

"Seth, wait. *Please.*"

I try to grab his arm, but he pushes my hand away and walks right up to Tanner.

"Why did you do it?" he yells.

Tanner nearly falls out of his chair in his effort to back away from Seth and stand up at the same time. "What?"

"Why did you do it?" This time Seth isn't yelling. He's broken. "You knew I liked her from the beginning. Things could have been great between us if you'd never gone for her. Why did you do it?"

Tanner rubs at his earlobe. "Look, I'm sorry." His eyes meet mine. "I like her too."

Seth looks close to tears now. "No. You don't cheat on girls you care about. And you don't screw over friends you care about."

He walks away before anyone can say anything else.

Tanner turns to me. "Why is he being like this? Did something happen?"

I can't even meet his eyes. I feel like such a jerk. "I kissed him," I say. "I kissed all your friends."

This isn't how I imagined Tanner finding out at all. I thought I'd be proudly announcing that I'd kissed his best friends while he realized how sorry he was. But this is horrible. *I* am horrible. How could I do that to Seth?

In the days that follow, Screaming Lemurs goes through an epic breakup. After their lead guitarist walks out and takes the band's lead singer with him, there isn't much the other three guys can do.

In the days that follow, Buck calls me Yoko really loudly in the middle of the cafeteria. I try to explain that Yoko Ono did not make out with all four members of the Beatles, but the culturally illiterate kids at my school don't get it and the nickname sticks.

Still, the nickname isn't the worst part. For the girls at my high school, me breaking up the band is nothing short of criminal. On Wednesday, I walk by a lunch table and hear "That Claire Jenkins goes through boys like she goes through the laundry." I have to force myself to keep walking and pretend I didn't notice. Gossip rolls right off me, usually. I'm used to hearing that my boobs are tiny or that I'm a bitch, but this is the kind of thing people say about Amberly or maybe Megan, not about me. When did I become that kind of girl?

On Thursday, I talk to Sam about it while we play video games in his basement. "So how does it feel to be the school Antichrist?" he asks, shoveling another Swiss Roll into his mouth.

"Is it really that bad?"

"For now," he says through a mouthful of snack cake. "Things will blow over, though. Eventually."

On Friday, a pack of girls I barely know pull me aside after the last bell rings. I'm trudging down the hallway under the weight of two AP classes' worth of books when they block my path. Four girls who are the less-hot equivalent of me and my friends glare at me with their arms crossed.

"We need to talk to you," says the blond one, who is obviously their leader.

"Yeah," says Amanda Bell, clearly angling to be second-incommand. "You just need to know that everyone hates you."

The blonde cuts in. "Because you're a slut. Amberly used to be the school slut, but now it's you."

"She is *not* a slut," I say.

Amanda snorts. "Yes, she is. But you're worse because you broke up Screaming Lemurs."

"They were the coolest thing to ever happen to this school, and you ruined everything," chimes in a girl with long black braids and a hot-pink shirt.

"All because you have to make out with anything with a pulse," says the blonde. "If you weren't such a slut, the band would still be together."

My eyes flash. I kissed four guys. Four. And I'm a slut? The average girl kisses seventy-nine guys before she finds the one she's supposed to marry. You'd think I'd screwed half the football team the way everyone is carrying on. I want to scream at them, *Hello. I'm a virgin!*

Instead I say, "How is this all my fault?" *Why does Tanner get to be innocent in all this?*

"Oh, we know your friends were involved. Everyone is pissed at them too," says the fourth girl, a cute redhead who talks with a lisp.

"That's not what I meant. Tanner—"

Amanda takes a step closer like a prowling animal. "Megan and Britney are the biggest bitches in school, and you and Amberly are the biggest sluts. And *everyone* is getting tired of it, so watch out."

"Yeah," says the blonde with a flip of her ponytail. "Y'all may not be the queens of the school for much longer."

"I don't care about that stuff. You're missing the point. Tanner. Cheated. On me. This whole thing started with him. And the other guys in the band are more than capable of making their own decisions. I didn't force them to kiss me back. I didn't force Seth and Tanner to fight. You guys act like it's okay to heap all the blame on the girl but let the guys off with a free pass. Don't you get how screwed up that is?"

But they *don't* get it. I can tell by their blank looks.

"Whatever," says Amanda Bell. "You're still a skank."

"Ho-bag," says Hot Pink.

I turn and stomp away, leaving their parting insults to ricochet off my backpack.

Whew. I managed to stay strong, and now I just have to keep it together until I reach Megan's car. But when I get there, I find Megan bawling like a baby.

"Everybody thinks I'm a bitch," she says as I plop down in the passenger seat.

"They got you too, huh?"

She nods and pours out the whole story. Amanda was right— nearly every girl in school hates us. So do the guys formerly known as Screaming Lemurs, especially Seth. It's hard to forgive when you've got Buck calling you Sloppy Fifths.

"What are we going to do?" Megan asks.

"We make a pact. Starting today, we fix our reputations."

She sniffs. "Yeah. And how do we do that?"

"I don't know." I bite my lip. "I guess we start by thinking about the problem. And your problem is that people, uh, think you're a bitch." I see the hurt flash in her eyes. "You're not a bitch," I say quickly.

She gives me a wry smile. "Thanks."

But then why does everyone think she is? She's fiercely loyal. She's fun. She's hilarious. She's completely honest about the things she loves and the things that terrify her. That's the Megan I see, anyway. I try to imagine the Megan other people see. Oh. I get it now. But if they could just see what I see— hey, wait! Maybe that's it! "You know how sometimes you act different around me? Like, you're not afraid to tell me how your parents make you feel dumb or how you like cooking more than breathing?"

"Yeah, I guess so."

"I think you should show that side to everybody else."

Megan sucks in her breath. "I don't know, Claire. That's, like, really personal stuff."

"I know, and I'm not saying you should be spilling your guts in front of everyone all the time, but you're so much more than just the cheerleader you, and sometimes I think that's all anyone sees. I think people would really like the real you. You could at least give it a try."

"That sounds scary." She starts cleaning up her makeup, which is a sure sign she's feeling better. "I'll think about it, okay? What about you, though? What are you going to do?"

I wrinkle my nose. "I already know what I have to do."

For me, this pact is about more than getting the girls at school to stop whispering about me behind cupped hands. I don't care if Amanda Bell thinks I'm a bad person. I care that hurting Seth's feelings and kissing a bunch of guys for revenge made me feel like I was turning into a person I don't want to be. The only way I can think of to fix things is to concentrate more on me and less on boys. Which mostly involves not flirting with guys or kissing anyone for all of junior year. Bor-ing.

It works, though. Plus, since junior year is crammed with SAT prep and every AP class under the sun, the lack of boy-like distractions helps keep my test scores high. Is it fair that I have to swear off boys while Tanner cheating on me seems to make him even more desirable? Nope. But I can only change *me*, not everyone else.

For Megan, it's a little more complicated. But she manages to pull off a public-image face-lift of epic proportions. She talks to everyone in school, even if it's just to say hi and smile, and you can tell by the way their faces light up that it makes them feel so special to be touched by Megan McQueen. She becomes the kind of popular girl that people actually like. And I couldn't be more proud of her.

chapter
13

Megan must be crushed after the breakup. But I don't call or visit. If she hasn't called, she's got to be mad at me. I don't know if our usual ice-cream-eating, picture-burning, revenge-plotting session is a good idea. So when her home phone number pops up in my cell window, I'm relieved.

"Hey. Is this Claire?"

"David?" Why is Megan's brother calling me?

"Yeah. Um, can you come over?"

I assume this has something to do with the Luke-Megan semipublic breakup. "Does Megan want me to come over?"

An awkward silence follows.

"She's barricaded in her room. She dropped the bomb about

culinary school this morning, and things got ugly, and she hasn't come out since. She needs you."

If David is calling me because he's worried about Megan's feelings, things must be serious. David doesn't do feelings. Getting straight As since the beginning of time, research on quantum dots, forgetting how to speak English in front of girls—these are things David excels at. Not feelings. I'm knocking on the front door of the McQueen house before we hang up the phone. David answers, his eyes big and scared.

"I'm so glad you're here. I don't know what to do."

He watches me, helpless, as I run upstairs to Megan's room. I knock but don't hear an answer, so I go in anyway. Megan sits in a nest of pillows in the middle of her bed, listening to music so loud I can hear it through her headphones. I look at her iPod. It's some scary death-metal song. On repeat.

"That bad?"

"It was horrible." She pulls off her headphones. "*They're* horrible. They keep trying to figure out 'why I am this way.' Like if they could figure out the sequence of events that spun me on this path, they could fix me. Like there's something horribly wrong with me. Well, there isn't. I like cooking and cheerleading and being popular. And I'm tired of being treated like that makes me defective."

I hop into her pillow nest and hug her. "What happened?"

"I told them about going to culinary school and how being a chef is my dream. They blew up. Just because I don't want to go to college. Mom even said I'm setting women back and solidifying gender stereotypes by wanting to work in a kitchen for the rest of my life. I tried to tell them most chefs are men and the schools I like are super prestigious, but they wouldn't listen. And they won't pay. So I don't see how I can go."

"They're brain-dead if they can't see how talented you are. You're a badass chef."

Megan giggles. "You just said 'badass chef.'" Then a new fountain of tears begins. "This is the worst week ever."

She pours out the whole story of the fight with her parents—every unfair detail. We throw around ideas about how to change their minds: maybe Megan could introduce them to a standout local chef, maybe she could make them an extravagant dinner, maybe she could pull a David and do a PowerPoint presentation on why she wants to be a chef so badly. It's tough. We're much better at concocting schemes against boys.

Eventually we get around to the breakup too. She tells me what I already heard through the door but mostly cuts out the parts involving me. It sounds like she blames him completely and not me, which makes me feel the strangest combination of guilt and relief. I feel heavy on the walk home. But also glad Megan and I are still friends.

Mama jabbers into the phone with her elbows propped on the kitchen table. She hangs up when I walk through the door, an ear-to-ear smile lighting her face.

"We have to plan a fabulous Christmas dinner this year. It's been too long," she says. "What do you want to make?"

"We can make anything you want," I reply.

This is awesome. Oh, how I've missed Christmas dinners. Honey-glazed ham. Squash casserole. Four kinds of pie. Yum.

"And guess who's coming for Christmas!"

"Who?"

"Sarah. And she's bringing her boyfriend." Mama looks like she might burst from the excitement.

"That's great." It's been forever since I've seen Sarah. And I can't believe she's bringing her boyfriend. She talks about him all the time (or she used to back when we talked more), but I've never actually gotten to meet him.

A week later, Sarah and Boyfriend arrive on our doorstep, looking so trendy and perky it almost makes me sick. The University of Georgia alums, Sarah with an exciting new job in the fashion industry, Boyfriend with a position at an advertising agency, are blissful as can be. He's very handsome, even if he does look like the kind of guy who plays golf in seersucker shorts. He and Sarah never stop touching. His arm around her waist. Her fingers gently scratching the back of his neck. You'd need Crisco and a crowbar to separate them.

I can't believe how much she laughs, how often she smiles. I wonder if I would look as happy as her if I could wipe the past two and a half years from my life. I drift through the house, checking in on Sarah as she helps Mama in the kitchen, watching her boyfriend play video games with Libby, peeking into my dad's study to see that he is hunched over papers and drawings as always. I just want everything to be okay. Having extra people for the holidays is a change, and we all know how well my family deals with that.

Then Christmas Day rolls around, and I play the happy daughter. And I don't have to try, because I *am* happy to have my whole family together for Christmas, acting almost like we did before. We open presents. We hold hands around the dining-room table while my dad offers thanks for our Christmas dinner. Sarah and Boyfriend gush about their fabulous life in Atlanta. I finally confess about wanting to go to Georgia Tech, and everyone teases me about being the renegade, but no one is actually upset about it. Libby brags about how well she's doing in school now. It is Hallmark-card perfect. You'd have to look really close to see the fault lines.

Christmas with my family was amazing. It really was. But it was also exhausting. I feel like I have to be the one monitoring everyone so I can step in if something goes wrong. The next day, all I want to do is play soccer and blow off some steam, so I text Sam to ask if he can meet me at the park.

I'm in fruitcake leftovers hell, he texts back.

I try a couple girls from the soccer team. No luck. I think about calling Megan or Amberly, but I need something active. Something physical. I try to think of any soccer guys I know well enough that it wouldn't be weird bugging them the day after Christmas.

Then I think of Luke.

Before I can angst out over whether or not I should be doing this and what his spectrum of possible reactions might be, I've already typed the message.

Need a break from the fam. Want to meet at the park for soccer?

I hit send and watch my phone like I'm expecting it to explode or something. It beeps a few seconds later.

Sure. Half an hour?

I change into workout clothes. I tell myself I'm just going to play soccer with a friend, but I know it's a lie. I wouldn't be putting on mascara if I were meeting Sam. I throw my hair in a ponytail, slip on a jacket, and step outside. The weather is perfect. Too cold for standing around, just right for playing soccer. The wind slips under my jacket collar and chills my neck as I jog to the park, but it feels great. Every footfall invigorates me.

Luke is already there, lazily stretching. He looks different now that he's not my friend's boyfriend. Or, rather, I can look at him differently. I've been keeping up a careful guard for so long. Making sure not to flirt with him. Trying never to look at him *that way*. But now that guard is down. I devour his dimples, his blue eyes, his masculine hands.

"Claire." He waves. "How's it going? Did you have a good Christmas?"

"Yeah. It was good. I mean, my big sister is home, and my

family is all together, so really everything is great. I just . . ." I trail off and stare at the field. It will sound so stupid if I start complaining—it's too complicated to explain.

"You'd rather do anything but talk about Christmas and your family?"

"Yes. Can we just play soccer for a while?"

Luke and I play against each other on one half of the field, taking turns trying to score on each other or defend the goal. We don't talk. We play a physical game with body checks and slide tackles and hands on each other's backs as we mark each other. I'm reminded of when we first met, although thankfully there are no bloody noses this time. I get a rush every time he touches me, even if it's just him throwing a forearm against my chest to fend me off. At the end of an hour we're panting and sweaty, so we collapse on the ground with our feet pointing in opposite directions but our heads right next to each other.

"I feel so much better!" I squeal.

"Good."

"So, how was *your* Christmas?"

"Pretty good. My parents haven't gotten in a fight yet." He fiddles with the zipper of his jacket. "I had to take Megan's present back to the store today. That was weird."

I prop up on my elbow and face him. "I'm really sorry. About the whole breakup."

"It isn't *your* fault."

"But if Megan never found us in the office like that, you might still be together."

"It was going to happen eventually. You didn't do anything wrong."

But I did. I liked you. I wanted you even though you were dating my best friend.

"Yeah, and I think Megan believes that, but she still broke up with you. I don't understand why she would do that."

"I do."

Now Luke sits up too. We're so close that when he breathes cloudy puffs into the air, I can feel the warmth of it on my cheeks.

"I like you," he says. "And I wasn't doing a very good job of hiding it."

At first I feel like flying. Luke likes me! Finally, a boy I like, a boy I can really talk to, likes me back. I can't believe he chose me over Megan. That's when the truth hits me like a sack of cement. It doesn't matter that he likes me. He's my best friend's ex-boyfriend.

"This isn't fair."

Luke snort-laughs. "Not the reaction I was expecting."

"I mean, we can't date or anything. You and Megan just broke up, and she's my best friend."

"So you do want to date me?" He smiles, and his dimples pop up and say hi.

I can't help it. I blush. "It doesn't really matter what I want, does it?" There is no way, *no way* this can end well. I shouldn't even be considering it.

"Just give me one date," he says. "We can see if it would be worth all the drama."

I shake my head. "Someone at school will see us. They probably have gossip phone trees set up for situations like this."

"We'll go on a date in another town. I promise no one will see us. What do you say? One date?"

I'm all ready to say no, but he's looking at me so hopeful.

"One date."

Kiss #14 _xoxo_

The Present

I need to meet Luke for our super-secret date in fifteen minutes. At the soccer field. We decided he couldn't pick me up at my house. Megan might see his car. I don't want to get sweaty on the walk over, so I pop into the kitchen, where my whole family, plus Boyfriend, picks at Christmas leftovers for lunch.

"Can I take your car to the park?" I ask Mama. "I'm going on that date, so it'll be a while."

Before she can answer, Sarah jumps up. "I'll take you."

"You don't have to do that. It's fine if I just take Mama's car."

"I know. I just want to."

I shrug and follow her out the front door to her sparkly new BMW. Everything is so easy for her. She got to go away to school and start a new life just when things were getting bad. Part of me hates her for abandoning us like that. The other part of me is jealous.

"Are you okay?" she asks. "You've been kind of quiet. Or tense, maybe."

"Oh, sure, I'm fine." I fidget with my lip balm, popping the lid on and off. "It's just . . . I just get so worried, you know? This was our first Christmas now that things are getting better, and I wanted everything to be great."

"It _was_ great. Don't worry so much. Do you know what Mama says? She says, 'I don't know if I ever could have made it through without Claire.'"

I drop the lip balm. "She said that?"

"Yes." Sarah pats my leg with her flawlessly manicured fingers. "She's so proud of you. I am too."

I feel my cheeks get warm. "Thank you."

But I don't really know what else to say, so we're both pretty quiet until she eases the car to a stop in front of the park. "Hey, have fun on your date. Are you sure you want me to just leave you here?"

"Yeah." I open the door and brace myself for the blast of cold air I know is coming.

"Okay. But call me if you need me to pick you up."

I nod and wave good-bye as she reluctantly drives away.

I have been told to wear "those black legging things that girls wear," tennis shoes, and warm clothes, which I decided meant my down jacket. Other than that, I have no idea what we're doing today. Right now I'm standing by the soccer field at the park and feeling very silly, but I only have to wait a few minutes before Luke arrives in a banged-up Jetta.

He leans over to open the car door from the inside. "Hey."

I jump in beside him and clap my mittened hands together. "Hey! Where are we going? I'm dying to know."

Luke grins. "Snow Mountain at Stone Mountain. We'll be two hours away from anyone we know."

"Sweet."

Luke passes me a pair of ski pants. "That's why I told you to wear the leggings," he says. "I figured you could slip these on over them. They're my mom's, so they might be a little short, but I think they'll work."

"Oh, yeah, I'm sure they'll be fine," I say, as Luke puts the car in reverse and heads toward Stone Mountain.

Stone Mountain is this mountain and park on the other side of Atlanta. Every winter the park uses snow machines to make *Snow* Mountain so Georgia residents can see, tube on, and play in actual snow. Well, manufactured snow. Which I am totally willing to settle for considering we haven't had so much as a flurry this winter.

When we get there, it's amazing—our very own artificial winter wonderland. Twelve snow-packed tubing lanes slope down a hill in front of an enormous rock face carved with the faces of Stonewall Jackson, Robert E. Lee, and Jefferson Davis. The rest of the world is green, so crossing the snowy perimeter is like stepping into a snow globe. The sudden temperature drop makes me shiver. Luke and I take off like excited little kids, throwing snowballs at each other and making snow angels. Before long, I'm having so much fun I forget to feel guilty.

The line for tubing stretches all the way down the hill, but the wait passes quickly because I'm with Luke. We watch as people whiz by on inner tubes. As we near the top, a couple of excited little kids cut in front of us.

Luke clears his throat. "Hey, guys, we were here first."

The kids' dad grabs them by their jackets and pulls them back. "Sorry," he says, smiling.

"It's okay." I smile back at the kids.

"We wanna sled first," the youngest kid whines.

Luke narrows his eyes. "Well, we've been waiting for twenty minutes, so no, you can't."

"C'mon, it's fine," I say, pulling Luke toward the front of the tubing lane. He's usually more chill, but I know waiting in line can make people cranky. "Let's go tube. Bet I can beat you."

He stops frowning. "Yeah, we should race."

We tube down the hill again and again. Then, with wobbly legs and pink cheeks, we go to SnoFire Point and drink hot chocolate by the bonfire. I take a deep breath, savoring the scent of dry leaves and burning pine.

Luke touches my arm. "I have something for you."

"Really? But I didn't get you anything."

"It's okay," he says quickly. "It isn't a Christmas present. It's more like a . . . well, you'll see."

He reaches into his inside pocket and pulls out a piece of thick cream-colored paper, folded up accordion-style. I can't believe he's had it tucked in his jacket all day. I unfold the flaps, puzzled, but when I realize what it is, I gasp.

"It's a map." Not just any map. A map of Europe. With a route drawn in black Sharpie and pictures cut from magazines. People dancing. *Macarons.* He didn't forget.

"It's our trip," he says. "I hope it's not weird."

"No, it's wonderful. I love it." I don't think anyone's ever given me something so thoughtful and romantic.

"Cool." Luke seems suddenly shy and embarrassed. "Hey, do you want to roast marshmallows?"

"Sure. And just so you know," I say, as we wait in line to purchase a s'mores kit, "I am a champion marshmallow roaster."

I skewer a couple of marshmallows and hold them over the fire, turning the stake slowly until they're golden brown on all sides. Perfect. Just like today.

Perfect enough to backstab your best friend over? a tiny voice inside me asks.

I shake that thought away. I saw him first. We were supposed to be together all along. I slide the marshmallows onto chocolaty graham-cracker sandwiches and feed one to Luke.

"Mmm. These are awesome," he says.

"It's the least I could do. This was a pretty perfect date."

He smiles. "You think?"

"Almost."

I'm thinking the only thing that could make it more perfect would be us kissing right now, and I think he knows it. We're standing on top of a mountain with our heads tilted toward each other. A light snow falls on us. It's fake, of course, but still totally romantic. The bonfire crackles and shoots out sparks that reflect in our eyes. Everything around us is begging for him to kiss me. I half expect to hear Sebastian from *The Little Mermaid* singing "Kiss the Girl."

And finally, Luke does.

When his mouth touches mine, a shiver that has nothing to do with the cold migrates down my back. He has the most deliciously full lips, and I want to kiss them again and again and again. He tastes like marshmallow, or maybe we both do.

I squeeze him closer, the layers of our down jackets squishing between us. The kiss is as blissfully right as everything else today.

"Now it's perfect," I say.

In fact, it's so perfect and so charged with emotion it scares me. I can't not have more. I can't give him up.

"Then what's wrong?"

"You and Megan just broke up. We can't do this."

"So you don't want to see each other?"

That is so not an option anymore after today. "No, I do. But what are we going to do? I mean, it hasn't even been two weeks yet. There's going to be so much drama."

"Let's just keep doing what we're doing right now."

When he squeezes my hands and smiles at me like that, I feel like anything is possible.

"What's that?"

"Dating." He kisses me again. "Kissing. And not letting anyone else mess things up for us."

"So we just won't tell anyone?" The idea of walking up to Megan and explaining I'm dating her ex-boyfriend makes me sick to my stomach.

"Not until you feel like things have blown over enough with Megan."

"But." I bite my lip. "Don't you think she'll be able to tell?"

He laughs. "Claire, I don't know if you've noticed, but Megan's not exactly the brightest crayon in the box."

She's not dumb, and I actually hate when people say things like that, but I let it slide because I'm relieved he doesn't seem to be harboring any feelings for her.

Luke pulls me into a hug and whispers in my ear. "Look. No one is going to find out. We can keep it a secret for as long as you want."

I'm a barrel of emotions at Buck's New Year's Eve party later that week. I'm hanging out with the girls, and Luke is nowhere in sight, but I cannot. Stop. Thinking. About. Him. Half of my thoughts are a Luke-Claire highlight reel—that afternoon in the park, our date at Snow Mountain, our texts from the past few days—all playing over and over and over in my head. The other half are devoted to arguing with myself about whether or not us secretly dating is a bad idea.

"B is the only one who has someone to kiss at midnight. How crazy is that?" says Megan.

"It sucks," I reply. I have someone to kiss, but even if he shows, there's no way I'll get to kiss him.

"Yeah," Amberly chimes in. She seems much more interested in texting.

"Having someone to kiss makes New Year's Eve so much fun." B gazes sappily at Buck, who is reenacting a football play using a taxidermied squirrel.

Could she at least *try* to keep the mushiness to a minimum? Her friend is in post-breakup recovery. Then I think about kissing Luke four days ago and know I'm a much crappier friend.

"Whatever. I'm glad I'm not with Luke anymore," says Megan.

I feel a little better.

"He always made me feel like I wasn't good enough. Or like he wanted something else and I couldn't give it to him."

I feel a whole lot worse.

She shakes her head and plasters on a bright smile. "Enough about Luke. I only have three and a half months to find another prom date!"

"Ugh. Do we really have to start thinking about prom dates already?" I hope Luke and I will be "out" by then. If we're still together.

"Well, Buck and I will be going together. I can't wait for us all to go dress shopping," says Britney.

Amberly doesn't say anything, even though I know she needs a date too. She's hunched over her phone again, trying to hide her smile. I lean back so I can see what she's texting.

I miss you too. Maybe I can come over tonight and show you how much.

"Oh my gosh. Are you sexting?" I read the name on her screen. *Mike.* "With Coach Davis?!"

"You're sexting a teacher?" Megan squeals, her expression horrified and excited.

"How did that even happen?" asks Britney.

"Well, I was taking care of his dog over Thanksgiving . . . ," says Amberly.

"Yeah, but he wasn't even there," I say.

"I know, but when he got back, I went over there so he could pay me. And he was watching a football game, so I watched the rest of it with him. And"—she blushes—"now we're kind of together."

"Wow."

"No way."

"OMFG."

"I can't believe you tapped Coach Davis," says Britney.

"Actually, we're waiting."

"Wait. Really?" I say.

Amberly rolls her eyes. "Yes. Really. I mean, we've done other stuff, but we're not having sex."

"Like, until you're married?" asks Megan.

"Hello, this is me we're talking about. We're just waiting until I graduate. But I think it'll make it special. Oh, and um, y'all can't tell anyone, because he could lose his job."

"Yeah," says Megan. "'Cause dating students is super creepy."

"He's only five years older, and he takes such good care of me. And we're so in love, you guys. We just have to keep it a secret until I graduate."

I've been learning all about the hardships of secret forbidden love. So even though the idea of her showing Coach Davis how much she misses him is gross beyond belief, I say, "If you're really in love, I hope it works out."

Amberly smiles. "Thanks."

Megan makes a face like she got kicked in the gut.

"What is it?" I follow her gaze to the kitchen, where Luke is removing his coat and slinging it over the back of a chair. "Oh."

"Are you okay? Do you want to leave?" asks Amberly.

"We don't have to stay," I add, partially for Megan's sake and partially because I'm uncomfortable. If my eyes happen to meet Luke's, the whole room will be able to see everything we did in that one look, I just know it.

Megan squares her shoulders. "We'll stay. I want him to see me having a fantastic time."

And we do have a fantastic time. We dance, we gossip, and a part of me almost forgets about Luke—until I get a text at 11:58.

Meet me in the upstairs bathroom after the countdown.

I delete the text, stat, and shove my phone back in my pocket. I know my face is turning red. I don't dare look at Luke, but I can feel his eyes on me. The butterflies in my stomach get bigger and bigger as the clock ticks down on the TV. A clip of the ball dropping in Times Square plays beside a clip of the peach dropping in downtown Atlanta.

Three.

Two.

One.

I jump up and down and squeal and hug Megan and Amberly. Britney and Buck engage in an incredibly sloppy French kiss. Someone throws confetti. Luke slinks upstairs, sending me into a flurry of anticipation and nervousness. I count to sixty.

"I have to pee!" I yell over the noise. Thank goodness no one tries to make it a group bathroom outing.

Sneaking upstairs to meet Luke makes me feel like a spy. A sexy and dangerous bad girl on a mission to have a secret make-out session with my secret boyfriend. I glance around as I touch my hand to the doorknob, the hairs on my arms standing on end, but the hallway is empty.

"Hey," Luke says when I open the door. "I was starting to get nervous."

"I had to wait a minute so no one would suspect."

I click the lock button on the door, and even as I'm pushing it closed, he jerks me toward him by the waist. Our first kiss was tender and sweet. Our second is hot-steamy-passionate. His body pins me against the bathroom counter as his lips close over mine. I never realized kissing was a skill, but the things he can do with his tongue could make you forget your own name. He picks me up by my thighs and sets me on the counter without breaking the kiss, and I reel him toward me with my legs and link my ankles behind his back.

He pulls his mouth away, sucking at my bottom lip. Then he nibbles at my earlobe and along my neck, sending a cascade of shock waves down my spine. He yanks my shirt to the side so he can get at my collarbone. A box of tissues is poking me in the ribs, and I so don't care. I rake my hands through his hair. I can't get enough of him. I pull his face even with mine so I can kiss him again. There are entirely too many layers of clothing between us.

Just as my fingers find the hem of his shirt, the door creaks open. I panic. I swear I locked it. I pull my lips away from Luke's just in time, because Amanda walks in, dragging Sam by the hand. But I'm still sitting on the counter in front of him. And my legs are still wrapped around his waist. Crap. I unwind them while Amanda glares at me, and Sam gawks.

"This isn't what it looks like," I say.

Amanda puts her hands on her hips. "It looks like you're a skanky bitch."

"Amanda—"

"I'm telling Megan. She needs to know some of her friends are still loyal."

Since when are they friends? She flounces away with Sam following. For a second, Luke and I stare at each other, our eyes wide with fear. Then we race after her. When I get to the bottom of the stairs, Amanda is already siphoning her poison into Megan. Megan's head jerks in my direction like she can sense me or something. She studies me. And then Luke behind me. Our flushed faces and messed-up hair seem to confirm everything Amanda is telling her.

"I knew it!" she screeches. The entire party goes silent. "You've been hooking up with my boyfriend. I never should have believed that bullshit lie you told me at Britney's party."

"We didn't hook up at Britney's party—"

"Just like you didn't hook up in the bathroom just now? Stop lying! You're a slut. And a bitch. And the worst best friend ever. You should leave. Now. No one wants you here anyway—all you do is act like you're better than everyone else."

She pauses to gulp back some tears, and Buck takes the opportunity to yell, "Yoko is back!"

Megan laughs a cold laugh. "Yeah. She is. So much for wanting to get away from your rep as the school slut."

I'm shaking and seconds from a sob. Everyone stares. I can feel their eyes like a million barbs catching my skin. I run out to the front porch to get away from it all, and Luke appears seconds later.

"Do I really act like I'm better than everyone else?" I blurt out.

Luke frowns and takes a long breath before saying, "That's the part that bothers you the most?" He's avoiding the question.

"So, that's a yes," I say.

"Only a little. And you are better than the people in there, so don't worry about it. Come on. Let me take you home." He puts his arm around me and kisses the top of my head. "I know what it's like to be on the receiving end of a public Megan meltdown. And just so you know, you're worth the drama."

chapter
14

If you got caught kissing in Naples, Italy, in the sixteenth century, you could receive the death penalty. Given what is in store for me when school starts back up, I think I'd rather be in sixteenth-century Naples. Megan wasn't home when I went by (her brother said), and she hasn't answered my phone calls (no surprises there), but neither have Britney and Amberly. And it's not just them. When I get to school, I realize the entire cheerleading squad is out to get me. Even though they go through drama with each other on a weekly basis, now that someone from the outside (me) has wronged one of their own, they've developed some sort of weird cheerleading solidarity.

While I'm drinking from the water fountain just after first period, two cheerleaders I barely know slut-cough me.

slut-cough *(verb)*

To cough into your fist while simultaneously saying the
word slut, *so that the word is disguised poorly, if at*
all.

(noun)

An act of slut-coughing

(synonym)

Whore-cough

While I'm walking to lunch, Amanda Bell bumps up against me in the hall, sending my books and papers flying.

"Oops," she giggles.

She's clearly loving this. After years of fruitless scheming, she finally has a spot at Megan's lunch table. My spot. I don't try to sit with them. I sit with the soccer girls, who are all pretty nice about things. The minutes tick by with excruciating slowness, though, and I eat my lunch on autopilot.

I pass Amberly and Britney on the way back to class.

"Hey," I say.

No response.

"Hey, Amberly."

This time her shoulders tense slightly, so I know she heard me.

"Seriously, can't you just talk to me?"

She turns and opens her mouth, but Britney stops her.

"No, she can't. Because she doesn't understand how you could do something like this to Megan. Don't expect anyone to be on your side."

She flips her brittle blond hair in my direction and stalks away. Amberly gives me this *I'm sorry, my hands are tied* look and follows behind her.

I go to soccer practice thinking the worst is over. At least none of the girls on the team have been sucked into the drama. The girls' locker room smells like the weirdest combination of overripe bananas and feet. The rusting lockers that no one even uses and the old wooden benches bolted to the floor are in sharp contrast to our crisp new Adidas duffels, the results of two car washes and a bake sale. I throw on my shorts and then my sports bra and T-shirt.

"Um, Claire?" Our goalie stares at me with a sad, uncomfortable look on her face.

"What is it?"

She points at my shirt. Other girls are looking now. Scrawled across the front, in what looks like black permanent marker, are five letters. *W-H-O-R-E.*

"Oh."

I try to pretend like it's not a big deal. I keep my chin up as I peel off my shirt and put it back on inside out. I only cry a little when we're out running laps and I don't think anybody will notice. I may not have proof, but it's obvious Megan's behind this. I don't understand how she could do this to me. She's my best friend. I knew she would be hurt, but this is more than just the silent treatment. This is wrong. And the worst part is I've lost more than my best friend. I've lost everyone. I keep thinking of

Amberly turning away from me in the hall. If I had trusted her, if I had let her in more, I wonder if she would have been standing with me instead of with Britney.

No one wants you here anyway—all you do is act like you're better than everyone else. Is that the real reason I don't confide in Amberly? Because I think I'm better than her? I've never felt like I fit in in Pine Bluff, but does wanting bigger things mean I think other people are smaller? I shake my head and run faster, but I can't get away from it. Megan said it, and everyone else thinks it. Even Luke agreed. But I don't know what to do about it, so I just keep running.

Things go on like this for the next few weeks. I'm dropping my book bag on my bedroom floor after another stellar day at school when I notice it. A sniffling just loud enough for me to hear in my bedroom. I tiptoe into the hallway. And there, at the end of the hall, the door that is always closed has been slung wide open. I walk toward the open door, toward the quiet weeping.

Timothy's room looks almost exactly the same. His choo-choo-train wallpaper chugs its way around the room. Baby-size corduroys and T-shirts hang in his closet next to a rack of impossibly small shoes. His crib is still made up with green-and-blue-striped sheets and bumper pads. Like any second now he'll be back to take a nap.

Mama sits hunched over in a chair, sobbing into her knee-caps. Another relapse, or will it be permanent this time? I can't ever be sure, and it kills me. Why didn't I spend more time with her when everything was okay? I stand in the doorway, frozen like a statue, taking in the horror of it all. Mama looks up.

"Oh, hi, sweetheart, I didn't realize you were there." She blows her nose and pats the ottoman in front of her. "Come sit down."

My legs move toward her coaxing as if independent of my brain. I sit stiffly.

"I was watering the plants today when I realized Timothy's tree had a flower," she says.

I stare at her blankly. Then I realize there's a black-and-white photograph in her lap. An extreme close-up of a single white cherry blossom in a sea of gray-black leaves.

"It's beautiful," I say carefully.

She smiles. "When I saw it, I ran inside to get my camera. I took a whole roll and printed this one out immediately." She runs her fingers along the edges of the photo. "I thought about where I wanted to hang it, and only one place seemed right."

"So, you came in here to hang that picture?" I'm still not sure what kind of sadness this is. I don't know what I'll do if it's the old kind.

"To figure out where to hang it once it's framed. But while I was looking around, I realized it's time to pack up his room now. And, well, I don't think that's something I can do by myself. Do you think you can get Dad and Libby and Sarah to help?"

"Of course." A deep breath floods my lungs, and my blood starts to move in my veins again. This is normal. *She* is still normal. And normal people sometimes shed normal tears when they're sad.

I jump in the chair with her and hug her so tight she lets out a little gasp. "Are you okay?" she asks.

"I'm fine," I say into her shoulder. "Everything is fine."

I make minute adjustments to the place settings at our dining-room table. I fuss with the vase of tulips on the buffet, even though two minutes ago Mama declared them "fabulous." I am an idiot. I never should have let Luke talk me into this. But I did. We were sitting on a rock at the park, and he asked if he could come over for dinner this Saturday, and then he ran his hand up and down my arm, and I stammered "yes." Idiot.

Maybe it will be okay. Sarah brought Harrison (who is a nice-enough guy to deserve an upgrade from Boyfriend) here for four whole days, and their relationship is still intact. And my family acts normal, like, at least 80 percent of the time now. So the chances of Luke making it through this meal unscathed are pretty good, right?

I scurry back to the kitchen to check my eggplant lasagna. The entire house smells like basil, and the cheese is just brown around the edges. Right on time. Mama and Libby chop vegetables for a salad. My dad hasn't emerged from his office yet. Everything seems fine, but I'm still wary.

"Luke will be here in fifteen minutes," I announce. "I think we need to have a debriefing or something. I'll go get Daddy."

But before I can leave the kitchen, the doorbell chimes.

"Crap. He's early." Why did I ever think this was a good idea?

"Sweetie, everything is going to be fine. Relax," says Mama.

I open my mouth, but she puts her hands on my shoulders. "Relax."

"Okay."

"Do you want to get the door or should I get it?"

"I'll get the door. You get Daddy. And tell him he has to talk during dinner."

Mama hides a smile. "I'll tell him."

It's going to be okay. *It's going to be okay.* Libby hasn't done anything feral in at least a month. Mama is dressed like a Stepford wife right down to her pink peep-toe pumps, which means she's having a good day—she's nearly always having them now and it's almost too wonderful to believe. As long as my dad isn't silent, we're good. I open the door.

Luke is wearing khaki pants and holding a bouquet of sunflowers.

"Hi," he says.

"Hey. Come on in."

I usher him into the kitchen, where my mom is picking lint off my dad's shirt until she sees us.

"This is Luke," I say.

My parents introduce themselves, Mama with exclamations over the flowers, Daddy with an awkward, no-eye-contact handshake.

"Wow, you don't look old enough to be Claire's mom," Luke says.

I can't believe he went with such a cheesy line, but of course my mom gobbles it right up. He's been in my house for less than two minutes, and he's already gotten her approval. Maybe I was worried over nothing. At least one of my family members is on Luke's side, and we haven't even started eating. Libby peeks around the corner at us, and I wave her over so I can introduce her. Luke shakes hands with her like she's a grown-up.

Dinner runs as smoothly as if I'd scripted it myself. The food is delicious—points for me. Luke asks Mama about her photography, and we chatter away without any lulls—points for him.

"What grade are you in, Libby?" he asks.

"Second."

"Really? I thought you were going to say third."

Libby sits up a little taller. Man, is he good with the ladies. Even ones who are eight years old.

"How do you like it?" he asks.

"It's pretty good. Except for this girl Kenzie. She's always making fun of me."

"Aw. I'm sorry."

"It's okay." Libby pops a bite of lasagna in her mouth. "I'm going to put chewing gum in her hair."

"You most certainly are not," says Mama. "We are going to get through the rest of this school year without another in-school suspension."

Luke leans toward Libby. "You could put a cricket in her lunch box, and if you're stealth about it, no one would know it was you," he whispers. "I can pick some up from the bait shop."

She grins from ear to ear. He's got Libby. Now all he needs is Dad. His chances don't look good, though. My father has spent most of the meal with his eyes on his dinner plate, speaking only when Mama and I address him directly and give him pointed looks. If I were Luke, I wouldn't bother. But he seems determined.

"Claire tells me you're an architect."

It takes my dad a second to realize this requires an answer.

"Oh. Yes. Yes, I am."

"I think architecture is a fascinating field."

"Thank you." Dad chews a bite of garlic bread with an agitated look on his face. "So, you're Claire's boyfriend?"

"Yes, sir."

"I'm just asking because I could have sworn I saw you with Claire's friend, Megan, who lives across the street. In her driveway."

What is he doing?! Of all the things I wouldn't want to talk about at dinner. There's a silence longer than the Mississippi during which you can hear bites of salad being chewed and silverware clinking against plates. I start to mumble a reply when Luke cuts me off.

"Megan and I used to date. I wanted to be with Claire since the day I met her, but Megan can be, well, persuasive. I'm so glad Claire's my girlfriend now." He holds my hand under the table. "I'm a lucky guy."

Then he flashes a dimpled smile at Mama and Libby, and they sigh in unison. My dad merely grunts and shovels in another bite of lasagna.

The rest of the meal passes without incident. We eat some key lime pie. Luke thanks my family for having him. I walk him to the door.

"I'll come out and say good-bye; just give me a second," I tell him.

I catch my dad picking at the remains of the pie.

"What was that about?"

He shrugs.

"Seriously, Dad! You didn't do that to Harrison."

"I don't know, Claire. There's something I don't trust about that boy."

"He didn't do anything but be nice to everyone."

"I know the difference between store-bought manners and being genuine. He says all the right things, but there's something off about him. Be careful, okay?" My dad is giving me one of his serious, *Trust me on this one, Claire-Bear* looks, the kind I haven't seen in ages, and it is so annoying because there were plenty of times when I needed him, and now—now that I don't need his help and just want him to be nice to my boyfriend—*now* he's decided to be Dependable Dad again.

I roll my eyes. "Noted."

I find Luke leaning against his car.

"Sorry about my dad."

"It's cool. Dads are supposed to be like that."

I love how he can take the worst thing that happened tonight and make it feel normal. Even with Dad's weirdness, tonight went better than I could have hoped for.

"I've never brought a boy home before."

"Did I do okay?"

"You did great." I kiss him lightly on the lips. "I love you."

I don't care that, per girl code, I'm supposed to make him say it first. I don't care that we haven't even been together a whole month yet. I know this is right.

Luke brushes a strand of hair behind my ear. "I love you too."

Best. Day. Ever.

The sounds of Gwen Stefani jar me out of a dream about ice-skating sumo wrestlers. I feel around the top of my nightstand for my cell phone. The number isn't one I recognize.

"Hello?"

"Hi, this is Karen Banks with *Seventeen* magazine."

I rub my bleary eyes with the back of my hand. "Um, what?"

"We're doing an article on backstabbing bitches, and we'd love to interview you."

I hear giggles in the background and a whispered "Shhhh!"

I am wide awake. "Very funny, y'all."

"Excuse me? I don't—"

"Britney, I know that's you." Her attempt to disguise her voice isn't so good now that I'm coherent.

"This is Karen Banks with—"

"Good night."

I hang up the phone. The pranking doesn't hurt nearly as much as the fact that I should be at the sleepover but I'm not.

To distract myself from the loss of all my best girlfriends, I cling to Luke and throw myself full force into soccer season. I love the soccer girls in a there's-no-I-in-*team* way, but being friends with them just isn't the same.

At least Luke is amazing. I roll out of bed on a sunny morning in blue pajama pants dotted with fat white clouds and stumble down to breakfast. I almost jump out of my pj's when I see Luke at our kitchen table. Two plates on two place mats with two sets of utensils sit in front of him. Heart-shaped waffles topped with whipped cream and fresh strawberries. A vase filled with red roses.

I knew Valentine's Day was today. I already bought him a present and everything. But I kind of forgot until just now. His surprise is so sweet and unbelievably romantic that I'll only tease him a minimal amount for bringing over a heart-shaped waffle maker.

My mom winks at me and wrangles Libby out of the kitchen. After they leave, Luke kisses me on the nose.

"Hey, beautiful. Happy Valentine's Day."

My hair is a tangled mess, my eyes are bleary and ringed with mascara, and I'm pretty sure my breath could kill an ox, but right now, I feel beautiful.

"Happy Valentine's Day to you, too."

He tries to kiss me on the mouth, but I playfully push him away.

"I'll be right back. I want to get your present."

I run upstairs, but instead head directly to the bathroom to wash my face and brush my teeth. I almost forget to grab his present on my way back to the kitchen.

"Here you go."

I hand him a featherlight box in glittery packaging. He makes a face and shakes it.

"Is there anything in here?"

The paper comes off in two rips.

"Hawks tickets. Nice! Open yours. Open yours."

It's a gigantic basket of Bath & Body Works stuff.

"Thanks. I love it."

It's thoughtful of him to exchange gifts with me before school. Carrying Luke's roses through the hallways would call about as much attention as stapling a red A to the front of my sweater.

I text Sam that I'll be getting a ride with Luke this morning. Now that Megan and I aren't speaking, he's been chauffeuring me to school whenever I can't borrow Mama's car. Luke waits for me in the living room while I get ready for school, this boy who comes to my house at the crack of dawn to make me breakfast. He sits there watching cartoons with Libby while she eats breakfast and I shower and get dressed. Then he drives me to school, holding my hand the whole way. He gives it a squeeze when we pull into the school parking lot.

"You look so beautiful today."

"Thank you."

"Maybe it's the shirt. I love it when you wear blue. Or maybe it's just you."

He leans over the console to kiss me.

"I love you, Claire."

"I love you too."

Being with Luke is like living in a fairy tale. And it stays like that for a while.

chapter
15

We're fooling around on the couch in Luke's basement the day things get weird. His parents are away at a dinner party, and we just got back from our own dinner to celebrate our two-month anniversary. It's February twenty-seventh. We count that day we kissed in the snow as the start of our relationship, even though he didn't officially ask me to be his girlfriend till later.

We're naked from the waist up doing everything we usually do, and today I decide I'm ready for us to be naked from the waist down too. When I unbutton his pants, his face lights up like a firework. I fumble with the waistband of his jeans, tugging it from side to side so it'll slide over his butt. How come stuff like this never looks awkward on TV? He pulls his jeans off the rest of the way by himself. They join our shirts in a pile on the floor. My jeans are next, and then our underwear, and then I am full-on naked in front of a boy for the first time.

"You look beautiful," he whispers.

"Thanks." I wish I could say the same for him, but penises look SO WEIRD.

"I have protection. We can—"

I freeze. "I'm not ready. Yet." I hope I wasn't sending signals that I was.

"Oh. Well, that's okay," he says. "Is there a reason?"

"Yeah. Um . . ."

I'm not ready because the last time I thought about being ready, my boyfriend was cheating on me. Because I'm scared it will hurt. Because I don't know how many girls you've slept with and you could be carrying chlamydia. Because I love you but I still haven't decided if you're the One.

"You don't have to explain right now. I don't mind or anything. I was just curious," he says. And then, after a pause: "Are you a virgin?"

My cheeks turn pink. "Yeah. Are you?"

"No."

"Do you mind if I ask how many?"

"Three."

I want to know if Megan is one of them, but I can't bring myself to ask. So we do stuff besides *IT* and then watch *SNL* reruns for the next two hours, and I'm mostly just happy he doesn't care that I'm not ready to have sex yet. But then in his car on the way home, he says, "It's funny you just now gave me a bj tonight."

"Why is that funny?" I ask, because I can't think of any other way to respond.

"Nothing. It's just Megan and I had already had sex by now."

He says it so casually, like he's making an observation about the weather. So many questions ping around in my head.

What does sex with me have to do with sex with Megan?

Does he compare me to her?

What if I'm not as good as her?

What if he compares how we look naked? Good Lord, I hope not.

I wonder if he ever thinks about her when he's doing stuff with me.

And why is he telling me this anyway? Is he trying to make me jealous?

Does he think it'll make me want to have sex with him sooner? He seemed so okay with waiting before.

"Well, I'm not Megan. And anyway, the last time I thought about losing my virginity, things went really badly, so I'm not wanting to rush into it again."

"Hey, it's okay." He reaches for my hand across the console. "I'm glad you're not her. I could never talk to her the way I talk to you."

Hearing him say that makes me feel warm all over.

"All we ever did was hook up."

And the warm feelings die.

I shake my head. "I don't want to talk about it, okay?"

"Why are you being like this? I said I'm glad you're not her. You don't have to be jealous. I love you now."

"I know. I'm sorry," I say.

But the thing is, I'm not.

* * *

When I come downstairs on the morning of my birthday, I half expect to find Luke in my kitchen. He's not there, though. Of course he's not. He wouldn't do the same thing again. But after Valentine's Day, I can't wait to see what he'll do for my birthday.

A horn beep means Sam is in my driveway, so I grab my stuff and run outside. A monstrous caramel latte and a cranberry-walnut muffin are waiting for me in my seat.

"Happy birthday!" says Sam.

"Aw, thanks."

Since I didn't have time for breakfast, I begin unceremoniously stuffing my face before he leaves the driveway.

"So, I was watching *Napoleon Dynamite* last night—"

"You know, I don't think I've seen that."

Sam practically veers off the road. "Wait. What?!"

"I've never seen it?"

"How have you never seen *Napoleon Dynamite*? It's only the funniest movie ever." For the remainder of our drive, Sam lectures me about how culturally illiterate I am. He keeps going even after he parks, and we stand in an empty space while I feebly defend myself.

"I can't believe I've never made you watch it before. You're coming over this Saturday. Bring kettle corn."

I see Amanda waiting for him by the back entrance. Her arms are crossed. She won't approach Sam while I'm talking to him because Megan or someone might see her and think she's talking to me.

"You better get over there or you're going to be in trouble." Man, that girl keeps him on a short leash. I'm tempted to say something more, but I don't want to bash his first real girlfriend.

He sneaks a glance at Amanda. "Yeah, I'll see you later."

I find Luke in the hallway on my way to class.

"Hey." I give him a hug.

"Hey. Happy birthday."

"Thanks. So, are we doing something after school today? Any special plans?"

"It's a school night."

"Oh."

My disappointment must be obvious because Luke quickly says, "Yeah, I guess we can do something. Want to meet me at my car after school? We could go get some ice cream or something?"

I plant a kiss on his cheek. "Ice cream or something sounds perfect. I have to be home in time for dinner with the family anyway."

I spend most of school daydreaming about how this is the best birthday I've had in years, and before I know it, the last bell is ringing and I'm winding through the halls to the back parking lot. Luke sits in his car with the windows rolled down. I wave, but he doesn't see me. I wave again. It's like he's in a trance or something. I reach my arms through the window and wrap them around his neck, giggling.

"You okay? You look kind of out of it."

He jumps. "Hey, I didn't see you."

He pulls my face toward his and kisses me until the parking lot disappears beneath my feet. His fingers brush through my hair, tracing patterns across my scalp. I come up for air, a light sigh escaping my lips, and through my half-shut eyes I see what Luke was looking at before I interrupted him.

Megan.

Perched on the back of her car and reapplying her lip gloss while she waits for Britney or Amberly or whoever, the afternoon sun glittering against her hair and the hood of the car. She's the only possible person you'd see if you were sitting in Luke's driver's seat and looking in that direction. I'm tempted to ask him about it directly, but I don't have the guts. He pulls out of the parking lot, slouching low in his seat with one lazy arm resting on the steering wheel, and I watch him to see if he'll look at her again, but he doesn't.

"So, have you talked to Megan recently?" I ask.

I scrutinize his face. Is he nervous or just surprised?

"No. Why?"

"Just wondering."

"Hey, I need to get gas before we go get ice cream." Luke pulls into Pete's, the combination gas station/convenience store/live bait shop, but doesn't get out of the car. "It wouldn't be the worst thing, though, would it? Us talking again? It would be good to smooth things over. For all of us, I mean—for you guys too." He sure is sweating a lot for someone who isn't talking to his ex-girlfriend.

"Yeah," I say. "I guess so."

Something about this whole situation doesn't feel right. So when he goes inside to pay for the gas, I do something I never thought I'd do. I see his cell phone, sitting in the console whispering my name. And I pick it up.

There's a text from Megan in his messages. That bastard! I can't open it because it's new and he'd know I did it, but the fact that it's there at all proves . . . something. When I replace the phone, taking care to make sure it's positioned exactly as it was before, I get a queasy sensation in my stomach. I'm one of *those* girls now. We have *that* kind of relationship.

But there was a text. From Megan. So obviously I was right to look. I shake my head. I can't even convince myself with that kind of logic. I know it wasn't right. But I also know this won't be the last time I check Luke's phone.

We get ice cream and everything is fine (well, as fine as it can be considering that text is all I can think about). Then he drops me off at my house and kisses me on my front porch and I try to find some sort of answer in the kissing, but it feels like . . . a kiss. A good kiss. A fun kiss. But it doesn't reveal the mysteries of the ages and it doesn't tell me why my best friend is texting my boyfriend or if he still has feelings for her.

I close the front door behind me and am immediately tackled by Libby.

"Open it! Open it!" she squeals.

She waves a letter over her head—it's from Georgia Tech. Holy crap, it's from Georgia Tech! I run my fingers along the seal but they're shaking and I'm clumsy and I practically rip the envelope in half trying to get at the letter inside. I gloss over the pleasantries and scan for the important part. "We are pleased to inform you . . ." I'm in!

"Libs! I'm in! I'm in!" I pick her up and twirl her around and then read over the letter again, savoring it this time.

This is more than just an acceptance letter. This is a ticket to a different life and a validation that everything I worked for was worth it and the beginning of a fulfillment of a pact I made two years ago. Something like longing clenches like a fist around my insides.

I wish I could call Megan and tell her.

"Claire," Mama calls from behind a rack of dresses. "What do you think of this one?"

The dress she's holding is fugly (periwinkle, huge crinoline skirt), but I'm so happy to have my mom take me prom-dress shopping I smile anyway.

"It's not really my style. I like dresses that are more straight and fitted."

She nods seriously and dives back into the racks. I keep going with the rack I'm working on, and a few minutes later she pops back out.

"What about this one?"

"Oh."

The dress is every shade of blue—it fades from a sky color at the top to a deep indigo at the hemline. The skirt is layers of sheer fabric that fall just above the knee, and the bodice is fitted through the waist with a slight flare at the hips. Wow. My mom can take direction.

"'Oh' good? Or 'oh' bad?"

"Definitely 'oh' good."

We add it to the pile of other potentials that is quickly taking over one of the dressing rooms. I rush to try on the other dresses first, saving it for last. The dress swooshes over my head. I zip it up and turn to look at myself in the mirror. It's perfect. It shows off my legs and how tiny my waist is, but it has this ruching across the chest that makes my boobs look huge (for me). I have never felt so beautiful in a dress before. It's like it was made just for me. I run outside to look in the three-panel mirror, and Mama agrees.

We're waiting to buy the magical dress when I realize the blond girl in front of me sliding a credit card across the counter is Megan. And she realizes it's me at exactly the same time, so neither of us can pretend to look away.

"Hey," I say.

"Hey," she replies. "So, you're here with your mom?"

I glance over my shoulder, but Mama is busy texting.

"Yeah."

"That's great." Megan smiles a sad smile at me.

I'm sad too, because I can remember a time when we would have been happy over it together.

"Is your mom here too?"

"No, I'm here with Amberly." She gestures to the doorway, where Amberly waves to me. "Listen, I have to go because B and Amanda are waiting for us at the food court."

With one last wistful look over their shoulders, they're gone. I see them again when Mama and I walk past the food court on the way to our car. They're with Britney and Amanda at a table, laughing, surrounded by colorful shopping bags. They're all eating salads (prom crash diet, I'm sure), and I'm not there to lecture them on the importance of protein in any weight-loss plan. Amberly says something, and Megan laughs so hard she grabs B's wrist with one hand and slaps the table with the other.

I stare at the four of them, Amanda sitting in the chair where I should be sitting. Where I *could* be sitting if I had never started dating Luke. And I start to wonder if he's worth it.

Kiss #15 xoxo

The Present

Megan deserves to win prom queen. I totally voted for her even
after everything that's happened. I have to pretend prom queen
is the most important thing in the world. If I lose my focus
for even a second, I might remember the other prom. I might
remember that prom is when little brothers die.

Seth, the senior-class president, makes a big show of
announcing the winners, waving his white envelope like it's
the Academy Awards or something. He'll announce king
first. I hope it isn't Buck. I still don't get why the 90 percent
of our class who spent four years under his reign of torment
would vote for him, but they will. People still voted Megan for
homecoming court back in ninth and tenth grade before the de-
bitch-ification process. That's how I know Buck will win too.

Seth finally rips open the envelope. "And your new prom
king is . . ." He reads the card inside. "Glennnnn Baker."

OMG. Glenn! The whole crowd screams for Glenn. I
whistle. Buck tries to play it cool, but he is so pissed. Ha!

Seth hushes the room. "And your new prom queen is . . . the
fabulously beautiful . . . the effervescent . . ."

"Just say it already!" someone yells from the back of the
room.

"Megan McQueen!"

Megan's cheers are, if possible, louder than Glenn's. I clap and yell along with everyone else, but I can't help frowning when she exchanges hugs with Amberly and Britney and even Amanda Bell, who holds on for a few seconds too long. I know I should hate her, but I kind of wish I were there to celebrate with her. Her winning prom queen means she completed her part of Pact #5. And I guess I did too. It just wasn't as fun as I expected.

Megan makes her way to the stage, her slinky floor-length red gown swishing with every step.

"I'm so glad Glenn won," I say to Luke as Seth gingerly places a sparkly rhinestone crown atop Megan's elaborate hairstyle. "It's unbelievable. Everyone at school finally wised up and didn't vote for the guy who made their lives hell. And Glenn deserves it so much."

Luke watches Megan and Glenn take their places in the center of the dance floor so they can share the requisite first dance. It's hard to tell whether he's looking at both of them or just her.

"So, you haven't said anything about my dress. What do you think?"

"Huh? Oh, yeah, it's really pretty." He takes another swig of his rum-spiked Coke—his third, I think—and turns back to the dance floor. "Have you seen Megan's? That slit up the side is so hot." His eyes devour her as she twirls under the spotlight, like he's planning to draw her from memory later. "And her hair looks so cool. How come you didn't do anything special with yours?"

"I'm not an updo kind of girl." My hands smooth my straight hair protectively. "Plus, do you know how much those things cost? I'd rather straighten it myself." I don't say, *Plus, thanks to you I'm no longer friends with Amberly, who would have done amazing things with my hair for free,* but I'm tempted.

He grunts in reply. Since he doesn't bother to look away from Megan, I figure he also won't notice if I leave him standing by himself, so I stalk off toward the ladies' room. Prom is being held in a ballroom at the Fabulous Fox Theatre, so it's one of those super-fancy bathrooms with overstuffed couches and real artwork. I scowl at my boring hair in the gilded mirror. Luke's at prom—with me. That means I won. So why don't I feel like a winner?

There's one thing I think could make me feel better, but I don't know if she'll talk to me. I know Megan's done some unforgivable things over the past few months. And I know finding out about Luke and me at a party in front of everyone must have been awful and humiliating. But I really miss my best friend. And it couldn't hurt to try.

When I come back to the ballroom, the first dance has obviously ended, because everyone else is dancing now. Including Luke. With Megan. I bump past dancing couples and trip over dress trains until I'm close enough to jerk Luke away by his elbow.

"Can we talk? Now."

Megan's eyes get big. "Claire, I didn't—he just—" I leave her there stuttering and yank Luke out of the ballroom, past the faculty members standing guard over the lobby, to a couch tucked into an alcove by the bathrooms.

Luke holds his hands in front of him, the universal gesture for *I have nothing to hide*. "I didn't do anything. She came up to me out of nowhere and asked me if we could talk about why we broke up. She wanted closure."

"Since when does closure involve freak dancing?"

"Oh, c'mon. It *wasn't* like that. Anyway, the only reason I danced with her is 'cause I couldn't find you. Why'd you walk off like that?"

I roll my eyes. "I'm surprised you noticed. You were so busy going on and on about Megan."

"I just said I liked someone's dress. You can't expect to have the best dress at prom or for other girls to never be prettier than you. Try not to be so insecure."

"Maybe if you'd stop comparing me to her, I wouldn't be."

"I'm not comparing you guys. I'm just stating facts."

"Oh, yeah? Well, your facts hurt."

He sighs like I am the most exhausting, annoying person in the entire world. Then he takes a drink directly from the flask in his pocket, because apparently I'm *so* annoying he can't stand to be around me without having some alcohol to take the edge off.

"Whatever, Claire. Prom is supposed to be fun, but if you want to ruin it by picking a fight with me . . ."

Me ruin prom? "You're the one—"

I stop because I hear noises coming our way. Luke shoves his flask in his pocket fast, but relaxes when a couple of junior girls breeze past our couch, giggling their way toward the bathroom.

He pulls it back out and takes a sip. I've never seen him have more than a couple beers, but he's a mean drunk. At least, I sure hope this is the alcohol.

"Look," he says. "I'm sorry I said that stuff about Megan. Can we just go back in and have fun now?"

I really wish it were that easy. "It's more than that. I think there's something going on between you two."

Luke's apologetic face disappears. "Are you seriously doing this right now?" He gets up and stomps across the alcove. "I broke up with her to be with you. How can you even say that?"

I follow after him and lower my voice. "You were dancing with her, and I know you guys have been talking again."

"No, we haven't. I don't know who's telling you this stuff, but they're lying."

I'd like to believe him, but I saw something like fear flash in his eyes before he answered. He's the one lying.

"I saw a text from her in your phone."

"*What.*"

"I looked through your phone one time when you were getting gas, and there was a text from Megan. I didn't read it, but—"

"What the fuck, Claire!" He moves toward me, his hands at his side like veiny claws, his face red with anger and rum. "I can't believe you went through my phone. It's the kind of thing Megan was always doing. First her. Now you. I'm so tired of dealing with this bullshit!"

And then it happens so fast. His left hand balls up and lashes out toward the wall, almost as if it's acting of its own accord. His fist passes so close to my cheek the flyaway hairs around my face spiral with the motion of the air. An angry thud echoes behind my ear. Did he really just punch the wall? But now he's shaking his hand in pain, and sure enough, there's a fist-size crater imprinted in the antique velvet wallpaper.

I back away from him like he's a wild animal.

"Claire, wait." He looks just as shocked as me.

I shake my head and run back to the ballroom, where other people are having fun at their senior prom. I flop into the first chair I find. My heart pounds against my chest, and I'm breathing like I just ran suicide sprints.

"Claire, are you okay?"

Megan hovers over me, looking ridiculously beautiful, even for her. She sparkles from head to toe, the top of her crown to the heels of her stilettos. Of course he wants her back.

"I'm fine," I say with my jaw clenched tight.

"I'm sorry about what happened before. With Luke."

"I bet you are."

"No, I am. I didn't mean for it to look that way. He came up and said he wanted closure and could we—"

"I already talked to Luke. I know you're the one that wanted the closure." I make air quotes when I say the word *closure*.

Megan's perfectly plucked eyebrows arch toward her crown. "No, I'm not."

"Well, I'm not about to trust someone who has done

everything she can to make my life miserable for the past four months."

"I know it was wrong of me to keep you closed out for so long. I'm sorry I did it."

"It was a lot more than that. The things you guys did . . . you tortured me."

Megan frowns. "What—?"

"No. You know what, I'm going to stop you right there. Some things are too big for sorry."

She opens her mouth one more time but then shakes her head and walks away.

Luke doesn't show his face for at least half an hour, and by then I've calmed down. He shuffles up to me with his head hung low.

"I'm really sorry. I was a jerk."

"Yeah. You were."

"But you know I'd never hurt you, right?" His blue eyes are wide and innocent, but I don't trust them anymore.

"Yeah, I guess."

A slow song plays over the speaker system.

"Do you maybe want to dance with me?"

I don't. But I also don't want to awkwardly dump my boyfriend in front of everyone at prom, so I'll do what I can until it's over. "Sure."

I take his hand reluctantly and follow him to the dance floor. In spite of what happened, my body molds itself to his, feet between feet, hips against hips, my head tucked under his chin.

I used to love how perfectly shaped we are for each other. To anyone watching, we must seem like this happy, totally-in-love couple sharing a romantic moment. But all I can think of is his fist swooshing past my cheek.

At the end of the song, he tilts my head up and presses his lips against mine. And like the traitors they are, my lips part until we're full on making out and my skin tingles with warmth and I'm hungry for more. Damn it. I know lots of people are into that whole passionate fight–passionate make-up thing, but I'm not one of them. The highs aren't worth the lows. Now if only I can convince my body.

Luke is overly attentive and gentle as a kitten for the rest of the night. He strokes the back of my neck while we take a packed limo to Buck's house for the after-party. He whispers in my ear how beautiful I am. It only makes what I have to do next that much harder. After the other couples exit the limo, I grab the sleeve of Luke's tux.

"Wait."

He slides back into the seat next to me. "What is it?"

Rip it off. Fast. Like a Band-Aid. Picture the wall crater. Let it be your strength.

"We need to break up."

"*What?*"

"You make me jealous and insecure. I make you punch walls. We're obviously not right for each other."

"Can't we talk about this?"

I scoot across the seat toward the door. "There's nothing to talk about. We'll just fight again."

I close the door to the limo and walk sadly into the party. Now I have no friends *and* no boyfriend. What I do have is a house full of people under various degrees of intoxication harboring various degrees of hatred toward me. It's time to start doing shots.

In the kitchen I find a shot taker's paradise—bottles in all shapes and colors supplied by Buck's older brother, who makes regular appearances at high school parties even though he graduated three years ago. Jimmy stands at the counter mixing drinks for a couple of sophomore girls who have apparently not been alerted to his legendary creeper status.

"Hey, Claire." His eyes light up. "What can I get you?"

I decide getting a drink is worth making a deal with the Grim Creeper. "Shots."

"Oh-ho-kay."

Jimmy whips up a line of shots, something with vodka and juices, and the four of us (me, Jimmy, the two sophomores) take them and slam the empty glasses on the counter. He immediately makes another batch, and when Sophomore #1 wimps out, I pound hers too. A hand squeezes my shoulder, and I turn.

"CJ, are you okay?" Sam asks, his brown eyes full of concern.

"I'm fine. I'm just having some fun."

He shifts from foot to foot like he wants to say something else, but before he can, Amanda drags him away for yet another photo op. I hop up on the counter, not caring that my dress gets wet in the process, and prattle away with the sophomores like we're BFFs. They don't seem to know they're supposed to hate me—that I'm a boyfriend stealer and a slut. Or maybe they're so excited to hang out with seniors they're not picky. Jimmy slips us a steady supply of fruity drinks while we talk, each one tasting stronger than the last.

"Be right back—I totally have to pee," I tell the sophomores. I jump down to the linoleum, barely sticking the landing. "And I totally have to take off these shoes."

I leave my heels in the kitchen and zigzag to the bathroom, which—miracle of miracles—is empty. When I open the door again, Jimmy stands in the hallway, waiting.

"Everything okay?"

"Yeah, I'm totally fine. Totally."

I take a step forward, wobble, and decide it would be easier to lean against the wall instead. Jimmy is suddenly close, really close, his breath hot on my cheek. The elk head mounted on the wall above me watches with glassy eyes.

"You sure are pretty," he whispers into my ear.

He kisses me, but I'm too drunk to care. I barely even feel it. My lips have gone numb. I press at them with my fingertips and giggle. There's a tug at my wrist, an arm around my waist, Jimmy dragging me up the stairs toward the door of a bedroom.

"What do you think you're doing?"

My eyelids flutter. Megan has stepped in front of Jimmy, blocking the doorway.

"Oh, uh, sorry. We can go somewhere else."

"You're not going anywhere with her."

"She wants to come with me." A whine creeps into Jimmy's voice as he backs away from her, pulling me with him.

"No. She doesn't." Megan's fingers pry his arm from my body. When I start to keel over like a doll that can't stand on its own, she quickly slides her own arm in place of his. I fall against her birdlike shoulder, and she staggers under my weight, taking tiny shuffling steps to lead me away.

Jimmy's face turns red between his goatee patches. "What am I supposed to do now?" He kicks the door. "Bitch."

"I don't care. But it won't be with her." Megan fixes him with her frostiest smile. "So you can go find someone else to molest, Creep Show."

Jimmy opens his mouth like he wants to say something else, but instead he stomps off down the hall. Megan and I half walk, half fall down the stairs, and by some magic she manages to get us to the first-floor bathroom in one piece. She leaves me on the floor, where I slump against the bathtub, which is nice and cool against my cheek. When the door opens again, she's holding a glass of water.

"Drink the whole thing." She shoves it into my hands, and I tilt it back. Some of it sloshes down the front of my dress. Megan sits behind me on the side of the tub and combs my hair away from my face with her fingers.

"What are you doing?"

"In case you throw up," she says.

"Thanks." Then I remember every awful prank and cold

silence for the past four months. "But . . . I mean . . . why did you pull me away from Jimmy?"

"Um, because he's the creepiest guy in the universe." She wraps an elastic around my hair.

"No, I mean, why are you helping me? I stole your boyfriend, and I just bitched you out at prom. You're supposed to hate me."

Megan kneels in front of me and holds my hands.

"Because, Pact number two, I couldn't let you make out with him. And, Pact number one, I don't hate you."

chapter
16

I go back to school on Monday wondering if things have really changed with Megan and me or if prom was a fluke. An alcohol-soaked dream. But then, at lunch, Amberly shyly asks me to sit at their table.

"I missed you," she says while we wait in line for sandwiches.

Everything inside me unknots at hearing her say that. "I missed you too."

"I'm sorry about not talking to you, but you know . . . my dad and everything . . ."

"It's okay. I was the home wrecker this time, so you stuck with Megan."

She smiles a sheepish smile.

"You have to know, though, I didn't do anything with Luke

until after they broke up."

"I believe you. I think Megan does too. I'm just sorry I couldn't get everyone to come around sooner."

I grab a turkey and Swiss on whole wheat. "That's okay. It means a lot that you tried. You probably tried to talk them out of the other stuff too, huh?"

My stomach clenches at her hesitation. *Please say you tried. Please say you weren't a part of it.*

"What are you talking about?" she finally says.

"I, um—" Could it really be possible she doesn't know? "Never mind. Let's talk about it later," I say, because we are rapidly approaching the lunch table, and Britney is already there with her seat scooted as close as humanly possible to Buck's.

"Hi," I say as I sit down.

She glances up for a second, says hi, and immediately goes back to mooning over Buck. If I didn't know better, I'd say she looked scared. Megan comes toward our table with a tray. She's staring right at me. I suck in my breath and have a strange urge to run, but then she smiles and sits next to me and bumps her shoulder against mine, and that one motion lets me know everything is going to be okay.

I don't know whether saving me from Jimmy cancels out the pranks they played. Or whether she's really forgiven me about Luke. But I'm willing to give our friendship another shot since she's so obviously trying. I have been given a second chance, and it feels great. It makes me want to give other people that same chance. And now I'm seeing people I've known my whole life in a new way.

I look closer at Amberly and see that she is really, truly in love with Coach Davis. And even though the idea of staying in our town and marrying someone from our high school makes me feel like someone is sucking all the air out of the room, I've been realizing that some people want that life, and it's okay.

I look closer at B and realize she's on pins and needles whenever I'm around, though I couldn't say why.

I'm scared to look closer at Megan in case it means our newly glued-back-together friendship has to fall apart again. We still haven't talked about Luke or formally apologized.

There are some shaky, awkward moments between us, but our friend group is approaching normal again. Except now Amanda Bell is a part of it. Hag. Okay, so maybe my inner-beauty finder still has some work to do where Amanda is concerned.

"I'm so glad you're back," Megan says to me on the way home from school one day. "Amanda Bell is no substitute."

"Did you really think she would be?"

Megan shakes her head. "She's so annoying. It's like she's so excited to be around us she just agrees with everything we say, especially me. And she's a huge bitch to everyone else. Even the girls she used to be friends with."

I smile. It's good to know I'm irreplaceable.

"So what are we going to do about senior trip?" asks Megan.

"What do you mean? I'm not going."

Every year the seniors from my high school go on a trip to Panama City Beach. I planned on going, but after things went bad, I didn't sign up, because what would be the point?

Panama City Beach (*proper noun*)
A beach town on the Florida panhandle where people in
the Southeast go for spring break/senior trips/any
other occasion that calls for sugar-white beaches and
thousands of rednecks.
(*synonyms*)
The Redneck Riviera, LA (Lower Alabama)

"Yes, you are. You have to."

"But who am I going to room with? No one will have spots open by now."

"You'll room with the four of us. We can get one of those fold-up cots. And if the hotel doesn't have any, Amanda can sleep on the floor for all I care."

I shrug. "Okay, I'm in."

"Sweet!!!!!!"

And then we're planning the trip together, just like old times. She and I are still fragile, though. I can tell by the way our friends are slightly on edge around us that they feel it too.

You know how sometimes people make up just so things can get back to normal and everyone else can be comfortable again? Well, that's kind of what happened here. Megan and I are best friends again. Technically. Officially. On the surface-ly. But underneath, nothing has really changed. We haven't talked about all the serious, dark stuff we need to talk about because we're both scared of what will happen. That our friendship might not survive that kind of major surgery. But you can't just slap concealer on a big giant zit and hope for the best. Because the bacteria festering just under your skin is still there. And sooner or later, that sucker is going to pop.

Before I know it, AP tests are over, we've graduated, and I'm at the beach. Amberly does my makeup while Britney paints her toenails on the balcony and Megan tries on fifty different skirts.

"I love that one even more," says Amanda. "You're so lucky. Everything looks *amazing* on you."

Megan raises an eyebrow at me, and I almost start giggling.

My phone buzzes in my pocket—a text from my mom. I open it to find a picture of a wall in Timothy's now-empty room painted with sample shades of orange, peach, and saffron. The text says they'll wait to pick a color until I get back because she wants it to be a family decision, but they wanted to give me a preview. I can't even believe how different his room looks without the choo-choo-train wallpaper.

"Hey, what's up? You look kind of sad," says Amberly.

"Huh?" I snap my phone shut. "Oh, um, it's nothing. I'm fine."

"Uh-huh. Well, close your eyes so I can do your eyeliner."

She traces and smudges and clucks over me and I let her. It's actually very relaxing.

"Done," she pronounces after what feels like no time at all.

I look in the mirror. My eyes are super smoky and sexy, just like I asked for.

"I love it. You're really talented, you know that?"

Amberly blushes. "Thanks. Some of the junior girls have already asked me to do their hair and makeup for prom next year. They even offered to pay me. It's crazy, right? This is the thing I love most in the whole world, and people are actually going to pay me to do it. And maybe if I get enough people interested, I could start my own business. Even have my own salon someday. That's the big dream, anyway."

"That would be so cool." I'm smiling, but I feel guilty. She's done it again. Spilled out her hopes and dreams to me like it's no big deal. Right after I shut her down like I always do.

I could say something back. But I let the silence grow. And it's the kind of silence that stretches out so long that it would be easy to let it go on just a second longer and avoid the moment completely.

"Hey." I fidget with my fingernails, unsure where to begin. "That text I got before was from my mom. And I was thinking, since you have such an eye for colors and all . . . well, my mom is finally redoing Timothy's room."

Her eyes widen at the mention of Timothy.

"And I was wondering if maybe you might want to help us pick the paint colors."

The idea of inviting someone, on purpose, to be a part of something so personal has me winding my fingers to resemble the knots in my stomach.

Amberly places her hands over mine and stops them. "I would love to."

Before I can say anything else awkward, Britney heel-walks into the room so as not to disturb her toenails and shuts the door to the balcony, cutting off the sea breeze.

"Let's get this party started!" she says, pulling five Coronas from the minifridge.

Amberly cracks open a bottle and starts to take a sip.

"Wait!" yells Megan. She leaps over a suitcase to stay Amberly's hand.

Amberly looks up from the bottle in surprise. "What?"

Megan grabs a lime and a paring knife. Only Megan thinks a paring knife is a necessary item for a trip to the beach. She deftly slices the lime, cutting through it so fast it makes me cringe. She slides a slice into the beer bottle and inverts it over her thumb.

"There." She hands the bottle back to Amberly. "That was close. Limes are critical."

After we finish our beers, we head to Club La Vela where everyone from our high school and every other high school is partying for teen night. We're close enough to walk, so that's what we do, because traffic on the strip has slowed to a crawl, turning the street itself into an ever-changing club. As soon as we get our hot-pink wristbands, we dance like crazy to hip-hop and techno.

I'm coming back from the bar with a water and checking the door for the eighty billionth time to make sure Luke isn't here, when Megan rushes toward me and clamps a hand over my wrist.

"We need to talk!" she yells over the music. "Now."

Uh-oh. What could she possibly be this upset about?

We find an upstairs patio where we can actually hear each

other talk. It's packed with smokers, but at least it's cooler than inside, and there's a clear view of the beach. I can smell that delicious salty coconut smell, even through the haze of smoke. I knew the moment where we get everything out in the open had to happen eventually, but I still don't feel ready for a conversation that determines the future of our whole friendship. Plus, I didn't expect her to look so mad.

"I need you to tell me what she did to you," she says.

"Who?"

"Britney. And probably Amanda too. I had a feeling they were doing stuff, but I pretended they weren't. I didn't ask because I was just so mad at you. And then I was talking to Amberly in the bathroom just now and I guess she confronted Britney about it or something and it sounds like it was a lot worse than a few bitchy comments, so I need to know."

Oh my gosh, she didn't know. The realization that my best friend didn't turn on me and try to ruin my life nearly sends me into tears. It's so wonderful I can't even believe it. Wait a minute. Do I believe it?

"Claire?" Megan is waiting.

"Um, yeah, so it was pretty bad." I need to be certain she's telling the truth. So I watch her. I tell her every last vicious thing that's been done to me since Amanda outed me on New Year's, and I watch as the shock registers on her face, and then I know, without a doubt, what the truth is. "You really didn't know, did you?"

And then she's shaking her head, and I'm hugging her like we haven't seen each other in years and crying into her shoulder.

"I'm so sorry they did all that horrible stuff to you," she says. And then she sits up straight like she's just realized something. "That's why you never apologized to me. I had wondered. I was so pissed because you were with Luke and you weren't even trying to make things right."

"I really am sorry, though." My voice comes out all garbled, and I daintily wipe away snot with a bar napkin. "I shouldn't have dated him right after you, or kept it secret. But I promise it didn't happen until after you guys broke up."

"I know," says Megan. "I believe you. I shouldn't have dated him either—I still ask myself why I did it." She stares out at the beach, where a couple of drunken frat boys are setting off Roman candles. "I think I was trying to show Chase I could be as happy as him. And also to prove to myself that I could. Because with Chase, and then again with Luke, I just felt like I had to work so damn hard to be lovable."

It's crazy that someone as amazing as her could ever think that. "You're lovable, with or without them. I love you. Everyone loves you."

She shakes her head sadly. "Everyone is afraid of me."

"That may have been true in tenth grade, but it isn't true anymore."

"Thanks." She smiles—the shyest smile I've ever seen from her. And then she looks suddenly serious. "Dating Luke really messed me up. I loved him and I thought he loved me too, but I think maybe he loved you all along. He would always say things about you and compare me to you. He made me feel like being pretty was my only redeeming quality."

It never occurred to me that she received the same treatment I did. I remember swelling with hope at Luke's compliments, but I never thought about what those compliments did to her. Now I know exactly how he made her feel.

Something about her story doesn't make sense, though. "I thought the whole reason you liked him was because he made you feel smart."

"He changed," she says simply. "He loved you for who you are. If I could have seen that from the beginning, I never would have gone for him."

"You're wrong. He didn't love me for me." Megan looks at me in surprise. "I felt the same way, like we were so in love. But then he would talk about how beautiful you are and make me feel like I didn't measure up. The worst was when he made me feel guilty for not having sex with him."

Megan squeezes my hand. "He knows *exactly* what to say when it comes to sex. When he wouldn't let me kiss him that time I was drunk, I think that was part of his game too. Because it made me feel really safe with him, so then on our second date when he totally switched gears and was really aggressive about taking my clothes off, I just . . . let him."

"I wish I had known all this sooner. I thought you were trying to get him back from me. That time at prom—"

"At prom? You mean when we were dancing? He came up to me and asked if we could talk. He told me he felt like we never got any closure."

"That's not what he told me." I shake my head. "I should have believed you. When he was with me, he wanted you. And when he was with you, he wanted me."

"So maybe he loved both of us."

"Or neither of us. You can't treat someone like that if you really love them."

"You're right. He's an asshole. I can't believe he almost ruined our friendship."

"I know. He so isn't worth it."

We swap horror stories about Luke until the sun dips low toward the ocean.

"Oh, I almost forgot. There's something I've been dying to tell you," says Megan. "I convinced my parents to check out the culinary school at the Art Institute of Atlanta with me, and I showed them the campus, and we met with the faculty, and they changed their minds. They're going to allow me a one-year trial run since it's so close to home, and they're going to pay for it and everything."

"Megan! That's amazing!"

"I know. And—" Her voice cracks. "And they said they're really proud of me. And you were the only person I wanted to tell, and it sucked."

"Me too! I mean, there's been so much I wanted to tell you too." Everything spills out at once. My acceptance letter. Stuff with my mom. Stuff about me trying to be a better, less judgmental version of myself.

"I missed you so much," she says.

"I missed you too."

We both go quiet, and I ask the question we're both thinking. "So, where does this leave our friendship?"

"I promise I'm a different person now. I would never let anything like this happen again."

She isn't just saying it. She seems different. Is different. It's like being around someone you used to know. She was always confident, but now it's more quiet. Like it's coming from deep inside rather than just a show she's putting on. And it isn't just her. I think about everything that's changed in my life over the past few months. "I'm a different person too."

"Does that mean we have to become best friends all over again?"

I smile. "That actually sounds like fun."

That night, Megan and I make another pact. Pact #6: We will never, ever let a boy come between us again. We pinky swear, like always, but then Megan says with a wild look in her eyes, "Let's do something extra to seal this pact."

"Like what?"

"I don't know. Something symbolic. I'm just so glad we're friends again. And I feel so free now."

I nod. I feel it too. I look around the deck at the guys in white tank tops smoking cigarettes. "Whatever it is we're going to do, I don't think we're going to find it here."

"You wanna go back to the hotel?"

"Sure."

We find the girls so we can let them know.

"We're leaving," Megan yells to Britney, who is dancing with Buck. I hang back because I don't trust myself to talk to Britney right now, but I can still hear Megan telling her they need to talk later.

"Okay," Britney yells back. She winces when she sees my face. *That's right. We both know what you did,* I tell her with my eyes.

I'm not going to turn this into a showdown, though. I don't want to make up with her either. Soon we'll be living in different cities and I'll have a whole new life and we can let this friendship fizzle out drama-free.

I don't see Amanda or Amberly, but Sam is nearby, standing by himself and half dancing, half rocking in that awkward way guys have.

"Hey! I think Megan and I are leaving now."

"Okay. So everything is good with you two now, huh?"

I can't believe he noticed. The difference in Megan and me since our talk must be more obvious than I realized.

"Yeah." I can't help but grin. "I'm so glad we're friends again."

Sam grins back. "Then I'm happy for you. And I'm happy you dumped Luke. You should hear the way that guy talks about girls. He's such a douche. If he ever starts on you . . ." He gives his head an angry shake.

"Thanks for looking out for me."

I give him a hug. A hug that doesn't go unnoticed by Amanda, who has just walked up holding two Diet Cokes.

"Hey. I was just coming to tell you we're leaving," I tell her. For whatever reason, Amanda's involvement in Operation Ruin

Claire's Life hurts a lot less. Probably because I never had any delusions she was my friend to begin with.

"Okay. I'm going to stay with Sam." She puts emphasis on his name, like it signifies her ownership of him, and latches on to his arm.

It's so beautiful outside Megan and I decide to walk home on the beach. I try to ignore everything I've ever heard about how dangerous that is for two teenage girls at night, but I still think I see muggers and rapists lurking in every dark shadow and behind every trash can. We make it back safely to find something even worse lurking in the hotel lobby: Luke. He's been attempting to burn his way through every girl in school since we broke up.

"Hey." He seems startled to see us, especially together. "So, you guys are friends again."

His speech is slurred. He's drunk.

"Yeah, we are." Megan grabs my hand as she says it. I can't tell if she's offering support or taking it, but it makes me feel stronger either way.

"You know, both you girls are so guh-reat. Sooo beautiful. I know I was a jerk, but you can't blame me for wanting both of you."

Megan and I glance sideways at each other. We're both annoyed.

"But thash the problem. There's both of you. Hey, I was just gonna go for a swim," he tells me. "Why don't you come with me?" he says to Megan.

Megan's eyes look like they could set something on fire.

"Which one of us are you even asking?"

"Either of you. Both of you." He shrugs. "I wanna make it up to you. I feel like we never got any closure."

My eyes narrow at the word *closure*. Before either of us can tell him we'd rather swim with open wounds during Shark Week, the elevator opens and out walks a girl who is as drunk as or drunker than Luke. Half of her miniskirt is tucked into her bikini bottoms. She stumbles over to him.

"Luke," she says in his ear, too drunk to realize her whisper is loud enough for us to hear. "Are you ready to go skinny-dipping now?"

"Sure."

He gives us an arrogant, lopsided smile (stupid freaking dimples) and walks off with his fingers tucked underneath her bikini straps.

"Did I tell you how pretty you look?" I hear him say as he holds open the lobby door for her.

"He did not just try to pick up both of us while he was waiting to go skinny-dipping with some chick," I say when the door closes behind them.

"Yeah," says Megan. "He did."

"Jerk."

"Loser."

"Ass clown."

We go on like this for a minute, calling him every name we can think of, when I have an idea.

"Let's follow them."

"What?!"

"Let's follow them and steal his clothes."

Megan's face lights up. "YES."

We hurry across the lobby and out the door, knowing they've got a head start. We peer around the pool area. Nope. The pool is crowded with people, including Glenn and a few other kids from school. They must be in the ocean. Pulling off our heels, we open the gate and run on tiptoes across the sand and take cover behind a lifeguard stand with our hands held in front of us to form fake guns. We peek around the wooden base of the stand, the sand digging into our knees.

There they are. Twenty yards away on the beach, stripping off their clothes. The girl falls over when she tries to pull off her skirt. Megan snorts and we both start giggling. Luke and his new friend leave their clothes a few feet from the surf and totter into the ocean bare-ass naked.

"How are we going to pull this off?" I whisper. "If we run at the clothes, they'll see us."

"I've got an idea. Just follow my lead."

Megan stands up, brushes the sand from her legs, puts her heels back on, fluffs her hair, and saunters over to where Luke and the girl are skinny-dipping. I follow a step behind her, and we stop just in front of the pile of clothes.

"What are *they* doing here?" The girl sinks lower in the water and looks up at Luke.

"I don't know," he tells her. "What's up?"

"Claire and I felt like swimming after all." Megan smiles her sexy vixen smile at him. I try to mimic her, even though I still don't get what we're doing.

"You did?" He coughs. "I mean, sure, come on in."

Megan catches my eye as she leans over to take off her shoes, stepping right up to Luke's shorts as she does so. It finally clicks. She's getting us closer and buying us time. I shuffle over to where his T-shirt sits discarded on the sand.

"Now," she hisses.

She snatches up the shorts, and I reach in every direction for everything else, a handful of boxers here, a T-shirt there. I try to grab the last thing, one of Luke's flip-flops, but it's too close to the surf and the ocean sucks it away from me.

"What the . . . ?" It finally dawns on Luke that he isn't about to be wet and naked with three chicks.

"Run!" yells Megan.

We bolt toward the pool area like the sand is on fire.

"I left a flip-flop!" I shout.

"It's okay. Keep going. He's after us!"

I glance over my shoulder to see Luke scrambling after us (still bare-ass naked), and in case you're wondering, a naked guy running is not an attractive sight. I think I see a flash of light, but I can't stop to see what it is. We make it to the gate, me first, Megan close behind, and he stops short. People will see him if he gets any closer.

"Give me back my clothes!"

"Nope. You deserve what you get," she says.

"Pleeease. I'm really sorry. Can you at least give me my underwear?"

I glare at him even though he probably can't see me in the starlight. "I wouldn't give you a Band-Aid."

"You stupid bitches. This is bullshit! Give me my clothes or I'll . . ."

"Or you'll what?" says Megan.

He doesn't reply.

"That's what I thought."

We prance inside and slam the gate behind us. Once we're safely within the confines of the pool area, I collapse on the cement, laughing.

"That. Was. The coolest thing we've ever done," I manage to get out between bursts of laughter.

"It gets better," says Megan. "I snapped a picture with my phone."

chapter
17

The next day Megan and I tell the story to the other girls in our room. Repeatedly. In detail. We do impressions of Luke and the girl. We show them the blurry picture of Luke naked and running. While we're laying out, we spot Luke a good ways down the beach from us. He has on swim trunks, so he must have managed to get inside eventually.

After sunset, most people trickle down to the pool to hang out because there's no teen night tonight. The other girls go to Buck's room with Britney, but Megan and I put on swimsuits and cover-ups and head downstairs.

"So, how did it go with B?" I ask. I saw them disappear for over an hour at the beach today.

Megan shrugs. "She gets that what she did was really screwed up, but she said she knew how much I really liked Luke and she was just trying to protect me. I know what you think of her, but I don't think I can handle cutting another friend out of my life right now."

I nod. I kind of knew that was what was going to happen. As we walk down the rough plank boardwalk, the kind that will give you splinters the size of coffee stirrers, drunken voices carry over the gate.

". . . got to second base in the bathroom of La Vela," says Jimmy Marcus to a chorus of whoops.

"I can beat that," says another voice. Luke's. Megan and I exchange frowns and let ourselves into the pool area, but he's surrounded by a crowd of people, mostly guys, so he doesn't see us. "Last night, I went skinny-dipping with this chick from Mississippi, and she is into some *freaky* stuff."

Jimmy slaps him a high five. "Aw, yeah."

"I thought I saw Megan and Claire go down to the beach right after you," says Glenn. "You must have seen them, right?"

"Oh, uh." Luke looks petrified, but just for a second. "I mean, yeah, they followed me down there. I don't know if they wanted to watch or what. Hey, it's been a long time since they've seen me naked, so I'm not . . ." He finally spots us. "Judging," he finishes quietly.

Most of the guys are laughing and nodding their heads, but Sam looks like he wants to murder Luke. His knuckles are white where he's gripping the stone table in front of him. Everyone watches Megan and me, waiting to see if we'll confirm or deny.

I put my hands on my hips. "You are so full of it."

"We pretended we were going to skinny-dip with you so we could steal your clothes," says Megan. "He chased us all the way back to the pool gate naked."

Some of the guys snicker.

"Oh, okay," Luke says. "You just came down there to 'steal my clothes.'" He makes air quotes with his fingers.

I glare at Luke. "We can prove it. Megan has a picture of you." I grab her phone and start scrolling for the photo.

"That only proves you wanted to see me naked. If a girl wants to take naked pictures of me, I'm not going to stop her."

Glenn clears his throat and takes a long pull from his beer. "Well, I saw you sneak in through the pool gate last night with a flip-flop over your pecker, so I'm more inclined to believe them than you."

Everyone laughs. Guys who doubted our story when it was Luke's word against ours believe us now that Glenn is on our side.

"Here," I say, waving the phone triumphantly.

"Fine," Luke says, standing up to get the attention back on him. "So you've got a naked picture of me. It's probably safer that way." He leans so close to me that we're almost touching, and I can smell the Jack Daniel's on his breath. "You wouldn't know what to do with the real thing, would you, virgin?"

The next few seconds are a blur. Sam stands so fast his chair flips over behind him, and before I know it, he lands a sucker punch across Luke's jawbone. Luke crumples to the ground. He rolls around, holding his face. One of the guys from the soccer team crooks an elbow under each of his armpits to help him up. Blood dribbles from the corners of his mouth and down his chin.

"I bih mah thung," he says as the guy walks him inside.

Sam shakes his punching hand. "Wow. I didn't realize that would hurt so much."

He sucks on one of his fingers. I rummage through a nearby cooler and scoop a handful of ice into my towel.

"Here." I lead Sam to a table in the corner, away from the crowd.

The pool light overhead fizzles in and out, dying a slow death while moths flutter around the carnage. I gently pull Sam's hand onto the stone table between us. His knuckles are swelling like sausages, but his fingers look normal and straight.

"Are you okay?"

He nods, but he can't help but wince when he flexes his fingers. "I don't think anything is jammed or broken. It just hurts."

"This'll help." I hold his hurt fingers with one hand and press the makeshift ice pack lightly against them with the other. He blows a slow breath out through his mouth.

"Thanks for sticking up for me," I say.

"How could I not? The guy's a douche." Sam's eyes get angry for a second, but then they soften. "You deserve better, CJ."

"Well, it means a lot to me. You're probably the only person I can always count on." I say all of this to Sam's hand. I didn't realize what a personal thing I was saying until it was already out there. It's true, though. Everyone else in my life has let me down at some point. Sam is the only constant. I've never thought about it quite like this. I always assumed I knew everything there was to know about Sam. But since this whole "digging deeper" experiment is working so well with everyone else, I decide to try it out with him too.

I glance up from my hands, still holding Sam's swollen fingers, feeling the calluses on his palms and his strong, bony knuckles. And I look at him. Really look. Something sparks when my eyes meet his. A feeling so big it makes me suck in my breath. I've felt that whacked-over-the-heart feeling with guys before, but never with Sam, and never this strong. I don't know what to do. This is Sam.

Sam.

My friend.

My buddy.

Not a guy I have feelings for. Except now maybe I do. My hand tingles where it touches his, and when Sam watches me pull it away, I can't shake this feeling I get from the way he's looking at me.

He knows.

I go back to the room with Megan and try to forget the way I felt when Sam and I looked at each other. He's just my friend. He's *just* my friend. And besides, even if I did like Sam (which I don't!), I'm done messing with other people's boyfriends.

Two hours later, Amanda comes flying through the door with mascara running down her cheeks.

"What's wrong, girl?" asks Britney.

"Sam broke up with me." She flops on the bed and sobs into

the tacky plaid comforter.

"Oh, no, honey." Amberly squeezes on the corner of the bed next to her and gives her a hug. "Why?"

"He says it's because we're going to school in different states, and he thinks we'd be better as friends. But the real reason he broke up with me is the same reason he punched Luke." She glares at me through her tears. "He's in love with *her*."

Kiss # 16 xoxo

The Present

Even though I felt that spark with Sam, and even though we're
both single, I don't do anything about it. I've had enough
romantic drama this year, and the last thing I need is to ruin my
oldest friendship on top of it. So we have a normal summer of
hanging out, watching movies, and playing soccer—except now
I sometimes get a fluttery feeling when he touches me.

The night before Sam leaves for the University of North
Carolina, and a week before I leave for Georgia Tech, there's a
knock at my bedroom door.

"Come in," I call. "Oh, hey, Sam."

"Hey, I let myself in. Where is everybody?"

"Tonight is third-grade orientation for Libby. But I really
needed to start packing."

I gesture around the room at the half-empty crates and
boxes. There's still so much I have to do this week. My desk
chair is piled with junk, so Sam sits on my bed.

"I leave for UNC tomorrow," he says.

"I know." I continue packing books into a cardboard box.
"Are you excited?"

"Yeah. I think I'll like my marketing classes. And it'll be nice
to start over in a place where nobody knows me as the fat kid."

"Aw, Sam. Things really changed this year, though. You
dated Amanda Bell."

"I know. But I think there are some people who will never see the new me." He looks so sad when he says it.

"Yeah. I'm ready to leave it all behind too."

I think about this year, and my reputation, and how I've been trying to think differently about people. I ponder this while I sort through my closet for summer clothes (pack) and winter clothes (leave). Sam's hand closes over my shoulder, and I try not to jump. I didn't realize he had gotten off the bed.

"Can I talk to you about something? It's important."

I stop pushing around hangers and turn to face him.

"Sure."

"I don't know if I should even be saying this, but there have been times this summer when you looked at me, and it made me think . . ."

He waits like he's hoping I'll interrupt him and rescue him from whatever he's about to say.

"Anyway, I'll regret it forever if I don't." His eyes are so scared, so vulnerable. They search mine like they're looking for an answer, but I don't know the question.

"I never stopped liking you," he finally blurts out.

Chill bumps pop up on every inch of my skin.

"You didn't?"

"Are you really that surprised?"

I kind of am. "I know you liked me when we were little, but you never act like that anymore."

"Only because you freaked out after that time at soccer camp. You didn't talk to me for three weeks. I was worried if

I told you, you'd cut me out again, and I wouldn't even get to have you as a friend."

"What about Amanda Bell?" I ask. I can't believe that while I've been hiding these growing feelings for a few months, he's been doing the same thing for practically forever.

"She's just a girl I had a crush on. She's not you." I am suddenly very aware of the fact that we are in my bedroom. Alone. He takes my hands in his. "I like you. I have always liked you. It's grown and changed as we've gotten older, but it never went away. I thought you were feeling the same way. But maybe I . . ."

"No, I—I think I might like you too." Sam's face lights up like the Fourth of July. "I started to realize it that day you punched Luke."

"Best punch ever." He grins.

Kissing Sam right now would be the easiest thing in the world. And I won't lie, I want to. But even though Sam and I have been thicker than thieves practically since birth, I'm hesitant. Nervous. This isn't some hot guy I just met. Then it would be easy to be bold. This is my oldest friend. And some things are more important.

I think Sam can sense my reluctance, because he takes a step back. "So, um, what are we going to do about this?"

"I don't think we should do anything." As much as it kills me to say it.

Sam looks at the floor. "Oh."

"It's just, our friendship is more important than anything else.

Plus, the timing is all wrong. Look at the facts."

"What facts?"

"Fact number one: we're going to school in different states. Fact number two: we just got out of serious relationships—your first, my most traumatizing." Sam looks amused, and I'm sure he will tease me about this later, but I keep going. "Starting college fresh and single is definitely the best thing for both of us. We still have a lot of figuring out to do, and if there's one thing I've learned this year, it's that friendships are permanent, but you never know about love."

I watch Sam, waiting to see if he'll accept a friendship when he wants a relationship. "It makes sense," he finally says. Whew. "But. What if the timing wasn't all wrong?"

"What do you mean?"

"I mean, so we don't date now, but what if later, say, when we graduate from college, neither of us is in a relationship? We could give it a try."

Works for me. "Dude. We should make a pact."

"Those things you're always making with Megan?"

"Um, yeah. They're *awesome*. Here's how it works: I'll say the pact, and you repeat after me. Okay?"

Sam looks like he is working very hard not to laugh at me. "Okay."

I clear my throat. Despite my having been friends with Sam for practically forever, this is our very first pact. "Sam-and-Claire Pact number one: If neither of us is seeing anyone when we graduate from college, we're going to try dating each other."

I nod at Sam, and he repeats the pact. "And that's it? That's all we do?"

I shrug. "Megan and I usually seal it with a pinky swear."

"I have another idea," he says.

The atmosphere, which was silly and fun when we were making the pact, is suddenly serious. He takes a step toward me, his green T-shirt and sunburned arms so close I could touch him in a second. His warm, brown eyes are locked on to mine, and he smells like grass and childhood memories. He's not supposed to kiss me. And if he does, I won't be able to stop myself from kissing him back. He leans down, and just when I think it's inevitable, he brushes his lips against my forehead, holding them there for just a moment. And somehow it is the most intimate thing that has ever happened to me.

chapter
18

"Y ou girls can start unpacking," says Mama. "Dad and I
will get the last few boxes."

They head back to the car, leaving Libby and me
to sort through a mountain of crap encased in cardboard car-
tons and plastic bins. I've already called my roommate (Katie B.
from Jacksonville, Florida), but she doesn't move in until tomorrow—which is good because I'll need all twenty-four hours to
make something of this wreck before she gets here. I open a
box labeled Books and start filing them on my bookshelf. Libby
moves around the room, touching a box here, a desk there, lost
in thought.

"Hey, Libs, you okay? You've been really quiet today."

She nods.

"You sure?" I turn back to the bookshelf and count to five. With Libby, it pays to be patient. One. Two. Three . . .

"It's just . . ." She sits down beside me and curls her legs to her chest. "I don't want you to leave me."

"Aw, sweetie, it's not going to be like that, I promise." I rub her back. "You can call me any time, every day if you want. And I'll visit a lot. And if Mama or Daddy starts acting weird again"— Libby's eyes grow fearful—"you let me know, and I'll come home and help, okay?"

Libby takes a deep breath and lets it back out. "Okay."

The door to my room opens again, and my dad waddles to my dresser, setting down the last couple of boxes with an exhausted grunt.

"How do you have so much stuff?" He leans against the wall and pants like a hound dog.

Mama laughs. "This is nothing. Have you forgotten what it was like with Sarah?"

His eyes get big, and he touches a hand to his back like it's seizing up at the thought. "You're right," he says. "This is child's play compared to Sarah's crates of shoes."

"You should have seen the shoe collection we moved into Megan's place last weekend. She is so lucky she has a real closet to put them in," I say as I hang clothes in a battered wardrobe that is slightly larger than the minifridge my dad is wrestling with.

Don't get me wrong. I'm really excited about the whole dorm experience. But that doesn't mean I didn't drool over the ginormous closet and non-communal shower in Megan's apartment.

Students at the Art Institute of Atlanta aren't required to live in campus housing, even as first years. Sometimes I worry her parents are still hoping she'll "get it out of her system." Little do they know we're already planning to be roomies in a fantastic off-campus apartment next year.

Dad rubs Mama's arm. "We should probably get going. Give Claire some time to settle in."

"All right." She hugs me so close I can't take a full breath. "I am so proud of you."

When she pulls away, she looks like she's about two seconds away from tears. Dad hugs me next.

"I'm proud of you too, Claire-Bear."

He's almost as tearful as Mama. Man, are they getting sappy. I'm so glad Katie B. is still in Jacksonville right now, instead of here in our dorm room witnessing these embarrassing displays of affection. I walk them to the car for more hugs and more sappiness, and okay, maybe I get a little sappy too, especially when I wave good-bye as they drive away.

Then it's back to my room for more unpacking. As I set up my laptop, my phone buzzes in my pocket. It's Sam!

"Hey!"

"Hey, CJ. How's college?"

"Great. I've been here two hours," I laugh. "How's UNC?"

"It's good, it's good. It's so weird not seeing you every day, though."

"Yeah, it is. Hey, fall break isn't that far away, though."

"Yeah." There's a pause on the other end of the line. "Hey,

you, uh, won't forget about that agreement thing we made?"

"They're called pacts. And no, there is no way I could forget about it." My phone beeps that I have a text. "Oops, that must be Sarah. She's bringing me some kind of surprise. I gotta go."

"Call me tomorrow?"

"Definitely." See? This whole friendship-with-Sam thing can work. I just have to refrain from hooking up with him when he comes to visit.

I check Sarah's text.

Outside your dorm. Come down.

I tear down the stairs like an excited kid on Christmas. Surprises do that to me. Sarah shuts the door to the car and wraps me in a huge hug.

"Whadya bring me?! Whadya bring me?!"

"You'll see," she says, stepping around me to pop the trunk with a flourish.

A gigantinormous plastic box is inside.

"A container from the Container Store?"

Sarah puts a hand over her heart like I have mortally offended her. "This is no ordinary container. This is my costume box, painstakingly assembled during four years of parties, mixers, and Halloweens. And now that I no longer need it, I'm passing it down to you." She says it with the seriousness of a priestess imparting a sacred rite. "I'll let you open it upstairs because I have to get back to work. Call me if you have time to get lunch this weekend."

She gives me one last hug, and I pick up the box. And nearly tip over into a nearby gutter, because it weighs as much as a small pony. Sarah was the social chair of her sorority at Georgia, and I remember seeing about a bazillion pictures of her with her sisters in ridiculous outfits. Now I know where those outfits ended up.

I stagger up the stairs—I swear this thing contains bricks, not clothes—and finally manage to make it to the door. Now to figure out how to get my key out of my pocket. I definitely need both hands to carry the box. But I don't want to put it down, because coating the top of the stairs is a nasty puddle that appears to be growing three kinds of fungi and some creatures from another planet.

"Need a hand?" says a voice from behind me.

Whew. I'm saved. "Yes, please."

I turn to look at my rescuer. Wow. There is one word to describe this guy, and it is *rugged*. Blond hair tumbles over a scar on his forehead, and his nose crooks slightly to one side like it's been broken. If I ask what he does for fun, I'm sure he'll say something like extreme mountain biking or night rappelling or catching trout with his bare hands. He grabs the box like it's empty and stacks it on top of the one he's already holding while I fish my key from my pocket and pull open the door, the metal bottom scraping through the grime at the top of the stairs.

Rugged Boy follows me down the hallway, and I can't help it: I imagine what it would be like to make him Kiss #17. I open the door to my dorm room and push a box out of the way so Potential Kiss #17 won't trip over it. Staring up at me from the bottom of the box is a photo of Sam and me at graduation. My heart feels all squirmy in my chest. I know I can date whoever I want, kiss whoever I want, and Sam can too. But maybe I'm not ready for Kiss #17 just yet. Though that doesn't mean it wouldn't be fun to have a friend who looks like he could be in an SUV commercial. Maybe he could teach me outdoor survival skills. Or maybe he's actually really into knitting.

The Potential Knitter strides across my room and sets my container on my bed (the only free space in the whole room).

"Hey, thanks," I say.

"No problem." He smiles a dazzling smile (his teeth are straight and white, but the smile is still somehow *rugged*).

I dig into my new treasure chest of clothes right in front of him because I'm too excited to hold back. Sarah wasn't kidding. There are knee-high boots in every color, angel wings, a toga, assorted animal ears, a marginally creepy blond wig, and so much more. The costumes make me think about how figuring out who you are is like dressing up in different costumes, and how college is the perfect place for me to do that, and a third reason Sam and I shouldn't date yet.

You can't start a relationship if you don't know who you are. Sam's not the fat kid anymore. I'm not the little tomboy. Or the girly-girl my friends tried to make me into. Or the slut everyone from high school thinks I am. Or the girl hiding the horrible secret behind the doors of her cookie-cutter suburban home. I have to figure it out. And I have to do it on my own—without a boyfriend. But I have a feeling I'll do fine.

"So, I guess I'll see you later, but if you need any help with anything else, my room is the one to the left of the elevator."

"Oh." I realize he is still standing there and that I completely forgot to introduce myself, and also that I am currently holding a feather boa and a pair of handcuffs. I shove them back in the box, ASAP. "Oh, sure, that would be great."

He holds out a hand. "I'm Troy, by the way."

I push off the bed and shake hands with Rugged Boy, aka Troy, aka Potential New Friend.

"I'm CJ."

Acknowledgments

I have so many people to thank for supporting me and this book!

Buckets of gratitude to my phenomenal beta readers: Chanelle Gray, Jamie Blair, Kierah Jane Reilly, Kellie Sheridan, Laurie Devore, Anna-Elizabeth McCloud.

To Krista Ashe, for helping me realize I couldn't shy away from having Timothy in the story.

To Melanie Kramer, because sometimes books need more work before you can send them out into the world and it takes a good friend to tell you.

To Debra Driza, for reading this manuscript so many times and for going through all my early agent feedback and helping me figure out how to fix things before sending it out again. Oh, and, you know, for referring me to my agent!

To Erin Brambilla, for being my brainstorming buddy, my cheerleader, my sender of kraken necklaces, my Hotel Onyx partner in crime. It's happening and you're next! Also, thanks for letting me use the smart half of the brain sometimes.

To the amazing writers at WN, OneFour KidLit, the AbsoluteWrite and Authonomy forums, and my Atlanta writer dinner crew. And to the LB's for brainstorming and hilarity and krakens and answering neurotic questions at all hours and letting me know what to expect from this mostly wonderful and sometimes scary roller coaster and in general just being the best people on the planet. I <3 you all.

To my agent, Susan Hawk (and everyone at The Bent Agency). Thank you for seeing something in my book and really "getting" it, for writing edit letters that make me excited to start revisions, and for making dreams come true. My husband is convinced you are actually a superhero named Lady Hawk.

To my editor, Jen Klonsky, for pushing this book to be better than I ever could have imagined, for writing the best emails ever, and for having room for both a genius and a teenager in your brain. I still can't believe how lucky I am to work with you. To Catherine Wallace, who is made of awesome. To Cara Petrus, Melinda Weigel, Lillian Sun, Karen Sherman, Christina Colangelo, Alison Lisnow, Susan Katz, Kate Jackson, and to anyone else at Harper who worked on my book in any way. You people are rock stars.

To my English teachers—Mrs. W, Mrs. D, Mrs. M, and Dr. H. And my other teachers, too, because teachers are awesome.

To my Georgia Tech girls: Laura, Katie, Nicole, Anya, Becca (my favorite person to discuss books with!), Bethany, Mahoney, Holly, and Rachel—for always supporting me, for talking with me about YA books and book ideas, for creating a lifetime's worth of book-fodder-worthy memories, and for never thinking I was dumb for wanting to do this.

To Alpha Gamma Delta, for changing my life and giving me

the confidence to reach for big dreams. The taxidermied squirrel on p. 242 is for you.

To Callie, Lisa, Jeanne, Sara, Kalynda, and the rest of the Emory neuroscience program—for being the kind of people who like to talk about science AND hold *Twilight* screening parties. You guys are the greatest!

To my family, for their unconditional love and support, especially my parents, and especially my mom, who took us to the library on countless summer Saturdays and told me to go read a book or go write something whenever I told her I was bored. To Maxie and Dennis, for being hilarious and supportive and watching Ansley so I actually had time to write.

To Ansley, for making each day a wondrous thing.

And to Zack Allen. Thanks for being my favorite person. And for reading this book and telling me when the boy parts sounded too emo. I love you.

EXTRAS

17 first kisses

17 First Kisses Who Would You Kiss? Quiz

Find out which guy from *17 First Kisses* is your perfect kiss match!

1. I prefer guys who are:
   (a) Athletes. The more muscles, the better. (Move on to question 2.)
   (b) Musicians. Especially the ones with soulful eyes. (Skip to question 6.)
   (c) Neither. (Skip to question 9.)
   (d) Both! I can't pick one or the other. (Go to answer #11.)

2. My favorite athletes play:
   (a) Football. There is no other sport. (Move on to question 3.)
   (b) Baseball. Nothing beats a day at the ballpark. (Skip to question 4.)
   (c) Soccer. I think it's the shin guards that do it for me. (Skip to question 5.)
   (d) Play? Real athletes run. (Go to answer #3.)

3. If people were making fun of me, my guy would:
   (a) Join in and push me down for good measure. (Go to answer #1.)
   (b) Make sure everyone knew the rumors weren't true. (Go to answer #2.)

4. Do you like guys who have beer breath and hairy

knuckles and speak almost entirely in bad sports metaphors?
- (a) Yes! Those are my three biggest turn-ons! (Go to answer #8.)
- (b) No. (Whew. Go back to question 2.)

5. How does your guy finally work up the courage to tell you that he likes you?
- (a) He leaves a note in your soccer bag. (Go to answer #5.)
- (b) After gratuitous amounts of flirting, he comes straight out and says, "I like you." After he dates your best friend. (Go to answer #14.)
- (c) The day before he leaves for college he confesses that he's been pining for you for years. (Go to answer #16.)

6. When you meet a guy who seems like a bad boy, you:
- (a) Are instantly drawn to him. (Move on to question 7.)
- (b) Can't run in the opposite direction fast enough. (Skip to question 8.)

7. The perfect song to describe your guy is:
- (a) "Sexy and I Know It" by LMFAO. (Go to answer #10.)
- (b) "Good Girls Go Bad" by Cobra Starship. (Go to answer #9.)

8. Your ideal guy has hobbies like:

   (a) Playing pool and video games. (Go to answer #12.)
   (b) Serving on student council and writing heartbreakingly beautiful poetry. (Go to answer #13.)
   (c) Picking his nose and wiping it on the bottom of his tuba case. (Go to answer #7.)

9. My idea of a dream date is . . .

   (a) A Winter Wonderland dance with punch and cookies and papier-mâché snowflakes. (Go to answer #4.)
   (b) Camping. (Go to answer #6.)
   (c) Knitting. Or night rapelling. Or knitting while night rapelling! My dream guy is so mysterious, he'd plan a date that would keep me guessing. (Go to answer #17.)
   (d) I don't care what we do as long as my date is a Creeper Extraordinaire. (Go to answer #15.)

Answers:

#1. Your kiss pick is Buck Bronson. He may look like an Abercrombie model (for a parallel universe Abercrombie that sells rebel flags and jorts), but he's kind of immature and he's got a mean streak, so watch out!

#2. Your kiss pick is Glenn Baker. Homecoming king and all-star receiver, this sweetheart is a total catch. Plus, he has creamy brown skin and eyes so clear and blue, you look into them expecting to see a bottom. Hawt.

#3. Your kiss pick is Ryan Bond. He seems pretty great, but let's just hope you don't get married because Chessa would make one scary sister-in-law.

#4. Your kiss pick is Amanda Bell's cousin. You are now the envy of seventh-grade girls everywhere.

#5. Your kiss pick is Alex Martinez. He's the best soccer player at camp, and also he's pretty adorable.

#6. Your kiss pick is Eric Masters. He's fun for camping sleepovers and he gives nice back rubs during lunch, but I wouldn't trust him at carnivals if I were you.

#7. Your kiss pick is Steven Lippert. If he's had Cheetos recently, I would run to the nearest drugstore and stock up on mouthwash. And dental floss. And possibly bleach.

#8. Your kiss pick is *the* Corey Collins, one half of The Collins Twins and Claire's ninth-grade prom date. Um, you should stay away from guys like this. I'm going to pretend you were kidding and let you take question 5 again.

#9. Your kiss pick is Tanner Walsh. On the upside, he's a rock star, which means his sweat has magical powers. On the downside, you may catch him cheating on you. Plus, his song lyrics suck.

#10. Your kiss pick is Lead Singer from the band Screaming Lemurs. Rumor has it he's pretty darn good at kissing, so if guys who rock eyeliner and tight leather pants are your thing, this guy's for you!

#11. Your kiss pick is Rhythm Guitar. He's in a band and he plays football, and while his kisses may have been known to chip a tooth and he does watch a lot of ESPN Classic, otherwise he's a pretty stand-up guy.

#12. Your kiss pick is Bass Guitar. He's sweet and nerdy and seems like he'd be a really devoted boyfriend.

#13. Your kiss pick is Seth Wong, lead guitar from the band Screaming Lemurs and senior-class president. He's funny and sensitive and writes amazing song lyrics.

#14. Your kiss pick is Luke Dawson. He's gorgeous and romantic, but this boy comes with a lot of baggage, so be prepared for a complicated relationship.

#15. Your kiss pick is the Creepiest of all Creepers, Jimmy Marcus. I think you should take question 9 over again. And maybe double knot your bathing suit straps while you're at it.

#16. Your kiss pick is Sam. Sigh. Sweet, funny, wonderful Sam. Way to pick a good one! ☺

#17. Your kiss pick is Rugged Boy—the height of mystery. We know almost nothing about this candidate other than that he is *rugged*. If you find out anything good, report back!

Claire and Megan's Ultimate Girly Playlist

"Girls Just Want To Have Fun"—Cyndi Lauper
"Perfect Day"—Hoku
"Fidelity"—Regina Spektor
"Breathe"—Michelle Branch
"Material Girl"—Madonna
"Be OK"—Ingrid Michaelson
"You Belong with Me"—Taylor Swift
"I Will Survive"—Gloria Gaynor
"Since U Been Gone"—Kelly Clarkson
"Your Love Is My Drug"—Ke$ha
"Supermodel"—Jill Sobule
"Just Dance"—Lady Gaga
"Super Bass"—Nicki Minaj
"Everytime We Touch"—Cascada
"Bad Reputation"—Joan Jett
"Ex-Girlfriend"—No Doubt
"I Love Rock 'n' Roll"—Britney Spears
"Ain't No Other Man"—Christina Aguilera
"Some Days You Gotta Dance"—Dixie Chicks
"Born to Fly"—Sara Evans

Alternate Kiss #13

I thought it would be fun to show an "alternate" version of Kiss # 13 to give you guys an inside look at how the editing process works. In the original version of the scene where Claire kisses Tanner's band mates, Seth isn't at the party and the kiss with him takes place in a separate kiss section. The party scene ends with Tanner trying to talk to Claire and her telling him "I just made out with all your friends" before flouncing out. And as she's flouncing, she thinks about how she's still a kiss short, which leads us to . . . the alternate kissing scene with Seth!

* * *

The very next night at the Saturday night football game, I get my chance to enact the fourth and final phase of Mission: Humiliate Tanner Walsh. Usually our games are on Fridays, but whenever we play Springville, our arch-nemesis, it's an all-out Saturday extravaganza. I just hope twenty-four hours wasn't enough time for Seth to find out about what happened at the party. I hover between the concession stand and the bathrooms, hoping I'll be able to catch him when he arrives.

A tap on my shoulder almost sends me into a frenzy. I whirl around.

"Seth!"

His shiny black hair is gelled into a faux-hawk. "Hey. What are you doing up here?"

"Oh, um, I guess I didn't really feel like watching the game."

He nods, pulls his jacket tighter around his neck against

the wind. "Want to take a walk?"

"Sure."

We amble around the perimeter of the school building and end up sitting on the hard stone steps at the front entrance, watching the leaves chase each other around the parking lot. Every now and then, a muted cheer travels our way from the stadium.

I'm tired of planning kiss-segue conversations, plus I'm super nervous, so this time I go right for the kiss. For a second, nothing happens, and I worry I'm about to be seriously embarrassed, but then his lips open and his tongue finds mine. One hand winds itself into my hair. The other splays across my back, pulling me closer. I can feel the tension in each of Seth's fingertips as they press against my ribs. There's a passion in his kissing that frightens me. He grabs my hand when I end the kiss.

"I knew you felt the same way," he says.

"What?"

"This whole time you've been with Tanner, I've been falling for you."

All I can do is sit there with my mouth hanging open. I didn't know he liked me. I didn't want to hurt anyone. Well, anyone except Tanner. I feel guiltier by the second about making him the fallout of my kiss warfare.

"And now I know you feel the same way." His grin falters. "Because, why else would you kiss me?"

"He cheated on me," I say to Seth's Converse.

I expect him to be annoyed. Or sad maybe. I don't expect him to wrap me in his arms and hold me.

"I know." He kisses my temple. "And I'm so sorry. But

11

you're with me now. I'd never do that to you."

Could this get any worse? I wiggle out of his embrace and stand on the stairs. He stands too.

"No." This time I look him right in his kind brown eyes. "I mean, that's why I kissed you. I kissed all four of you guys to get back at him."

His face looks like it's having a fight with itself.

"All *four* of you? So, this was just . . . And you don't . . . Damn it!" He kicks over a trashcan. It clangs against the sidewalk, sending crumpled balls of paper careening across the lawn like little white tumbleweeds.

"I'm sorry." I feel like the worst person in the world.

"It isn't your fault. He knew I liked you from the beginning. Things could have been great between us if he'd never gone after you. It was all him."

And with that, he stalks off toward the football field.

"Seth, wait. *Please.*"

I try to grab his arm, but he pushes my hand away and continues toward the stands, all the while muttering a string of unintelligible swear words. I should realize what's going to happen next. But I don't. So I don't think to stop him from leaping over the top rung of the bleachers like a track-and-field hurdle. I can't keep him from plowing through band kids, sending them toppling into one another like blue-and-orange dominoes. I can't do anything but watch as he grabs Tanner by the tasseled front of his band uniform and punches his face so hard his goofy hat falls off.

Tanner tries to recover, but with his snare drum in his hands, he doesn't stand a chance. Seth hits him again and again. Only about half the band is still attempting to play at this point. His fist connects with Tanner's nose with a sickening crunch that sends him flying, his drum taking out Steven Lippert in the process.

In the days that follow, Steven Lippert shows everyone his black eye and tells anyone who will listen how his tuba mouthpiece jammed into his left eye socket during the fight.

In the days that follow, Screaming Lemurs goes through an epic break-up.

Edit Notes:

My editor, Jen:
Given that she already kissed Tanner's other friends, why is this still important? Didn't she make her point at the party?

More about what she thinks . . . how revenge doesn't always work and she ended up using the guys and hurting Seth's feelings.

Me:
For the part where she kisses Seth—I agree that she made this point to Tanner at the party already so it seems strange that she still feels like it's important to kiss Seth too. Should I combine the sections so this kiss with Seth happens at the same time as the other kisses? And then when she sees how hurt he is she could instantly feel horrible about all the revenge kisses?

Jen:
That would be awesome!

13

(Side note: That's right. My editor says things like "awesome" and "woo-hoo" and uses plenty of smiley faces and exclamation points. Do you see why I love working with her?)

So, what do you think? The fight in the middle of the band section in the old version was funny, but I love the new version so much more. It's more emotional and I think Seth's actions are truer to his character. I also love that it provides an opportunity for Claire to reflect more on how her actions have hurt other people, especially Seth.

Megan's BFF Chocolate Soufflé

M: Hi, I'm Megan.

C: And I'm Claire.

M: Today I'm going to teach all of you how to make the soufflé that started our friendship.

C: And I am going to painstakingly record every last detail of what she does so I can scientifically prove she uses voodoo magic to make soufflés.

M: I do not! Just because I make ultra-fabulous soufflés every single time does not mean I practice dark magic.

C: (coughs) Mmm-hmm. I'm just gonna copy down the ingredients.

5 egg whites and 3 egg yolks
¼ cup heavy cream
¼ cup plus 1 tablespoon granulated sugar (or vanilla sugar if you're fancy like Megan)
5 ounces bittersweet chocolate (cut up)
1 stick (1 cup) unsalted butter (melted and then cooled)
2 tablespoons unsweetened cocoa powder
Powdered sugar
Voodoo magic

M: First, you separate the egg whites and yolks into two

separate bowls while the eggs are still cold. No egg yolks in the egg whites bowl! This is key! Every time a molecule of egg yolk makes it into the egg whites, God kills a kitten. Write that down, Claire!

C: Egg yolks = dead kittens. Got it.

M: Then, we want to give the whites a chance to warm to room temperature, so we'll do some other stuff.

Preheat the oven to 350°F. Line four 1-cup ramekins with two coats of butter and one coat of granulated sugar.

Do it just like how Curtis Stone does it with the 2-minute refrigeration in between. Find his baking tutorials online. The man is a genius.

C: Plus, let's be honest, watching a hot chef with an accent cook chocolate desserts is eight different kinds of bliss.

M: Combine chocolate and cream in a small saucepan or double boiler, stirring occasionally until smooth. Then transfer to a large bowl to cool.

Whisk yolks and cocoa powder together and then combine with the chocolate mixture until smooth.

In a large bowl, beat the egg whites with an electric mixer until they look foamy. Then gradually beat in the ¼ cup of sugar.

Make sure to beat the eggs long enough so that peaks form on the beaters when you lift the mixer. (lifts electric mixer) See?

C: That looks highly unnatural. But I'm still gonna lick those later.

M: Fold two scoops of the egg white mixture into the chocolate mixture using a rubber spatula. Then fold in the rest of the egg white mixture.

You have to be super gentle here. And you definitely don't want to over mix or you'll lose all the air bubbles that make the soufflé puff up in the oven. If there really is voodoo magic in this soufflé, it's hiding in those air bubbles.

C: I knew it!

M: Put an equal amount of soufflé batter into each ramekin, making sure the batter comes to the very top of the dish without going over.

Bake 10–20 minutes.

Baking time really varies by oven. You want the soufflés to puff out the top of the dish, but you also want them to be moist in the middle. I suggest sitting in front of your oven the first couple of times and watching them. Every. Single. Second. The perfect soufflé takes trial and error. If you don't cook it long enough, it falls. If you cook it too long, it falls.

C: If you talk above a whisper or make sudden movements or give it the stink-eye, it falls.

M: Sprinkle powdered sugar on top and pour on chocolate sauce (made from more chocolate and heavy cream in the double boiler). Serve immediately to your new best friend.

C: I feel like the "immediately" part is unnecessary. Anyone who wouldn't shove this in their mouth immediately is not someone I want to be best friends with.

M: Word.

*Note: This recipe is adapted from Easy Chocolate Soufflé (p. 173) from *365 Great Chocolate Desserts* by Natalie Haughton and Curtis Stone's *The World's Best Chocolate Soufflé* video.